P9-EMG-584

Praise for
KATHRYN SPRINGER'S

"Kathryn Springer's refreshing writing style
and sense of humor make this story sing!"
—Neta Jackson, bestselling author of
The Yada Yada Prayer Group

"A tender, insightful read and a great debut—
I want more from Kathryn Springer!"
—Judy Baer, author of *Million Dollar Dilemma*

"A delightful package of humor and gentle truths,
Front Porch Princess is poignant and honest,
a compelling, well-written story that will find
the nooks and crannies of your heart and linger
long after the book is done. Highly recommended!"
—Susan May Warren, bestselling author of
Chill Out, Josey!

"Springer's combination of humor,
family values and longing will reach out from
the pages and touch readers' hearts."
—*Romantic Times BOOKreviews,* Top Pick!

PICKET FENCE
Promises

KATHRYN SPRINGER

Steeple
Hill
Café™

Published by Steeple Hill Books™

If you purchased this book without a cover you should be aware
that this book is stolen property. It was reported as "unsold and
destroyed" to the publisher, and neither the author nor the
publisher has received any payment for this "stripped book."

STEEPLE HILL BOOKS

ISBN-13: 978-0-373-78602-2
ISBN-10:   0-373-78602-6

PICKET FENCE PROMISES

Copyright © 2008 by Kathryn Springer

All rights reserved. Except for use in any review, the reproduction
or utilization of this work in whole or in part in any form by any
electronic, mechanical or other means, now known or hereafter
invented, including xerography, photocopying and recording, or in
any information storage or retrieval system, is forbidden without
the written permission of the editorial office, Steeple Hill Books,
233 Broadway, New York, NY 10279 U.S.A.

This is a work of fiction. Names, characters, places, and incidents are
either the product of the author's imagination or are used fictitiously,
and any resemblance to actual persons, living or dead, business
establishments, events, or locales is entirely coincidental.

This edition published by arrangement with Steeple Hill Books.

® and TM are trademarks of Steeple Hill Books, used under license.
Trademarks indicated with ® are registered in the United States Patent
and Trademark Office, the Canadian Trade Marks Office and in other
countries.

www.SteepleHill.com

Printed in U.S.A.

This book is affectionately dedicated to Indiana Jones and the "Thursday Girls." For five years, we've broken bread together and shared our hearts and our lives. I can't imagine being on this journey with anyone else—but then, God does have a sense of humor! Looking forward to our next adventure down the narrow road...

Now to Him who is able to do immeasurably more than all we ask or imagine, according to His power that is at work within us.
—*Ephesians* 3:20

Chapter One

There is an old saying that a person's past will eventually catch up to them. Mine was a bit slow because it didn't find me until I was forty-five years old. When it did, it didn't tiptoe up and give me a discreet tap on the shoulder, either. A gentle, *Remember me?* Of course not. My past rolled down Prichett's Main Street in broad daylight. In a black stretch limo.

It was a good thing that my two best friends, Elise Penny and Annie Carpenter, were with me or I probably would have hijacked the next pickup truck lumbering down the street and ended up somewhere in Canada.

Annie, who'd been catching snowflakes on her tongue, grabbed my hand and held on. Annie may be twenty years younger than me but what she lacks in age she makes up for in wisdom. She's the kind of person who always seems to have one ear tilted toward the sky, as if she's expecting at any moment God is going to whisper something in it. And I'm convinced that He does on a regular basis.

I tried to work up enough saliva so that I could talk, but my mouth had gone as dry as the fields in the middle of July. If you live in Prichett long enough you begin to think in farm metaphors. It started happening to me about three years after I'd moved here, and I look at it as a permanent condition—like crow's feet…or cellulite.

"It can't be *him*." There it was. My voice. Well, a reasonable facsimile anyway. It must have come out at a slightly higher pitch than normal because a flock of blackbirds in the tree over our heads began to rustle around and protest. "Someone must have rented the limo for an anniversary or something."

There was no other reason that a limo could be stopping…right in front of the Cut and Curl. Which happened to be the beauty salon that I owned.

"If there was an anniversary, it would have made the marquee," Elise said. She grabbed my other hand and leaned forward, staring intently at the sleek black vehicle that was now purring alongside the curb.

This was wishful thinking on Elise's part. Her name had been on the marquee for three months now. The marquee was a sacred relic and it hung off the old theater on Main Street like an arm with a compound fracture, announcing all the news that Mayor Candy Lane decided was noteworthy.

Elise had been a contestant in the Proverbs 31 Pageant and had recently won the state title. So far, she'd set a record for having had her name on the marquee the longest. Because she didn't like the attention, I knew she was secretly hoping that someone else would have something happen to them that was *noteworthy* enough for the sign to be changed.

"Not possible," I muttered, staring at the ground. I was beginning to have memory flashes. You know, those little things buried so deep inside that only a reality explosion will bring them to the surface.

And right now I was remembering that Phoebe Caine, a former acquaintance in my life D.A.—During Alex—would spill Everest-size amounts of delicate information when bribed with Godiva chocolates. And this was the woman I'd spoken to on the telephone a month before, making her promise that she wouldn't tell anyone that I'd called.

But this had nothing to do with the limousine. Did it?

"You better go talk to him. He's looking this way," Elise murmured.

"Who's looking this way?" Denial. It's a pitiful thing. You'd think after this many years, I would have figured that out. But no. It had become my first weapon of defense.

"Alex Scott." Annie said the name so matter-of-factly that she could have been talking about Mr. Bender at the hardware store instead of one of the biggest names at the box office.

There was no way he could recognize me at this distance. I'm a hairstylist. I see my reflection in the mirror all day and it's nowhere close to the one that looked back at me when I was in my early twenties. More wrinkles. Not to mention the rest of me. There was more of that, too.

I had the weird, surreal feeling that I was watching one of his movies. The driver, who looked like he was moonlighting from his other job as an NFL linebacker, got out and started unloading luggage from the trunk. Luggage. People were starting to pause in midstep and stare. Limousines in Prichett just weren't that common. Now if someone had parked a combine in front of my shop, no one would have blinked an eye.

I swallowed to dislodge my heart, which had wiggled its way into my throat and was beating ten times faster than usual.

God, can You explain this? I mean, what is this!

Talking to God is something new in my life and it is getting easier and easier for me, thanks to Annie's influence. I'm trying to settle into *listening,* too, but somehow that isn't as easy. I frequently remind myself that God gave me two ears and one mouth and there must have been a good reason for that divine design. But just because I was spending time with God and starting to make peace with my past didn't mean that I wanted to work things out—face-to-face—with it. I hadn't let myself think about Alex for…oh, all right, at least twenty-four hours, which is ridiculous because the last time I'd seen him was ten years ago. I was hit with the sudden urge to escape into a quart of Ben and Jerry's, and never come out. Hiding. I'd turned it into an art form. Esther Crandall, a friend of mine at the Golden Oaks Nursing Home who practically oozes wisdom from every pore, told me that one of God's favorite words is *surprise* and I am now a card-carrying believer that it's true.

The proof was standing next to a black limo. Alex Scott was in Prichett.

Surprise!

He was staring in our direction, his shoulders slightly hunched against the chill in the air. That might have had something to do with the fact that he was dressed for *California* in late October, not for Wisconsin. We knew better. My winter coat was already on red alert, hanging on a hook beside the door with my wool gloves tucked into the pockets.

I could feel Elise and Annie looking at me. My toes suddenly curled inside my shoes as if they'd formed their own survivalist agenda. My brain picked up the signal. *Make a break for it.* Unfortunately, Annie's fingers were still woven into mine. I couldn't run without dragging her along with me and she'd just found out a month ago that she was pregnant with twins. It probably wouldn't be fair to the little newbies to get them involved in my mad dash out of Prichett.

I could tell the second he recognized me. His hand lifted in a hesitant wave and he started walking toward the park, which up until five minutes ago had been a quiet retreat from a stressful morning in which I had to use scissors and half a jar of peanut butter to get a package of bubble gum—chewed—out of a four-year-old girl's hair while her mother watched in an almost catatonic state.

"We'll talk to you later," Elise said, peeling my hand away from hers.

"You can't leave me alone with him." *Breathe, Bernice. In. Out. In. Out.*

"You'll be okay," Annie said, but there was a shadow of a frown between her eyebrows.

"You called him," Elise reminded me.

I had called him. Right before I'd chickened out and told Phoebe, his publicist, *not* to tell him that I'd called.

"I called him but I didn't expect he'd show up here! Where am I going to *put* him?" I demanded. "There is nowhere in this town that I can hide him. Candy probably has a five-pound sack of birdseed with his name engraved on it already."

As I'd said before, Candy Lane was Prichett's mayor. Somewhere in the fine print that outlined her mayoral duties, it must have said something about hunting down unsuspecting tourists and gifting them with a bag of birdseed—she also owns the feed store—or sending them to Sally's Café for a piece of pie. On the house. They had to pay fifty cents if they wanted it à la mode.

My breath stalled again because Alex was a hundred feet away and closing in fast. It isn't fair that some men are hurt-your-eyes good-looking. And it wasn't fair that the years had carefully chiseled character into the lines on his face while they'd used a jackhammer on mine. His hair was shorter than I remembered, but still as dark as espresso. His skin was evenly and disgustingly tanned. And his eyes didn't need tinted contact lenses to make them any bluer. He looked the same...but different.

There were too many years separating us. And every one of them disappeared the second he smiled. "Hi, Bernice."

* * *

Alex Scott was one of those things that happen to other people. Beautiful people. People who are ushered to the head of the line and accept that it's their right. People who own houses scattered all over the world.

But somehow he became something that happened to me. Our paths crossed when I worked in Los Angeles as a hair-stylist for the rich and infamous. Nell, my boss, had been called to a movie set for a hair emergency and as her stylist-in-training—I handed her the curling irons, combs and scissors—she'd made me come along. It turned out the hair emergency belonged to an actress who had tried to trim her own bangs. She'd cut it when it was wet and hadn't allowed for proper shrinkage, so when her hair dried it had climbed up to the top of her forehead.

She was crying and carrying on, and I watched for about ten minutes as everyone tried to alternately encourage, sympathize and cheer her up. Even Nell, who was used to this sort of thing, looked as though *she* was about to cry.

The whole situation was ridiculous and if no one else was going to point that out, then I figured it was my civic duty. "Oh, please! It's not your arm or your leg you cut off, it's just *hair!*"

There was complete silence as everyone in the room gawked at me. Then, someone clapped. Loudly. Deliberately.

It was Alex Scott. I recognized him the minute he'd stood up, unrolling his six-foot-two frame from a chair in the corner. He gave me a mischievous wink. "She's right. Let's speed this up a little, okay? I have a dinner date tonight."

The actress harpooned me with an evil look and then pouted up at him. "A date? You didn't mention that before."

He'd shrugged and I'd tried not to stare. Alex Scott's career was just starting to take off and it occurred to me that the set we'd been called to was for his latest movie.

I shot a nervous glance at Nell. I'd only been working for her for six months and I knew I was dispensable. There were only a few hundred people willing to thank me for my stupidity and jump into my shoes.

The actress was still fuming but at least it was a silent tantrum now. Nell was smiling.

I wondered if she smiled right before she fired her assistants.

"Go ahead and see what you can do," she told me.

Instead of firing me, she handed me her scissors.

The actress began to fuss and fidget, obviously as doubtful about this sudden turn of events as I was.

"You aren't queasy at the sight of blood, are you?" I asked her.

Her eyes narrowed. "Why?"

"Because if you don't sit still, I might accidentally cut your earlobe off or something. I'm new at this."

She sat still.

Working with Nell, I never ceased to be amazed at what constituted a crisis. An extra two pounds from a weekend of pasta overload. A blemish erupting on a forehead. These were the things that normal women lived with every day and they had to pluck their own eyebrows besides. I started to wonder if I had the patience to deal with this kind of thing on a regular basis the way Nell did.

"You see, with the shape of your face you could be bald and still look beautiful," I told her, hearing the frustration creep into my voice. *Yup, that tone will win friends and influence people, Bernice.* As far as I was concerned, she had no right to complain about her looks, shrunken bangs or not. Not when some people—present company included—had features that were put together like a human Picasso. "You don't need the bangs anyway. Watch this."

A half hour later there was a crowd of people in the

trailer and a very happy actress admiring her reflection in the mirror.

I turned to give Nell her scissors back. She shook her head.

"You keep them, sweetie. I have a feeling that you're going to need them." Laughing, she walked out the door.

"Yeah, famous people love to get yelled at," I muttered under my breath.

"So, how about dinner?"

I heard the question but continued to pack away my toolbox full of supplies.

"You do eat, don't you?"

I looked up and there was Alex Scott, standing two feet away. And he was looking right at me. "You're kidding, right?" I said the first words that came into my mind. "Does it look like I pass up that last piece of cheesecake?"

"Happens to be my favorite, too. So what do you say?"

What do I say? What do I say to Alex Scott—*Alex Scott*—asking me out for dinner? I say that I somehow got sucked into an alternate universe, that's what I say.

But even in an alternate universe, I'm sure that the beautiful people only ask other beautiful people out for dinner. "Why?"

"Because I've been forgetting some things that maybe you can help me remember."

"Um, Bernice?"

With that first date flashing before my eyes, I was only dimly aware of Elise squeezing my hand to bring me back to reality.

And the reality was that Alex had found me. Again.

"Annie, you did need some help with those curtains this afternoon, didn't you? We better scoot." Elise had to use one hand to peel the other one away from the death grip I had on it.

"I do need help." Annie was trying really hard not to grin.

Everyone looked at me, waiting expectantly. Introductions. I could do those.

"Alex, these are my friends, Elise Penny and Annie Carpenter," I said, squeezing every drop of polite etiquette into my voice instead of screaming at him. *Whatareyoudoinghere?*

"It's nice to meet you. I'm Alex Scott."

Honestly, was it even necessary to say it? Thanks to cable, everyone with a television set knew who he was.

"I thought we were going to pick out fabric together," I said, narrowing my eyes at Elise and Annie. Subliminal message coming through. *Don't you dare leave me!*

"You two probably have a lot of catching up to do," Elise said.

"You've got that right," Alex said cheerfully.

As if on a silent cue, we all fell into step together. Bless their hearts, Annie and Elise could sense that I was still poised to bolt and they positioned themselves protectively on either side of me as we walked toward the salon. I was on my lunch break and my next appointment was in forty-five minutes. I calculated the time it would take to push Alex and his luggage back into the limo and finish what was left of my tuna sandwich. I'd probably even have a few extra minutes to clean out my comb drawer.

"I'll call you two later." *As soon as I get rid of him.*

"Sounds great." Annie linked her arm through Elise's and she did a funny hop-skip step as they walked away that reminded me of Dorothy in *The Wizard of Oz. Lions and tigers and movie stars. Oh, my!*

Now we were alone. But not. Alex was oblivious to the attention we were getting as he looked up and down Prichett's Main Street, absorbing his surroundings. I tried to see it through his eyes and wondered if he'd be able to appreciate it. For the past ten years, this was the view I saw out my window every day, both from the salon and my upstairs apartment. It wasn't perfect but I loved it. Maybe that's *why* I loved it.

Prichett is one of those blink-and-you-miss-it towns. At one point in time, it had been a thriving little farming community but now it was gasping for air, its respirator a farm-implement factory that employed half the town in some capacity. Even though at least one business a year closed its doors and took a piece out of the town's heart, I never got the feeling that it affected the town's soul. There was a *sameness* to Prichett that gave me a sense of stability.

"So this is where you've been hiding." Alex shook his head.

Hiding? That was the trouble with Alex. He always seemed to know things about me that I hadn't quite figured out for myself.

"I know what you're thinking…" At least I thought I could make a pretty good guess. "You're thinking I could have picked a better spot."

"Are you kidding? I'm thinking that I'm insanely jealous."

My palms were clammy and I shoved them into the pockets of my jacket. This was not good. Increased heart rate. Sweaty palms. Alex was having that curious effect on me again. The one that should have short-circuited and died about twenty years ago but instead was looking more like it was outfitted with the same batteries as a certain pink, drum-banging bunny. It just keeps going.

Lord, Mayday! Mayday!

We were still the objects of everyone's attention. People were pretending not to stare, which just made it more obvious that they were pretending not to stare.

"So, what's it going to be, boss?" the limo driver growled at us. I'd forgotten he was there.

"I'll catch up with you later, Digger."

Digger? Some parents have a lot to answer for, that's all I can say.

The driver's gaze did a swift once-over down Prichett's

Main Street, just as Alex's had a few minutes ago. "Are you sure?" he asked doubtfully.

"I'm sure."

With a disdainful snort that should have gotten his fancy hat taken away, the driver jumped into the front seat and the limo cruised away. Leaving the luggage on the sidewalk. Leaving *Alex* on the sidewalk.

"Wait a second. Where is he going?"

"I assume back to Chicago."

"But you're still here." All right, I have a genius for pointing out the obvious.

"I'm due for a vacation." Alex's eyes had a funny glow in them. For a split second, the glow settled over me. Warmed me. Then I shook it away so I could think straight.

"In Prichett?" I squawked. "Why?"

"Because you called and wanted to know how I was doing."

"So?" Another squawk. I should have been cast in a pirate movie. *The part of the green-and-blue macaw will be played by Bernice Strum....*

"So I came to tell you."

Chapter Two

Without thinking, I snagged Alex's hand and pulled him into the salon.

"This is crazy—"

"You own this place?" Alex immediately began to prowl around, forcing me to follow him. His movements were easy and relaxed, while I did the jitterbug in his footsteps.

"Don't change the subject—"

"How many people work for you?"

"Three. Me, myself and I," I said, exasperated. "Now will you just pinch me and wake me up from this dream I'm having so I can go back to my ordinary life, minus the handsome celebrity?"

"Mmm, a dream. That's promising. You could have said nightmare. And where would you like me to pinch you?" He grinned.

Shields up!

"Aggha." That's all I could manage and I know that the spell check on my computer could never have found that particular word.

He grinned. "You look a little shocked, Bern."

"That's because, number one, Phoebe said you were in

Australia, and number two, she told me she wouldn't mention that I called. I can't believe she hasn't retired yet, by the way. She was ancient when…"

When we met. I didn't want to revisit the past. Denial, remember? It works for me.

"Phoebe *is* retired, but she house-sits for me when I'm on location. What a coincidence, huh? That she was there when you called?"

I felt a sudden urge to visit Esther at the nursing home. Maybe she could make sense of this. For the past few months I'd been visiting her at the Golden Oaks and she'd been helping me sort through and discard things in my past that were weighing me down. I knew now that there was no such thing as good luck or bad luck or coincidence. But this was just too…I don't know what. Terrifying, that's what it was. Had I missed something? Wasn't the Christian life supposed to be about tranquility and peace? The twenty-third Psalm, right? "He makes me lie down in green pastures. He leads me beside quiet waters."

I need my green pastures and quiet waters right about now, Lord.

"No coincidence. I just called because I wondered how you were doing," I said defensively.

"After you ran out on me twenty years ago. Wait, that would have been the first time you ran out on me. The second time was ten years ago in Chicago, wasn't it? This must be like a ten-year-class-reunion type of thing for you, Bern. It got me curious. Why you called out of the blue like that."

I knew why I'd called him. It would have been hard enough to talk to him over the phone with a few thousand miles separating us, but with him right here in front of me, it was next to impossible. How was I supposed to tell Alex he'd fathered a child that I'd given up for adoption? And that she was now part of my life and might eventually ask about her birth father?

"So you decided to travel from L.A. to Wisconsin to find out." The sudden urge to launch myself into his arms was overwhelming. I knew if I closed my eyes, I'd remember how they felt around me. I was on dangerous ground, that was sure, scrambling for a toehold.

I grabbed on to God. What had I done without Him all my life? With all the times over the past few months that I'd clung to Him like a baby opossum, I wondered if He was getting a little tired of it. Annie would probably say no. Well, that was good, because if He was going to continue to tip my life upside down, He had to know that I was going to hang on to Him for dear life, right?

"I told you, I'm on vacation. Where did you find these hair dryers? They look like they belong in Dr. Frankenstein's laboratory." He poured himself a cup of coffee. "Is this decaf?"

"No, it's regular," I said through gritted teeth as he shrugged and drank it anyway.

"I haven't eaten since five o'clock this morning."

"Really."

"I saw a café down the street."

"Absolutely not." He couldn't go to Sally's. I'd seen what the town did to Elise when she was a contestant for the pageant. Parades. Billboards. What on earth would they do with someone like Alex? They'd probably empty the town bank account and bronze the entire sidewalk where he'd walked.

"I'll be back."

Wait, wasn't that Schwarzenegger's line? *Stick to your own movies, buddy.*

I hurried to catch up with him as he headed out the door and almost tripped over the suitcases still on the sidewalk. "You can't leave these here."

"They'll be fine. This looks like a town filled with honest people."

Honest, yes. Desperate in their need for something that would lift them out of obscurity, absolutely. I couldn't guarantee that Alex's possessions wouldn't end up on eBay by the end of the day. Just to generate some attention.

Like a beagle on the trail of a bunny, Alex lifted his nose and started down the street. Every Tuesday morning, Sally makes homemade cinnamon rolls and sells them for fifty cents apiece. It sounds reasonable, but she also raises the price of coffee seventy-five cents. The whole town smells like a bakery and we respond like Pavlov's dogs and eagerly pay the difference. Donald Trump could learn a few things from Sally Rapinski.

I pushed the luggage out of the way with my foot as I jogged to keep up with him. Just the sight of that luggage— and not one overnight bag but a whole matched set—added another reason why Alex Scott could not vacation in Prichett.

"There isn't a motel in town. Where are you planning to stay on this alleged vacation?" I panted. My lungs were reminding me that they weren't used to this. Exercise always ranks either one or two on my list of New Year's resolutions every year, sliding dismally to the bottom by mid-February, only to disappear completely by Easter. Too many chocolate bunnies and marshmallow chicks to compete with. Why even try?

He didn't break stride. "No motel? Really?"

He chuckled and my palms started to sweat again.

I had a sudden epiphany. "There *is* a bed-and-breakfast. Not four-star or anything like you're used to, though." Desperate times called for desperate measures so I squashed a twinge of guilt for mentioning the only place open for guests in Prichett during the off-season.

Everyone in town referred to it as the Lightning Strike Inn. Charity O'Malley owned it and she had to be as old as the Victorian itself. Prichett's houses were mostly modest one- and two-story structures but the Lightning Strike was on the historical register because it was a true painted lady from eons ago. The first banker had built it for his new bride, when everyone thought that Prichett would someday be the capital of Wisconsin. Delusion rears its ugly head!

Charity's husband had passed away before I moved to town but from what I've been told, instead of selling the house and buying a condo in Florida, she had the upstairs remodeled with two guest rooms and a bathroom, hammered a sign next to the mailbox by the road and started advertising it as a bed-and-breakfast in the *Prichett Press*. The Weeping Willow Inn was what she'd named it, although there was no weeping willow in sight. There *was* a twisted-looking crab apple by the front steps.

The bed-and-breakfast may have been a good idea except for two things. The first thing was a rumor that Charity had adopted a noisy bird that allowed the guests to get as much sleep as Ebenezer Scrooge on Christmas Eve. The second thing was that the house kept getting struck by lightning. So far, it had happened three years in a row. The farmers that lined the counter at Sally's Café tried to guess which storm was going to produce the next strike that would singe Charity's steepled roof.

"Bed-and-breakfast?" Alex's hand reached toward the door to Sally's. "Sounds good to me."

I summoned the adrenaline that I knew was lounging around somewhere inside me and pushed in front of him. "Are you sure you want to do this? It isn't a vacation if you have hundreds of people clamoring for your autograph or picture, is it? I have half a tuna sandwich in my shop. I'll share."

"Hundreds of people? In a café the size of my living room?" Alex's eyebrow lifted. "Right. And you should have offered the tuna fish ten minutes ago. I would have taken you up on it."

We took our first step together and got wedged in the

doorway. I rotated one hip and let him through, sure that my face was as red as my jacket.

Sally was standing behind the counter with a pot of coffee in hand. Lined up in front of her like canned goods in a pantry were the retired farmers that made the café their second home. She didn't even glance our way.

Neither did the farmers.

Neither did the other people sitting in the café, absorbed in their newspapers and cinnamon rolls.

"I hope I have enough ink in my pen," Alex whispered.

There was something wrong with this picture. Sally should already have Alex's picture on the Prichett's Pride and Joy Wall by the coffeepot, ready and waiting for his autograph. Mayor Candy should be standing nearby, ready to greet us with a bag of sunflower seeds tucked under her arm. Maybe they were planning an ambush. As we were sitting down, someone was probably organizing a parade and an ice cream social....

"What can I getcha, Bernice?"

Sally was like me, a control freak who not only owned her own business but made sure she was there from the time it opened until the last customer left in the evening. She grudgingly employed waitresses only because arthritis was slowing her down and she couldn't move as fast as she used to. There was a time when she'd operated the café completely on her own, just as I did the salon.

"I'll have a BLT and a chocolate shake."

"Sounds great. Make mine on wheat, please." Alex smiled and Sally finally looked at him. Like he was a bug who'd turned up in the oatmeal.

"Wheat." She repeated the word.

"Or whole grain."

Alex, Alex, Alex. Why don't you just ask for a veggie burger and a smoothie made with organic bananas and tofu?

He had no way of knowing that Sally still put a pat of real butter on every hamburger that landed on the griddle in the kitchen. This *is* the dairy state, after all. Judging from the expression on Sally's face, I knew he was going to get a BLT on white. And he was going to like it.

What was going on? My town wasn't acting like my town. Sally's life centered around the café but I know she went to an occasional movie. She had to recognize Alex. She pivoted sharply and did her own interpretation of *stomping* back to the kitchen. And I was officially in an alternate reality.

"Friendly little town," Alex murmured.

I saw the sparkle in his eyes but refused to get caught up in a humor-fest with him. That's exactly what had launched our relationship the first time and now I could recognize the signs. Honestly, Alex Scott should have a Surgeon General's warning tattooed on his arm.

This man may be dangerous. Any contact with him could have long-term effects on a woman's heart…including but not limited to sweaty palms, rapid pulse and the loss of her ability to think straight.

The door to Sally's opened and ushered in a gust of cold air. I glanced up and bearing down on us like a torpedo in plaid flannel and denim was Prichett's mayor.

Sally may have acted strange but I could count on Candy to pull me back into reality. Funny, though, no bag of birdseed tucked under her arm…

"Are those your suitcases cluttering the sidewalk by the Cut and Curl?" She stopped right next to our table and glared down at Alex.

"I thought they'd be safe there while we grabbed some lunch," Alex said, smiling up at her.

"Alex, this is Candy Lane, Prichett's mayor—" I tried to interject.

"Of course they're *safe* there." Candy looked thoroughly offended. "But they're a hazard to pedestrians. If you don't get rid of them, I'm going to have to cite you for violating ordinance number B31, section eighteen."

Alex laughed. Candy didn't.

"Candy, you can't be serious." I tried again but Candy shifted her weight and didn't crack a smile.

"I'll give you fifteen minutes to remove them or they'll be *confiscated.*" With a short nod at me, she swept out. Do not pass go. Do not collect your bag of birdseed.

The temperature in Prichett may have been chilly but now it was downright arctic. Not exactly a warm place to vacation. And I had no idea why. As far as I knew, no ordinance B31, section eighteen even existed. Maybe Candy had written it on the way to the café.

"I have no idea what's going on," I muttered, feeling strangely embarrassed. Maybe a tad more embarrassed than I would have felt if the whole town had been waving paper and pens in his face.

"I do. They're protecting you."

"Protecting me? Don't be silly. Everyone knows that I don't need to be protected." I'd been living on my own for…well, a long time. And only in Prichett for the past ten years. My roots weren't nearly as deep as most of the people who lived in the area. For the first five years I'd lived here, I was regarded cautiously, like a strange weed that had popped up unexpectedly in their little garden. I guess at some point they got used to me.

Alex stood up and for a second I thought he was going to leave.

"Um, could I have everyone's attention, please?" he said. Loudly.

The stools at the counter swiveled on cue as the farmers

swung around to face him. The rest of the people sitting at the tables all looked in our direction.

"I just want to know right now how many guys I'm going to have to arm wrestle to take Bernice Strum out for dinner tonight?"

Hands shot up around the room. I stopped counting at eight. Closing my eyes, I prayed once again for those green pastures and quiet waters that God had promised me!

"Now do you believe me?" He sat down just as Sally marched back with our food. I dared a look at the plate she dropped in front of Alex. BLT on white.

"That's the palest-looking wheat bread I've ever seen," he said, winking at me.

His milk shake was a bit on the anemic side, too. In fact, it looked suspiciously like vanilla. Sally was giving a whole new meaning to the term *food fight*.

"Okay, what have you been doing? Using a poster of my face as a dartboard? Why is everyone circling you like a wagon train under attack?"

The sip of shake I'd just taken took a quick detour from my esophagus into my lungs. Nothing had prepared me for this. A phone call was one thing, but to be sitting two feet away from Alex with only our BLTs separating us, was a whole different story.

Alex was right. Incredibly, annoyingly, unbelievably right. And suddenly, as if someone yanked the curtain in my brain to the side, I knew what was happening. I knew why Sally was probably in the alley, stirring a barrel of hot tar and why everyone would gladly part with some of their ruffled feathers to roll Alex in before he was chased out of town.

The only thing that made sense out of the way people were reacting to Alex's arrival was that they'd taken one look at him and connected the DNA dots. Heather. She looked like him.

She may have inherited my green eyes, but his genetic code had waged war with mine and fortunately his had won. Heather was beautiful. Not only on the outside, but on the inside, too.

And just this past summer, Heather had used all the brand-new Internet technology at her disposal to find her birth mother. Me.

Chapter Three

But I couldn't tell him that. Not yet. After so many years, how did a person drop that bombshell into a conversation? *By the way, remember when I left twenty years ago? I didn't realize I was pregnant. I decided not to tell you and I gave the baby up for adoption. I didn't think you were serious about me...about us...and I was too scared to take the risk.*

"Alex, why are you here? Really?" The tangled threads of the past, the ones that God and I had been painstakingly snipping over the past few months, were starting to wrap themselves around my feet again, threatening to trip me up.

"I told you—"

"You're on vacation," I finished, rolling my eyes. "Well, those of us who *aren't* on vacation need to go back to work. I have an appointment in five minutes."

How could I get rid of him? Maybe a case of frostbite from Prichett's cold shoulder would discourage him from staying.

"I'll tag along. I have some suitcases to move before they get confiscated. Ordinance B31, section eighteen."

It wasn't fair that he had a sense of humor about all this. I searched for mine and realized it had probably left at the same time the limo did.

Alex paid the bill and left a generous tip for Sally. The skittering up my spine told me that everyone was watching us as we walked to the door. Alex thought that everyone was protecting me, but I realized that I was protecting him, making sure that he was in front of me on the way out. One never knew when a rogue dinner roll could fly out of nowhere and hit someone in the back of the head. I wasn't going to take any chances.

"So where is this bed-and-breakfast you were telling me about?"

"The Lightning—um, the Weeping Willow? It's three blocks down, turn right and it's the last house at the end of the street." Another twinge of guilt but I rationalized it away, reminding myself that it was too late in the season for thunderstorms. At least if he wasn't safe from Charity's bird, he was safe from another lightning strike. I could live with that.

"So, how about dinner?"

Why was it that I couldn't remember where I'd left my car keys or why I'd walked into the kitchen, but I could remember that those had been the exact words Alex had said to me the day we met? Another question to ask God when we finally met face-to-face. I'd started a list.

"I can't."

"You have a date."

I almost laughed. A date. *Oh, those gross brown fruit things that look like crayfish with no legs? Because that's the only kind of date Bernice Strum is familiar with….*

"No, just plans I can't change."

"Where do you live? Maybe I can stop by later this evening."

"Look up."

"What?"

"Up." I repeated the word patiently, even though my heart

had just shifted into high gear. I didn't want him to stop by later. Stopping by meant conversation. Conversation would lead to questions like, *What's been happening in your life?* Which would lead to answers like, *Our daughter found me after twenty years and she's smart and beautiful and she has your smile....*

Alex was looking around, trying to figure out if I was nesting in one of the oak trees in the park or maybe on the roof of the post office.

"Do you see those windows? I live there. Above the salon."

"I thought you always wanted a house with a picket fence."

Something snagged in my throat. It took a minute before I could squeeze some words out around it. "It made sense to be close to where I work."

"This town is the size of a nine-hole golf course," Alex pointed out helpfully. "I can't imagine that anywhere you lived would be that far from work."

The house I'd had my eye on for years wasn't for sale but I wasn't going to tell him that. I couldn't pay rent on the building plus make a house payment. Even with some creative stretching, my budget couldn't perform those kinds of fiscal gymnastics. When I'd moved to Prichett and opened the salon, I told myself the apartment would be temporary but somehow it had become my "temporary" home for the past ten years.

"Well, your suitcases are still here. All five—" how long was he planning to stay? "—of them." Again, stating the obvious is a gift of mine but I hoped Alex would take the hint.

"There probably isn't a taxi service here, is there?"

"Munroe has one but it's half an hour away. By the time they got here…"

Alex's hand lifted. "I get the picture. Small town. No extras."

"Prichett has plenty of *extras*." I had to correct him because the snowflakes returned as if on cue. Tiny white parachutes that drifted down and got caught in Alex's hair. "Just not the kind that you expect."

"Intriguing." Alex's box-office smile surfaced for a moment and he gathered up his luggage. "I'll see you later."

I had just enough time to unlock the door and turn the lights on when the bells jingled and Mindy came in.

"How are you today, Bernice?"

For Mindy Lewis, this was not a polite greeting. She wasn't inquiring about my overall emotional well-being, either. *Thank goodness.* No, Mindy wanted specifics. Do I have an upset stomach? A low-grade fever? The sniffles? In other words, do I have anything wrong with me that has the potential to jump track via the germ train and get her sick?

"I'm fine. Have a seat, Mindy." I smiled and patted the chair by the sink. Snapping the cape around her neck, I fought the irresistible urge to cough.

Be a grown-up, Bernice.

"I saw a man dragging a bunch of suitcases down the street," Mindy said. "But I didn't get a good look at him. From the direction he was headed, it looked like he was going to the Lightning Strike."

If grapevines had taproots, Prichett's would be Mindy.

I tried to postpone the inevitable by changing the subject. I wasn't about to tell Mindy that Alex Scott had chosen Prichett over the French Riviera for his vacation. "How's Greta doing these days?"

Greta is Mindy's niece, her brother's youngest daughter. There aren't many teenagers like Greta in Prichett. She dresses in black from head to toe, but that's just to throw people off. She designed Elise's dress for the pageant and I know she has a colorful soul.

"Tired lately. Senior year, you know. She's supposed to

find out any day now if she's been accepted by that college in New York."

The door opened and Jim Briggs stepped inside. Mindy began to bounce up and down so much that I was tempted to make her sit in the elephant chair. It came equipped with a seat belt for rambunctious toddlers but there were many times I was tempted to stuff fidgety adults into it, too.

If there were an eligible bachelor in Prichett, it would be Jim. He'd sold the family farm and started an excavating business, which must have been successful because a few years ago he built a brand-new, two-story house just outside the city limits. I tried really hard not to drool over the picket fence.

Jim and I had met shortly after I'd moved to town. He'd shocked me by stopping in at the salon even though the majority of the men in Prichett seem to regard personal grooming the same way a stray dog would. When they got too shaggy, they'd go to the barbershop, which had the macho name of the Buzz and Blade. I never confessed to anyone that that was the reason, in a moment of attempted wit, that I named my salon the Cut and Curl. The trouble was, no one got it. So much for being witty.

For reasons that I didn't want to question, Jim had passed the Buzz and Blade that day and stopped in to see if I had time to cut his hair. His reason became obvious while he was in the shampoo chair. His warm, chocolate-brown eyes stared up at me as he'd tried to woo the new girl in town. I may have been flattered, except that his unique brand of romance was telling me that since we were both over twenty-one and single—and because I had a past the town could only guess at—maybe we should *get together.* As an afterthought, he mentioned pizza.

So I dyed his hair green.

He ran all the way to the Buzz and Blade and I don't quite

know what happened after that. All I know is that Jim has avoided me ever since and no one else—the cowards—had asked me out on a date since.

And now here he was, shaking snow out of his hair and pouring himself a cup of coffee.

"That's regular," I told him.

He made a face. "Is there anything else?"

I'd seen Jim in church just this past Sunday. Elise told me he'd been attending for a few years now but I wouldn't have known that because I just started to go to church a few months ago myself.

"Is there something I can do for you?" I asked cautiously. *Wax your eyebrows? Dye your hair green?*

He smiled. "Two things."

Uh-oh. For his sake, one of those things better not be pizza. I could tell by the way that Mindy's body had gone completely still that her brain was already set on Record.

"I just joined the PAC and Candy told me I should talk to you about what subcommittee to serve on."

PAC was the Prichett Advancement Council. Candy had started it shortly after she was elected mayor. Most of the businesses on Main Street were represented, the Cut and Curl included. Candy had finagled me into serving as vice chairman right at the beginning and ten years later I was still the vice chairman. Not because I was such a great vice chairman but because no one else wanted the job. The other committee members had the responsibility of bringing brownies or making sure there were disposable coffee cups for the meeting. I had to convince everyone that change was a good thing. Brownies were definitely easier.

"We don't have subcommittees." What was Candy thinking? "We all just kind of pitch in and do whatever needs to be done."

"She mentioned there was a new committee forming because of the grant the city received last week. Something about the arts?"

"We got that grant?" I couldn't believe it. Prichett was barely a dot on the Wisconsin map and we'd actually received the grant that Candy had applied for two years ago?

"So she says. She's pretty excited about it."

I could only imagine.

"A grant for what?" Mindy interrupted.

Sorry, were we talking too fast for you to take mental notes?

"Candy applied for a special state grant that pays for something in the area of the arts. If we got the grant, we decided to put a sculpture in the park."

"That's a good idea." Mindy's head bobbed enthusiastically, almost dislodging the clips I'd put in her hair. "Especially since we're getting new playground equipment in the spring."

The new playground equipment was compliments of Elise. When she won the pageant, she received a check to donate to her favorite cause. Since the playground equipment had been in the park before the invention of a neat little thing called plastic, it definitely needed replacing.

"What's the sculpture going to look like?" Jim poured himself another cup of coffee. I was tempted to tell him that I hoped he had a good book handy, because with that much caffeine speeding through his system, he wasn't going to fall asleep until Saturday.

"We haven't decided yet." Honestly, the chances of receiving the grant had been so small we hadn't even discussed it. "I suppose that's why Candy wants a separate committee."

In a way that was good because our PAC meetings lasted three or four hours as it was. It may have had something to do with the fact that Prichett's idea of advancement was one step forward and three steps back. As vice chairman, it was up to me to nudge them into taking the one step forward. Sometimes the nudging took months.

"If you don't mind, I'll put myself on that committee, then," Jim said. "It sounds like fun."

Fun? The words "PAC" and "fun" just couldn't exist in the same sentence as far as I was concerned.

"I will, too," Mindy chimed in.

"You have to be a business owner to be in PAC," I reminded her. I took out the blow dryer and glanced at Jim before I turned it on. "You said there were two things?"

"Yeah, I also need a trim. Do you have a few minutes between appointments?"

I could tell Mindy wanted to linger and find out if there was something going on between me and Jim by the way she counted out my tip in change instead of parting with the five-dollar bill I saw peeking out of her purse.

"Oh, Greta needs an appointment to get her hair done for the Senior Tea," Mindy remembered. I may have denial down to an art, but Mindy has perfected delay tactics.

I checked my appointment book. The Senior Tea was one of the highlights of the year and my schedule was always tight that day. According to legend, *The Tea* started years ago as the final exam for a chapter on etiquette in the home economics class. Somewhere along the way, finger sandwiches and punch served in foam cups evolved into its present-day extravaganza—a rite of passage for the senior girls that gave them the chance to wear formal dresses, have their hair done and sip tea out of bone china cups in Charity O'Malley's music room.

It had gotten so popular that I had the girls calling me over the summer to book their hair appointments but I knew I would squeeze Greta in.

"I'll schedule her at seven-thirty before my first appointment. It's on the early side but otherwise I'm booked solid," I said.

"I'll tell her." Reluctantly, Mindy took a slow, measured step away from the counter. Jim was already in the shampoo chair. A trim, huh? Where was the hair dye? Maybe orange this time, to coordinate with the Thanksgiving napkins…

The bells jingled mournfully as she left and I walked over to Jim.

"Okay, spill it. What's going on?"

"On?" He frowned up at me, his expression way too innocent.

That was it. Two attractive, overly confident men in one day were plenty. More than plenty. "Take your pick—green or orange?"

Panic flared briefly in his eyes. "I just want you to be careful. That's all."

"Careful?" I was confused. "About what kind of sculpture we should have for the park?"

"About that guy you were with at Sally's."

Alex. He was warning me about Alex?

"And this would be your business…*why?*"

"I can put two and two together."

And come up with eight.

"Or should I say one and one?"

Under normal circumstances, if someone would have shouldered their way into my life and given me advice that I didn't want, I would have spun the chair around so many times that he would have experienced a g-force. Now I felt a familiar nudge inside and I knew Jesus wouldn't approve.

I sighed. "You're talking about Heather."

"I saw you in church with her a while back. She looks like you. And him. Listen, Bernice, I know you're right and that this is none of my business, but I always thought somewhere down the line someone broke your heart."

"So, the little pizza party you invited me to when I moved

to town was supposed to be a Band-Aid?" I asked, surprised that that little wound still hurt.

"I'm sorry about that." Now Jim sighed. "I was just being stupid. You wouldn't believe how many times I've regretted that. But…just be careful. Now, go ahead and dye my hair green if it makes you feel better."

He was being protective of me. Just like Candy and Sally and the retired farmers in the café, who all went to the Buzz and Blade but knew who I was. There was a warm and fuzzy chenille feeling inside of me at the thought.

"How about a nice trim? We'll skip the dye for the next time you ignore my No Trespassing sign, okay?"

After he left, I still had one more appointment and then I had to drive over to the Golden Oaks Nursing Home. Once a month I donated a few hours and cut the residents' hair and then ate dinner with them. It also gave me a chance to spend more time with Esther and her husband, John.

Should I check on Alex? I chewed on my bottom lip as my brain and my heart tried to come up with an acceptable compromise. The irony of Jim's warning came back to mock me. He'd assumed that Alex had broken *my* heart. Assumed that for someone like Alex to have fallen for someone like me would have been impossible. I'd assumed the same thing, which was why I'd left him. Knowing my heart was going to get broken, I'd simply saved him the trouble and done it myself.

Chapter Four

I sat in my car for fifteen minutes trying to decide if I should stop by Charity's. Hard to believe that when I woke up this morning, I thought the most challenging part of my day was going to be Mindy's one o'clock appointment.

I put the car in Drive and inched my way down Main Street, pretty sure that I saw a kid on a tricycle pass me on the sidewalk.

"Fine." I huffed the word out loud and made a quick right turn at the last second onto Lily Road.

Charity's house was a bright spot of color, even surrounded as it was by the faded colors of fall. It was painted a cheerful buttery yellow, its gingerbread trim accented with a soothing ivory coupled with soft shades of sage and ochre. What gave it an unexpected touch of whimsy was the crimson front door that greeted her guests where the cobbled walkway ended.

Weirdly enough, right before I pressed the doorbell, I heard it ringing inside the house.

"Bernice!" Charity opened the door and greeted me like a long-lost relative. She was small and birdlike, her entire body enveloped in a lavender tasseled shawl that hung past her knees. She wore blue eye shadow and there was a brush of peach face powder on her cheeks, like a fine layer of dust on a piano. Pulling me down to her level, she brushed her face against mine. I caught the unmistakable scent of rose water.

"Bernice?" Alex suddenly darted into view farther down the hallway. He looked slightly rumpled and extremely glad to see me. And extremely handsome. Once again awe struggled with irritation. I mean, think about this. Does a woman really want to be with a man who's better-looking than she is?

"I just stopped by to make sure you were settled." Yes, I was defensive. Call it self-preservation against the pair of gorgeous blue eyes locked on me.

Charity chuckled. "Of course he's settled, dear. I gave him my best room. The one with the fireplace. He's from *California*, you know."

At least Charity seemed to be treating him well. Maybe the grapevine hadn't sent out runners to the side streets yet. Somehow, though, I sensed that it wouldn't make a difference to Charity. She didn't have many honest-to-goodness guests at the Lightning Strike—oops, the Weeping Willow and…

"'Blessed are the poor in spirit, for theirs is the kingdom of heaven.'"

The words blared out of nowhere and I jumped. Charity put a calming hand on my arm.

"Come in and sit down. Murphy and I were just having tea with Mr. Scott." I glanced at my watch as Charity shuffled past me.

Alex was at my side in a heartbeat. "You have time for *tea*, right, Bernice?" he whispered in my ear, his fingers wrapping around my elbow.

"Enjoying your vacation?" I whispered.

"Mrs. O'Malley is fine," he whispered back. "It's Murphy that I'm not too sure about. But then, he's probably the reason why you sent me here instead of the Super 8, right?"

"There is no Super 8," I reminded him under my breath.

"You're looking very pretty today!" The words were chortled loudly just as we reached the doorway to the old-fashioned sitting room.

"Is he talking to you or me?" I murmured.

Alex's response was to lightly pinch my arm. I yipped in surprise.

"Murphy, you're such a charmer," Charity chuckled.

I looked around the room for Charity's other guest but all I saw was a grouping of empty watered-silk furniture swathed in plastic.

"'Charm is deceptive and beauty is fleeting,'" the invisible Murphy shouted disapprovingly.

"And my beauty fled years ago!" Charity laughed agreeably.

I headed toward an oversize chair by the fireplace but just as I was about to sit down there was a flash of white and a rush of air several inches from my face.

"Blessed is the man who does not sit in the seat of mockers."

I froze in place and blinked. There was an enormous white cockatoo sitting in the exact spot that I was just about to claim. His feathers lifted to create a huge ruffle around his face and he clicked his enormous gray beak.

"You're paraphrasing again, Murphy," Charity said with a disappointed shake of her head. "You're supposed to be working on the Beatitudes now, not the Psalms. Please concentrate."

Charity's noisy bird was apparently not a rumor, after all. I'd imagined something…smaller. Like one of those little blue-and-white parakeets. Something in a *cage*.

"You can sit over here, Bernice." Charity patted the cushion next to her. Alex, I noticed, had picked the chair farthest from Murphy.

"I only have a few minutes," I said, watching out of the corner of my eye as Murphy took little marching steps up the arm of the chair. A bird who had more Scripture memorized than I did. It wasn't fair. I loved reading the Bible and I valiantly tried to memorize verses—there were three-by-five cards taped to practically every surface in my apartment—but so far all I had down was a whopping three. Annie cautioned me not to make memorization something to beat myself up over—did she know me, or what?—and said to think of them as "grace graffiti."

"Are you going over to the Golden Oaks, dear?" Charity asked.

How did she know that? Was my daily schedule posted somewhere in town? It was definitely worth looking into.

She lifted a beautiful china teapot and poured hot tea into a cup for me, then carefully refilled the other two on the tray. I'd never been a tea drinker—I drink coffee out of a mug that could double as a thermos—but there was something so quaint and sweet about a dainty cup decorated with tiny violets that I was momentarily swayed.

"What is the Golden Oaks?" Alex accepted the cup she offered and snagged a sugar cookie off the tray on the coffee table to go with it.

"The nursing home outside of town." Charity answered Alex's question before I could. "Bernice goes there a few times a month and gives free haircuts."

"Really." Alex smiled slightly.

I could read his mind. Future ammunition.

"So how long have you been Bernice's beau, Mr. Scott?" Charity asked.

"Bernice's beau!" Murphy repeated, and then made a noise that sounded like he was choking on a cracker.

"He's not—" Without thinking, I took a quick, very undainty swallow of tea, which burned a path all the way down my throat.

Charity's eyes were as bright and unnerving as her cockatoo's as they searched my face. She smiled benignly. "You make a lovely couple."

Alex lifted his cup and waved at me with his pinkie finger.

I had to run away. But this time, I knew I couldn't go very far. My roots in Prichett weren't as deep as some, but like it or not, they were anchored there by my responsibilities and I couldn't just pull them up, shake them off and relocate to an Alex-less place. But at the very least, I could leave Charity's.

"I really should go. They're expecting me by five." Probably breaking several unwritten laws about proper tea etiquette, I downed what was left in my cup and stood up, smoothing wrinkles out of my skirt that weren't there. I still hadn't called Elise and Annie, and I knew they'd be beside themselves with curiosity about Alex.

"'The Lord bless you and keep you,'" Murphy intoned, then cackled delightedly and belted out, "Bye-bye, baby!"

"I'm going with you," Alex decided.

"Take your time, Mr. Scott. I'll leave the door unlocked until ten, then you'll have to climb through the basement window around back."

"'Enter by the narrow gate...'" Murphy began.

I didn't hear the rest because Alex practically pushed me out of the room.

"You can't come with me," I grumbled as he towed me toward the escape door at the end of the hallway. I discovered that digging my heels in on a polished hardwood floor was an exercise in futility.

"I can tell that bird doesn't like me. Animals *never* like me."

I stopped so quickly that Alex bumped into me. He smelled a bit like lemon furniture polish and rose water. "Oh, please. Don't give me that," I said, annoyed with him. "*Everyone* loves you. Babies. Second-graders. Elderly women. You can charm the birds out of the trees."

"Not all birds," Alex said darkly. "I won't get in your way. Scout's honor."

"Don't try to tell me you were a Boy Scout." I rolled my eyes.

"I played one on TV?"

I wasn't going to laugh. Laughter led to… Well, in our case it had led to *like*…and like had skipped right to love. At least it had for me and I had the scars to prove it. Alex was in Prichett on a mission to…to what? Tell me how he was doing? That could be taken care of with eight simple words. *I'm fine, Bernice. See you in ten years.* No, he obviously had a more sinister agenda.

I slid into the front seat of my car and before I could put it into gear, Alex was buckling himself in next to me.

My car decided to add to my torment. The engine gargled too much gas and quit. There was a ritual that I had to perform whenever this happened and it wasn't pretty.

"It died," Alex pointed out helpfully.

I turned on the brights and the radio and the windshield wipers, pumped the gas pedal several times and then turned the key in the ignition again.

Alex leaned across me. "You have over a *hundred and fifty thousand* miles on this vehicle."

"And she's still going strong." I patted the dash as the engine hiccupped and then settled into a rough purr as I eased the car into the street.

Just as I saw the long row of lights from the nursing home, my cell phone rang from the depths of my quilted purse. Which happened to be in a heap at Alex's feet.

"It's probably Elise or Annie," I muttered. "Can you just pick it up and say hello and tell whoever it is that I'll call them back? My voice mail is messed up."

Alex dug deep and found it on the third ring. "Hello? This is Alex Scott, playing Bernice Strum's answering service. Bernice is unavailable at the moment but she loves to hear from her fans. Leave a message and she'll call you back."

Cute. I mouthed the word at him and yanked the phone out of his hand. Now I had some serious explaining to do with whoever was on the other end. "Hello, I'm sorry about that…"

"Bernice? You have the funniest messages on your phone. I just called to find out what's new."

Heather. And she thought that Alex's voice was a recording! A hysterical giggle formed in the acid churning in my stomach. I sucked in some fresh air to diffuse it. "Ah, not much new happening here."

Ruthlessly, I stuffed all my emotions into the vault in my heart that I'd let Jesus clean out. I didn't know what else to do with them at the moment. Heather was the *new* that was happening in my life and I didn't take a breath during the day without thanking God that she'd found me after twenty years. But, Alex…he was the something *old*. He'd been the main ingredient in a stew of insecurities that I'd kept warm for years. What was I supposed to do with him?

He started to hum the song "Unforgettable." Even in the gloomy interior of my car, I could see that his eyes were closed and he was smiling.

Chapter Five

"I'm just pulling up to the Golden Oaks," I said, pressing my chin against the phone so Heather wouldn't hear Alex in the background. "It's my night to cut hair."

"I won't keep you then, I just want you to start thinking about the holidays. What are your plans?"

I never made special plans for the holidays. They just kind of…happened. Elise and Sam always invited me for Thanksgiving and after dinner, Elise and I would waddle into the living room with our second piece of pumpkin pie to watch *It's a Wonderful Life*. It's one of Elise's favorite movies and that's the only reason I pretended all these years to enjoy a movie about a man who was given a second chance—even though I knew that never happened in real life. Now, since Heather had reappeared in my life, I was beginning to believe.

"I'm not sure just yet." I answered her question cautiously and glanced at Alex.

"I'll call you tomorrow and we can figure something out. Mom and Dad know I want to spend some time with you and they said they're flexible."

"Sure. That would be great." Make room, stuffing more emotions!

"Is something wrong?" There was a touch of uncertainty in Heather's voice and I glared at Alex. Which was wasted because his eyes were still closed.

"No, not at all. I'll talk to you tomorrow." I scraped up some cheerfulness and injected it into my voice.

"Bye…Mama B."

Mama B. My throat tightened and I blinked away the tears that scratched the backs of my eyes. Where had that come from? Not that I minded… I just felt totally humbled by the honorary title. I certainly didn't deserve it.

Alex followed me into the Golden Oaks and I was relieved to see that Audrey Cooke, the receptionist, wasn't sitting behind the desk to greet people. Maybe it was possible to smuggle a celebrity into a group of senior citizens without any fallout.

"I always stop by to say hi to Esther and John first," I murmured.

"Relatives?"

"Friends."

I navigated Alex through the corridors until we came to a room near the end of the hallway. "I should mention something, although you'd probably figure it out soon enough by yourself. John is blind."

"Okay."

"Don't act weird around him, though, because he has a sense of humor about it."

"How can someone have a sense of humor about being blind?"

"You'll see." I rapped lightly on the door. "Esther?"

"It's Bernice," I heard Esther say just before the door opened.

She and John must have set a record for the oldest pair of newlyweds. Their summer wedding was held right at the nursing home and I'd even fixed Esther's hair for the occasion. It was a day I'd never forget because it was the day I took a deep breath and faced the past. Although, it had been a little easier when part of it wasn't warming the air beside me.

"Hi, Esther." She put out her arms and I hugged her, resisting the urge to lift her off her feet and swing her around the room. She is so petite she could get lost in a group of fifth-graders and I feel like a giant next to her.

"Come in, come in." Esther linked her arm through mine and noticed Alex hovering in the hall. "Is he with you?"

No. Yes. Argh. Complications. How was I supposed to introduce Alex?

"I'm Alex."

I exhaled. Problem solved.

"One of Bernice's old flames."

I was going to kill him. Wait a second, there was a commandment about murder, wasn't there? Maybe I could dye his hair green… And what was this about being *one* of Bernice's old flames? Like I'd had a buffet to choose from?

John, sitting in his wheelchair by the window, laughed. "Both of you, come in. Alex, let me take a look at you."

Alex glanced at me, clearly puzzled.

"I warned you," I whispered.

"Do you live nearby?" John asked.

"California."

A sudden thought hit me like shrapnel. Esther always asked about Heather when I visited her. That was because in a sunny window one afternoon I'd spilled out my life story to her. But I wasn't ready to tell Alex about Heather yet. It wasn't a good time. Not that there was any empty space in my appointment book that I could fill in to make that announcement.

"Bernice?" She looked at me and the compassion in her eyes broke straight through to my heart. She knew who Alex

was. Was there *anyone* in Prichett who hadn't figured out who
Alex was? Still, relief cut a sweet path through the panic.

"I lived there for a few years. Near Monterey," John was
saying as he reached out and took Esther's hand. "I can't
compare it to living here, though. I'm spoiled by the changing
seasons. We know we're going to get winter, but what kind of
winter? The kind that yanks your breath out and steals it away
or a mild one that dumps huge drifts of snow outside the
windows? And spring, is it going to be warm and green or gray
and muddy? If I lived anywhere else, I'd miss the variety, that's
the truth. Even when I was in New York, I'd remember this
area and it pulled me back like high tide. Now I know why."

Esther blushed an adorable pink. "Sounds like it's the
seasons you love, not this old lady," she teased.

"I love you both." John winked. "How long are you staying
in Prichett, Alex?"

"I have some vacation time."

"A week?" Esther asked the question that I had been
afraid to.

I could deal with a week if he really insisted on staying in
Prichett. I worked every day except Sunday and could avoid
him on several evenings when I had other commitments. He'd
be long gone before Thanksgiving.

Alex smiled. "Actually…I have three months."

I lost sight of Alex an hour after I started cutting hair for the
residents. The last I'd seen him, he'd been talking to a woman
named Althea, who thought that he was her son, Henry, who'd
finally come for a visit. No one had said anything about having
a celebrity in their midst. In fact, half the people in the family
lounge probably thought that Alex *was* Althea's neglectful son.
Once in a while, I saw one of the nurses give Alex a specula-
tive glance but no one approached him.

"Three months," I muttered under my breath.

"That's if I decide to go back," a voice said behind me.

I'd lost sight of Alex but apparently he hadn't lost sight of me. *If he decided to go back?* What did he mean by that? "You can't just *step* out of your life."

"Why not?"

"Because you're Alex Scott. People like you can't just decide one day that they're not going to be famous. You picked your life and now you're stuck with it. If you wanted this—" I poked a comb in the air "—you would have chosen it a long time ago. After what you've gotten used to, you'd go insane in a small town like Prichett."

"You seem pretty sane."

Ha. The fact that he thinks so only shows how good an actress *I* can be. The truth is, I'm only coasting next to normal and like every good daughter, I blame my mother.

"Henry?"

Althea wandered up to us and I saw Alex's expression change. His face softened and he put his hand on Althea's arm to steady her. "I thought the nurse told you it was time to go back to your room now," he reminded her, his voice so low and warm that it brought another dormant memory to life. Alex was a good man. I'd assumed that by now he'd be cynical and self-absorbed, and knew it would be easier on me if he was. I didn't want to see him being kind to little old ladies who thought he was their long-lost son.

Althea looked at me, and then her gaze shifted back to Alex. "I just wanted to be sure you'll come back to visit me. Don't be gone so long next time."

"I won't."

"Henry is my son," she told me, her voice faltering slightly. "I'm lucky to have a boy like Henry."

"Good night, Althea." I watched as the nurse came to take

her to her room and then I glanced at Alex. "I'm almost done here. I can give you a ride back to Charity's."

"Just give me five minutes. I'll meet you by the reception desk."

"What are you going to do?"

"I'm going to call Henry."

I took advantage of the few minutes I had to duck back into Esther and John's room. John was already asleep but Esther was sitting in a chair by the bed, knitting.

"I'm starting early. I'm going to have to make two, you know."

"You're making blankets for Annie's babies?" I reached out and touched the whisper-soft skein of mint-green yarn. Twins might not be such a big deal anymore when women all over the place were having triplets or quintuplets, but these were *Annie's* twins.

Esther nodded, the knitting needles gently clicking together as the blanket grew in her lap. One of the things I loved about Esther was the way she didn't feel the need to crowd the air with words. She knew I had something to say and she gave me the time and space I needed to say it.

"Thank you for not mentioning Heather. I'll tell him. I'm just not sure when. Soon." The thought suddenly occurred to me that if I wanted him to leave, revealing that particular bit of news just might do it. But why? I felt a ripple of unease. Over the years I'd convinced myself that I'd done him a favor by removing the baby and me from his equation, leaving him a famous, wealthy entity while saving myself from the rejection that I knew would eventually happen. I couldn't let myself imagine that Alex and I might be celebrating our twenty-fifth wedding anniversary in a few years if I'd made another decision.

"And are you going to tell Heather?"

"I don't know yet." That was something else that I didn't want to face. I felt the urge to run away again. *God, could we just rewind the last twenty-four hours and start over with a new script?*

"God is bigger than this," Esther said quietly. "Don't forget that."

"I thought the Christian life was supposed to be peaceful," I said, hearing the faint whine creep into my voice. I never whine. I blamed Alex. "You know, like a nice scenic riverboat ride."

"A riverboat ride." Esther tipped her head thoughtfully and the knitting needles fell silent. "I think it's more like…oh… bungee jumping off a bridge? Skydiving…?"

"I get the picture! Why didn't someone tell me that?" *Bungee jumping?* She had to be kidding. I got dizzy if I ran up the stairs to my apartment too fast.

"This is what you have to remember, Bernice. Peace isn't necessarily a warm, fuzzy feeling. It isn't even something we can grab and hold on to. Peace is *Him.* It's God Himself. So when you hit the rapids on your nice, scenic boat ride, you don't run away, you run *to.*" The needles began to click again. She gave me a wide smile and a wink. "It's an adventure, but you can trust Him."

"You aren't really going to leave me here, are you?"

When I pulled up in front of Charity's B and B I didn't even put the car into Park, I just put my foot on the brake to hold it steady for the two seconds Alex would need to open the door and get out. "Yup."

"You don't have to sound so cheerful about it."

"Oh, you'll be fine…with Murphy for company." I couldn't resist.

"You're trying to get rid of me."

"I'm not very good at it."

Alex twisted around in the seat. "You were," he said. "But you aren't going to get away this time. You aren't just passing through Prichett, you *live* here. I've got you cornered. See you tomorrow."

He started humming again when he got out of the car and strolled up to the door, which Charity was holding open for him.

I slapped my hands against the steering wheel and howled silently. Why was he doing this? Being funny and charming and kind? It was killing me.

I had forgotten to leave a light on so I had to blindly bump my way up the outside staircase behind the Cut and Curl in the dark. When I flipped the light on, the first thing I felt was absolute, total relief that I hadn't let Alex come up.

My apartment gave the term "shabby chic" a whole new meaning. I have a weakness for tag sales and it shows. I've convinced myself that one day I'm going to convince Lester Lee to sell me the little place he owns a few miles out of town. I will then take up my hobby of choice and refinish furniture in my spare time, which is why, over the past ten years, I've collected a staggering number of old wooden chairs, interesting side tables and an antique buffet that stretches the width of my living room. And happens to be covered with my collection of snow globes—another weakness. I tried to see my apartment through Alex's eyes and what I saw was an odd assortment of furnishings that wouldn't make sense to anyone but me. And then I caught sight of my reflection in the antique mirror. It wasn't even centered on the wall—I'd hung it on the only nail large enough to support it while it waited patiently for its true home. The one with the picket fence.

Then I tried to see *me* through Alex's eyes. I leaned closer to the glass and peered at the lines fanning out from my eyes. Anchoring two fingers on each side of my cheekbones and my thumbs against my chin, I pulled back on the skin that had loosened over the years, like I was retucking a fitted sheet that was beginning to lose its shape. It didn't help. Now I looked like I had at the age of six, when my mother braided my hair too tight. I let go and gravity prevailed once again. For a few seconds I wished I was aging as beautifully as Elise. But then, Elise had started out beautiful, so maybe that was the secret.

And though my parents had done their best to shake me off our branch of the family tree, there was no denying that I was their child. A mixed-up concoction of Strums and Corbins that ended up with me looking like the final product of a potluck casserole. My insecurities saw an opportunity and came rushing back but at the moment I was too tired to fight them off. I collapsed onto the sofa and felt something crinkle underneath me. One of my three-by-five cards.

I love you, O Lord, my strength.
The Lord is my rock, my fortress and my deliverer;
My God is my rock in whom I take refuge.

My strength. My fortress. I wasn't in this alone. The thought bloomed inside of me. Esther was right. He was the one I needed to run to. And Alex was wrong. He thought I was backed into a corner, but actually I'd taken refuge in the one who'd created me. Ha.

Chapter Six

"You don't look like you slept much."

I shot Elise what I thought was an evil look, but I must have failed because she laughed instead of fleeing for her life. "I watched one of those home-shopping channels until three in the morning. I think I may have ordered something, although I can't remember what."

Elise settled into one of the chairs by the window and shrugged out of her coat. "Are you okay?"

"No."

"Is he still in town?"

"He's at Charity's. At least he was last night when I dropped him off. He wanted to have dinner with me, I told him no because I was cutting hair at the Golden Oaks. He met Esther and John, and Esther told me that being a Christian is like bungee jumping—*thanks so much for warning me about that*—and unless Charity's bird perched on Alex's poster bed last night and recited the Ten Commandments, he's probably lurking around somewhere, ready to pounce on my unsuspecting self. Oh, and Heather called and he answered the phone..."

"Okay, stop right there. My brain can't take your version of shorthand. Heather *talked* to him?"

"Sort of. He pretended he was my voice mail. It wasn't a real conversation. He said he has me cornered. I went back home and decided I'm *never* going to let him see my apartment."

"I like your apartment. It's unique, like you."

Best friends. Their loyalty is deep but strange.

"I don't think I'm going to get out of dinner, unless he has to arm wrestle Jim Briggs, then there's a chance. Alex could probably beat the farmers but Jim has arms like wooden posts, have you noticed that?"

"Why would he arm wrestle Jim Briggs? Never mind. How long is he staying? And why is he here?"

"Answer to both questions—no idea." I glanced at my appointment book and saw Jill Cabott's name scrawled between the black lines. Jill always ran a few minutes late. "I'm not even sure how he *found* me. He said he wanted to tell me how he's doing."

"So he came in person. From California."

"I guess." Seeing Elise's expression, I shrugged. "It doesn't make sense to me, either."

"Does he want a relationship with you?"

Elise's words may have been soft but they hit hard. "No!"

"You sound pretty sure."

"He didn't ever want a relationship with me."

Elise frowned. "But you told me that you left him."

"I did."

"So, doesn't that mean *you* were the one who didn't want a relationship?"

"I can't have this conversation without coffee."

Elise smiled. "I'm just trying to understand."

"Get in line."

In the ten minutes of privacy we had before my appointments started, I filled her in on what happened at Sally's and how Candy threatened to confiscate his luggage and that Jim Briggs wanted me to be careful. By the time I finished, the normally unflappable Elise Penny was looking a bit dazed. I was glad—I'd hate to be the only one.

"So people aren't falling all over him?"

"Maybe if they're armed with pitchforks."

"He's not going to make the marquee then." Elise looked disappointed.

"Maybe he will…only it'll say Go Home Alex Scott."

"You're handling all this pretty well."

I was? "I am?"

"You aren't falling apart. You aren't packing your suitcase. You aren't eating handfuls of Tootsie Roll."

I've learned to dispose of the wrappers. But she was right. "God reminded me of something last night. I don't have to run away anymore. Now I can run *to.*"

Elise didn't flinch or look surprised when I mentioned God. She was getting to know Him better, too. I came across a verse recently that said something about *God-chosen lives* and what splendid friends they make. Elise was that kind of friend. So were Annie and Esther and John.

There was a flash of color outside the window and the door swung open. "Good morning, ladies."

Alex. And he looked like he got a decent night's sleep, too. And he looked like he'd been…running? He was wearing black sweatpants and a gray T-shirt and tennis shoes that would have cost me a month's rent. His hair was messy and his face flushed with color. And he still looked gorgeous. Honestly, could he be any more annoying?

"You remember my friend, Elise?"

Alex nodded and smiled. "Hi, Elise."

The day before, I'd been so shocked when I'd seen him that

I couldn't even remember introducing him to Elise and Annie but now I watched him carefully to see his reaction. Usually when men see Elise for the first time, they get a little tongue-tied. Elise is truly beautiful. If God hadn't planted her in Prichett, Elise could have been as famous as Alex.

The first time we met, I really wanted to hate her but Elise is totally un-hate-able. In the first place, she isn't one of those beautiful women who flaunt their beauty. And she doesn't pretend she isn't beautiful, either, which can be just as irritating. She accepts it just like I accept the way my hair has a stubborn wave that can only be tamed with a curling iron the size of a rolling pin.

My favorite thing about Elise is that there's more to her than pretty packaging. We've been friends for ten years but it wasn't until Heather contacted me and I started to unravel that I realized that true friends are right there, winding you back up and tucking in the loose pieces of your heart.

Alex was polite but his eyes didn't linger on Elise, like a tourist getting his first glimpse of the Mona Lisa. What on earth was wrong with him? He was looking at *me*.

"I almost woke you up to go running with me this morning."

Elise was too polite to laugh but out of the corner of my eye, I saw her shoulders jiggle. "Well, I better start my day. Sam and I are going over to Munroe to pick up some parts for the tractor."

"How is Annie feeling?" Mindy would be thrilled that I'd tried out her delay tactics but I really did want to know. I'd been so wrapped up in my own troubles that I hadn't even thought to ask until now.

"Anxious to start the nursery. With the holidays coming, she's going to be busier at church." Elise moved toward the door just as Jill Cabott pushed it open.

"Elise!"

Jill hugged her and Elise disappeared momentarily in the depths of Jill's sheepskin coat. When she reappeared, she was smiling. Wonders never ceased. A few months ago I practically had to hide my scissors when the two of them were in the same room together. Elise had blamed Jill's son, Riley, for her daughter Bree having second thoughts about going to college. But Bree and Riley were taking their romance slowly and she was in Madison—at least for the next four years—so Elise could breathe a little easier.

"Hi, Jill. All set?"

"Just let me hang up my coat."

Elise gave me a little wave that promised we'd get together soon and slipped out the door. Alex was sitting on a chair, his hands clasped behind his head and his legs stretched out in front of him with a cup of coffee wedged between his knees. Right next to the coatrack.

I knew the second Jill realized who Alex was because her sudden gasp sounded like a blown-out tire.

I hustled her over to the chair and sat her down. "Now, what do you want me to do today?"

"The same as always. Trim a little off the sides. It's getting a little shaggy. Better go shorter because with Thanksgiving coming, I know I won't have time to come back before the middle of December."

I tried to ignore Alex but it wasn't easy. Especially when he jumped up and prowled over to the chair. Jill's eyes got so wide I was afraid they were going to roll out of her head.

"Wait a second. You're telling her what to do?" He leaned over until he was eye to eye with Jill, who shrunk farther into the chair.

"Alex!" I snapped out his name but he ignored me.

"Yes…" Jill obviously thought it was a trick question.

Alex looked at me and shook his head. "They have no idea, do they?" he muttered.

"You're not helping," I said through gritted teeth. "Have some more coffee."

"Tell Bernice to cut your hair the way she sees it," Alex said.

I stepped on his foot, wishing that I'd worn my one pair of stilettos, an impractical impulse buy that lurked in the back of my closet but I didn't have the heart to part with. "Alex, Jill just wants a trim."

"What do you mean, the way she sees it?" Jill was confused but willing to be enlightened.

"You aren't supposed to tell *her* how to cut your hair— she's supposed to tell *you* how your hair should be cut."

"She is?" Jill glanced at me. "You are?"

"Jill, I'll cut it any way you want me to."

Alex said something under his breath that made Jill gasp again but she swallowed bravely. "Go ahead."

"Jill…"

"I mean it, Bernice. Do whatever you think you should."

Alex grinned and stalked back to the row of chairs. "My work here is done."

The work of messing up my entire day? And he was willing to do it for free. How *sweet.*

An hour and a half later Jill was staring at her reflection in the mirror, touching the ends of her hair with shaky fingertips. Every four to six weeks for the past ten years I'd been trimming a conservative inch off Jill Cabott's puddle-brown blunt cut, knowing that the style was hopelessly outdated and didn't show off her features to their full advantage. I had to admit that I went a little crazy with the unexpected power I'd been given.

"I… Old Dan is going to faint when he sees me," Jill whispered.

Old Dan is Jill's husband and he isn't that old. Unfortunately, his firstborn son was named after him and to differentiate between the two, they had to split into Old Dan and Young Dan. People should really think these things through in advance, if you ask me.

"He's going to buy you roses and take you out for dinner," Alex, the eavesdropper, said.

"I'm sending this bottle of gel home with you…" The tears in Jill's eyes stopped me cold. "Jill, I'm sorry. What can I do? Do you want me to take the highlights out?"

"No, I love it. I look…like I always wanted to." In a daze, she wrote me a check with a tip big enough to pay my monthly cable bill. She even gave Alex a timid smile as she walked out the door. Oh no, his first convert.

"Thanks a lot." I grabbed the broom and started to sweep the floor, resisting the urge to use it to chase him down Main Street.

"Do these people know anything about you, Bernice?"

"They know what I want them to know."

"I get it. You'd rather pretend that all you know how to do is follow directions. If they knew who you are, what you can do, it would wreck your whole small-town *beautician* persona, wouldn't it? You might not feel like you fit in after all."

Without knowing it, Alex ripped a Band-Aid off a wound I'd been trying to keep covered for years. I *knew* I didn't fit in with Prichett. All the years I'd lived and worked here and no matter how hard I tried, I just couldn't blend in with the natives. But why did Alex have to see it? And why did he feel the need to point it out?

"Don't even think you know me. That was twenty years ago. We were practically *kids* when we met. Don't think for a minute I'm still the same person."

"You haven't changed that much." He actually had the nerve to laugh. "You still aren't afraid to tell me what you think."

"Somebody has to. Honestly, just because people are

gorgeous and have money doesn't mean they shouldn't get yelled at once in a while." I absolutely wasn't going to smile.

"Bern...why aren't you married with ten kids?"

My heart stalled suddenly. Alex was still standing five feet away from me but suddenly he felt much closer. It astounded me that he could even ask the question—I mean, was his eyesight that bad? My looks were as plain as my name.

Since I couldn't tell him the truth, I gave him the grim statistics instead.

"If you must know, Prichett has a population of less than two thousand people and out of that number there are only *six* eligible men. Out of those six eligible men, four of them are afraid of me and the other two are forty-year-old brothers who still live with their mama."

"Afraid of you?"

"There are totally unfounded rumors that I'm...difficult."

"No kidding?" Alex stretched and rubbed the back of his neck with one hand. I immediately focused on the coffeepot instead of the expanse of tanned abdomen that he'd uncovered with that casual movement. Alex really was a health hazard. "Hard to imagine. So, are we on for dinner tonight?"

"I have a PAC meeting." Yes. Finally a reason for its existence.

At Alex's blank look, I filled him in. "The Prichett Advancement Council. Don't laugh."

"Not in a million years. But just to warn you, I'm not leaving town until you have dinner with me so the more excuses you come up with, the longer I'll be here."

My ten o'clock appointments—the Graley sisters—were crossing the street. I couldn't take the risk that Alex would say the same thing to them that he'd said to Jill. As it was, I couldn't imagine what kind of fallout there would be when people saw her new look. I figured I might have to beg for a job at the Buzz and Blade.

Chapter Seven

The PAC meetings were always held at city hall, which was a tiny brick building on the corner of Main and Ripple streets, which was named after one of the town's original founders and had nothing to do with the fact that the street resembled the sole of an old work boot. City hall shared quarters with Prichett's minuscule police department, whose part-time officers worked a normal nine-to-five shift. If any criminal activity happened after that, the county sheriff's department stepped up to the plate.

Candy was already setting up for the meeting when I arrived, late because my last appointment had said, and I quote, "Cut my hair the way you see it," which proved that the Prichett grapevine had been working like the well-oiled machine that it was.

"I'm glad you're here. I've got an addition to the agenda." Candy barely glanced at me as she stapled papers together. She must have come right over from the feed store because she was still wearing dusty overalls and a heavy red chamois shirt. And the ever-present baseball cap.

I snuck a look over her shoulder at the agenda and if it

hadn't been right in front of me in black and white, I wouldn't have believed it. Written neatly in black ink was one word. Junebug.

"Junebug is coming to the meeting?" Junebug happened to be Lester Lee's Holstein and Elise's bovine nemesis. Lester had talked Elise into posing with Junebug for the annual county agriculture calendar and she'd been quite the prima donna. Junebug, not Elise.

"I wouldn't put anything past Lester these days," Candy snorted. "I liked it better when he let Carolee do all the talking for him. If Mindy Lewis isn't talking one of my ears off, he's working on the other one. He thinks that cow of his is the town celebrity…" She gave me a pointed look. Which I ignored. I wasn't going to be lured into a discussion about celebrities. Not after the day I'd had.

"But what does the advancement council have to do with Junebug?" I couldn't connect the dots here.

"I have no idea. He just called and told me to put Junebug on the agenda for this evening." Candy finished stapling and I decided, as vice chairman, that I should pitch in to help. I reached for the pan of brownies on the table.

"Don't cut those, it's not your job. Denise'll have a fit."

I knew better than to argue. She was right. Denise *would* have a fit. I sat and waited for everyone to wander in. Mr. Bender, from Bender's Hardware, shuffled in with Jim Briggs patiently at his heels, and Sally rushed in a few seconds later, still wearing her apron. Denise was late and we were all hungry, so there was a unanimous decision to cut the brownies without her. But Candy still wouldn't let me do it.

Lester Lee sidled in, cap in hand and alone, which was a small wonder because usually his wife was attached to the hip of his Carhartts. His hair was slicked back and he was wearing a tie. No sign of Junebug. Candy and I exchanged relieved glances.

For the first half hour, we had our yearly argument about when the Main Street Christmas decorations should be put up, before Thanksgiving or after. Denise wanted them put up before because she was already getting Christmas merchandise in at the variety store. She claimed she couldn't unpack it unless she could look outside and see evidence of the holiday and feel the glow. Whatever that meant. Our decorations didn't glow. They were supposed to be bells but they looked more like the orange cones used to separate traffic in construction zones.

The second half hour was spent trying to figure out a time when all the downtown businesses could participate in a Christmas open house.

"Why don't we have it the same time that Faith Community holds their live nativity?" Denise asked suddenly. "That would be perfect. People are out and about anyway and we could all have extended hours those evenings, maybe serve hot chocolate and cookies. Do something creative in our own stores that might generate more business."

This was easy for Denise, who had boxes of decorations at her fingertips, but a total stressor for me, whose holiday decorations fit in a shoe box. I wasn't counting my snow globes because there was no way I was lugging all fifty of those down to the salon to be lifted and shaken by kids who'd been clutching gooey candy canes.

"That's a good idea," Candy said. "Denise, you and I will form a committee to plan that."

Denise sat back with a satisfied smile on her face while I silently formed a committee of one to work on a way to get *out* of the holiday open house.

"Any new business not on the agenda… Lester, we'll get to you in a second. You're on the agenda. We may be small but we do things properly in here."

No one said anything.

"Okay, Lester, you have the floor." Candy took advantage of the moment to winch a brownie out of the pan with the end of her ballpoint pen.

"I want to be on the committee for that new grant we got," Lester said.

"You'll have to talk to Bernice and Jim about that," Candy said. "They're the ones heading it up. We already decided to use the grant for a sculpture in the park—"

"And the sculpture should be a cow," Lester interrupted.

The dots suddenly connected. *Let me guess. A cow modeled after, oh say, Junebug?*

"A cow?" Denise wrinkled her nose. "There's nothing special about a cow. I thought the sculpture should reflect the spirit of the farmer, something abstract…"

I want off this committee. Please, let me make snowflakes out of craft sticks instead. Let me hot-glue thousands of sequins onto felt Christmas stockings…

"It should be a cow," Lester insisted stubbornly.

"You mean, it should be *your* cow!" Denise shot back.

Candy held up her hands like she was directing traffic, and used her mayor voice. "Lester, we haven't decided on a sculpture. That's what Jim and Bernice are going to look into. If everyone agrees, we'll table this discussion until the next meeting."

We all wanted to go home. We all agreed.

The sleeve of my coat was stuck in the folding chair but I didn't realize it until I tried to put it on. I had one arm in one sleeve and was yanking on the other when suddenly I was free, compliments of Jim Briggs.

"Thanks."

Jim smiled and for the first time I noticed that he had a rather appealing dimple in his cheek. "It's not that often I get to rescue a damsel in distress. When should we get together to talk about the grant?"

"I'll need to check my calendar." At the moment, I couldn't come up with an empty square. I always ended up working longer hours during the holidays because everyone wanted to look their best.

"I think Lester's right," Jim whispered.

"About the cow?"

Jim nodded. "It does reflect what we're all about. This is a farming community."

I hated to admit it, but he had a point. "Let's just look into all our options. I mean, do we really want Junebug's head to get any bigger?" *Or Lester's?*

"Bernice, she's a cow. I don't think things go to her head."

"Have you met her?"

"Met her?" Jim laughed. "No, I can't say that we've been formally introduced."

"Until you do, keep your opinions to yourself. We're not talking about your ordinary everyday cow here."

"If you say so." His dimple flashed again but suddenly he glanced away from me and focused on the reproduction of the Constitution that was taped to the wall. "Are you going to the chili supper at church tomorrow night?"

"Is that tomorrow night?" I groaned the words. I'd promised Annie that I'd be there. Stephen's youth group was hosting it and there was going to be a free-will offering taken for the mission trip to Mexico they were going on at the end of June.

"Tomorrow night. Six o'clock."

And I was supposed to have dinner with Alex. My stomach knotted at the thought. *Lord, I've got that bungee-jumping feeling. Don't let me go!* Just as I surfaced from my frantic SOS, I heard what Jim was saying.

"…sit together if you're going alone."

"I've got to bring Alex." Did I say that out loud?

"He's still in town?"

"Somewhere, yes." Even though I hadn't seen him all day. I admit it. I was concerned.

"Well, I guess I'll see you…both…tomorrow night then. Give me a call when you come up with a time we can meet about the grant." Jim looked like he was about to say something else but he shook his head instead. "Take care."

Jim left and I stood there, still distracted by the reminder of the chili supper. If I put off another dinner with Alex, he'd just be in Prichett that much longer. I knew he was bluffing about staying longer. There was nothing for him here and he knew it.

"Bernice? I've gotta lock up." Candy looked impatient to go and I didn't blame her. She'd put in a long day just as I had and, other than the brownie, she probably hadn't had supper yet, either.

"Sorry."

"Be sorry while you're walking out the door, okay?"

I knew better than to take Candy's gruffness personally. That's what happened to independent women. They got…independent. "'Night."

"Next meeting is the first Tuesday in December."

"I'll write it down. By the way, Candy, is there really an ordinance B31, section eighteen?"

She didn't crack a smile. "There is now. And if you need any more, let me know."

There was an ordinance against parking cars on the streets overnight from November to April so maybe Candy could actually add one that would make it illegal for celebrities to take up residence in Prichett. It was worth remembering.

I walked back to my apartment, zipping my coat up to keep out the chill. It was past the town's bedtime and the only thing open was the gas station on the outskirts of town. Even the grocery store closed at seven. For a few minutes I soaked up the silence around me and watched each breath turn into a puff of frost every time I exhaled.

When I walked past the Cut and Curl, I couldn't resist pausing outside the window for a minute to press my face against the glass, just to make sure I'd turned the coffeepot off.

Then I remembered the look on Jill Cabott's face when she saw her reflection in the mirror after I'd finished drying her hair. I hadn't felt that kind of satisfaction for a long time. I'm not sure why I hadn't advertised the fact when I moved to town that, once upon a time, I was a "stylist to the stars," but just the fact that I'd moved to Prichett without even having so much as a shirttail relative here was cause for suspicion. If Prichett's population changed, it was because someone moved *away*. Since I started out as an oddity, I didn't want to mention my previous job and seal the deal for the rest of my life. Even if it meant cutting Jill's colorless brown hair in a conservative bob for ten years. And perming hair that looked better straight. And touching up the dark roots on women who wanted to be blond but should have stayed brunette.

Now, thanks to Alex, I was going to be a slide under the microscope once again.

"Need a ride home?"

There was no mistaking the voice but when I turned around, Alex wasn't standing behind me. He was sitting in the cab of a huge black pickup truck. How that thing managed to pull up behind me without making any noise was beyond my comprehension. Especially because the hood was so wide there were probably two engines tucked underneath it.

"Very funny. I am home."

"I bought a truck."

He sounded like a six-year-old on Christmas day who'd just opened his first toy tractor. I pressed my lips together to flatten a smile. "Nice."

"Do you want to go for a ride?" There was so much boyish enthusiasm in his voice that I hated to be the one to squash it.

"I'm tired. And hungry." I wondered if there was any other woman in the world who would have used those two flimsy excuses as reasons not to jump into a shiny black pickup with Alex Scott.

"Just a spin around the block. You know that will only take thirty seconds. You can even time me."

God, why does he have to be like this? So annoyingly friendly. So...here. I just don't think my heart can take a round two with Alex Scott. Can't You just make him disappear?

"It's got leather seats."

Apparently not.

"Five minutes."

He jumped out of the driver's side, came around and opened the door for me. If there hadn't been a step-up into the cab, I would have needed a ladder.

"It's as big as an elevator in here." I could smell new leather and the faint scent of pine, probably coming from the cardboard evergreen dangling from the rearview mirror. This was the free gift that every new truck owner received with the purchase of a new vehicle at Prichett's only dealership.

"It has four-wheel drive."

"I hate to remind you, but you live in the city. You don't exactly *need* four-wheel drive."

"Listen to this engine. It purrs like a kitten."

"So that's what you did today after you wrecked my day. You went to the dealership and made someone else's."

"I wrecked your day?"

He sounded so innocent that my back teeth ground together. "Customers are going to expect *wow* and *vavoom* from now on when they go to Bernice Strum to get their hair done, thank you very much."

"You can do *wow* and *vavoom*. I don't see a problem."

He wouldn't. "This is *Prichett*." Maybe if I talked slowly, enunciating the word, he'd see the problem! "There isn't exactly a need for *wow* and *vavoom*."

"I'd say that that's a reason right there. You're just mad because I ripped the cover off your disguise."

"When did you have time between movies to get a degree in psychology?"

Alex laughed. I caught a glimpse of the billboard with Elise and Junebug's picture on it. We were heading out of town.

"Wait a second, I thought you said we were going around the block."

"I have something I want to show you."

Suddenly the cab began to shrink. "Did you or did you not hear the words 'hungry' and 'tired' come out of my mouth a few minutes ago?"

"I always keep an appetizer in the glove compartment."

I flipped it open and found a package of dry-roasted peanuts. "This will go really well with the brownie and diet soda I had for supper."

"I bought them for Murphy because Charity mentioned that they're his favorite, but go ahead. I think you need them more."

I was running out of options. It was obvious that neither frantic prayer nor sarcasm was going to make him go away.

"We take a left here and we're almost there."

"Almost where?"

The truck sailed around a corner and a sudden, overwhelming feeling of unease ricocheted through me.

"I didn't just buy a truck today…"

I closed my eyes and pretended that I didn't feel the truck slowing down. In the same exact spot that *I* slowed down every time I drove out this way.

I couldn't speak. Couldn't open my eyes. Couldn't swallow the three peanuts I'd just eaten.

"You can't see it very well in the dark…"

Oh, I didn't have to see it. I already knew what *it* looked like. It was adorable. In a previous age it had been a country church, small and quaint with an elegant roofline and an honest-to-goodness steeple. Somewhere down the line, someone had turned it into a house but had wisely decided not to tinker with perfection. They'd remodeled the inside but left the outside intact. It had two outbuildings with fieldstone foundations and a crescent-shaped pond that attracted migrating geese in the spring and fall. There was a hedge of lilacs that bloomed with wild abandon in the spring. The house also sat on the very corner of Lester Lee's property, the intersection between fields and five acres of hardwoods. It had stood empty for as long as I'd lived in Prichett because Lester was either too stubborn or too sentimental to sell. Until now.

"There isn't a lot of real estate around here, unless I wanted to buy a farm."

"You're…renting it?"

"No, the guy—Lester—wouldn't rent it to me. I bought it. So what do you think?"

"I'm never going to talk to you again."

"What?"

"You bought *my* house."

Chapter Eight

"You're really *not* talking to me, aren't you?"

I flashed Alex an impatient look. "That would be immature. I'm processing."

"Processing?"

"Yes, *processing*. I'm processing the fact that you bought a truck with four-wheel drive and a *house*…in *Prichett*. For a *vacation*. You have way too much money. No one does that, Alex."

"I suppose." He didn't sound too sure, which made the already gaping abyss between us widen. The people he knew probably did this kind of thing all the time.

"Listen, my first appointment is at eight tomorrow morning. Can you take me home now?" I couldn't prevent myself from glancing at the house one more time. It really was adorable. The only thing it needed was a picket fence.

I don't know why Lester had sold it to him, unless he had some sort of underhanded plan to use Alex's influence as a means for Junebug to become the next animal movie star.

"I was hoping you could help me fix it up a little. The inside needs some updating."

Updating. All I had to do was show Alex my avocado-green oven and my collection of snow globes and he'd be flying in an interior design team from Los Angeles. Not to mention the irony in the fact that he was asking for my help to fix up the house he'd stolen from me!

"Why don't you just give me a nice paper cut and pour lemon juice in it?" I muttered.

"*The Princess Bride,* right?"

Rats. He'd heard me. I had a habit of quoting lines from my favorite movies and usually no one picked up on it. It occurred to me suddenly that that was another thing that probably underlined my strangeness to my fellow townfolk. I spoke a completely different language. *Scriptese.*

"Home."

"Fine, I'll take you home. What time are we having dinner tomorrow night?" Alex may have admitted defeat for this particular battle but he obviously needed to remind me that he was still in the war.

"Do you like chili?"

"Sure."

"Then dinner is at six-thirty."

At four in the morning, I finally gave up pretending to sleep. My brain refused to shut down. After Alex had dropped me off—and watched to make sure I made it to the top of the stairs safely—I discovered four messages on my answering machine. One from Annie. One from Heather. One was a woman I'd never heard of who insisted that I squeeze her in the next day for a "Jill Cabott"—whatever that was—and one from my mother.

The last one had clinched my sleepless night.

My parents still live in California and we have a system. We exchange one phone call per month on a Sunday afternoon when the rates are cheapest and talk for ten minutes about absolutely nothing. Once a year, on Mother's Day weekend, I close up the salon and fly out to see them. A two-and-a-half-day bracing reality check as to why living so far apart works for us.

Her message had been brief.

Bernice, it's Mother. Where are you this late at night? I'll call back tomorrow. I'm going to bed now. It's late.

So half the night I tossed and turned, wondering why she'd called on a weeknight and why, at my age and with many miles between us, my stomach still twisted like a pretzel when I heard her voice. The other half I spent wondering why Alex was in Prichett and knowing that the time to tell him about Heather was getting closer.

Call me a coward, but I was thankful that the chili supper would delay the inevitable. It's not as though we could have a serious conversation in the fellowship room at Faith Community Church. I'd already been to one potluck supper there since I'd become a Christian and the acoustics in the basement were terrible—the silverware clinking together sounded like band practice at the high school. Add that to the loud hum of conversation that made you think killer bees weren't just a myth and all you could do was eat tuna casserole and smile at the person next to you. It was perfect.

I looked at the clock that had been flashing digital numbers at me for the past seven hours. Five-thirty. Finally, I could justify getting up. I slipped on my bathrobe and tried to focus my blurry eyes on the three-by-five card taped to the bathroom mirror.

I sought the Lord and he answered me, He delivered me from all my fears.

I wanted God to deliver me from my fears. I really did. But just when I thought I was free, they returned in a sneak attack. Or in a stretch limo.

Alex. He'd been my best dream and my worst nightmare all rolled into one. After that first date, when he'd asked the waiter to bring us cheesecake while we decided what we wanted for dinner, I knew that I wasn't going to come out of the relationship with my heart intact. I'd never been in love before and I struggled against it, sure that I was a novelty for someone like Alex. We spent hours together, talking about everything from our favorite brand of peanut butter to our political views, but the fact that he didn't like to take me to public places made me realize that women like me and men like him didn't end up with a happily-ever-after. Especially not in the type of business he was in, where beautiful, confident women were constantly sashaying into his life. I finally got to the point where I couldn't wait anymore for him to sever our relationship. Less than a month after I'd left, I found out I was pregnant.

Not knowing what to do, I'd gone back to my parents. That was when my mother's words hacked away at my already rough edges, causing permanent scars. I shook away the conversation we'd had just as it began to seep back into my mind. I didn't want to relive that day.

"Lord, I don't want to live like this anymore. You gave me a new heart. Promised me that I'm a new creation now. Why is all this coming back now? I want to be free from all those feelings," I whispered.

Choose.

The single word brought me up short and I searched the verses again. The word "choose" wasn't even there.

Did You just talk to me, God?

I was afraid to even ask the question—afraid that I'd suddenly hear a "yes," or that I'd hear a "no." What I heard was silence and I felt a little silly. Maybe I'd imagined it.

Okay, if God was trying to impress something on me, and if I took His advice, what would I choose?

I would choose to listen to His voice instead of the voice from my past. That's what I'd choose.

And suddenly, like someone wrapped a puffy comforter around my shoulders, I felt *loved*. And *safe*.

I went down to the Cut and Curl an hour early because I didn't want to be surrounded by my four tiny walls and remember that Alex had bought my dream house. With a granola bar clamped between my front teeth, I started the coffee, and the bell on the door, which I'd forgotten to lock again, suddenly jingled an intruder alert.

Candy was standing just inside the door, her cheeks pink from the cold. "Your sign says you take walk-ins."

"Yes…" My sign did say that. But why she was pointing that out at seven o'clock in the morning was a mystery.

"So I'm walking in."

Candy had never come in for a haircut. Ever. In fact, I don't think I've ever *seen* Candy's hair because she always had it hidden under a grungy baseball cap.

"Now?" Honestly, I had to give up coffee. I was positively simpleminded until I felt that first jolt of caffeine.

"Am I here now or what?"

"Fine, I'm opening a little early this morning anyway." I flipped on the rest of the lights and then noticed that Candy was still standing by the door. "What's the matter?"

"I saw Jill Cabott last night at the gas station. After the meeting. She was with Dan. He'd taken her out for dinner. And bought her flowers."

Of course. The skimpy mixture of brown-tipped carnations and wilted roses stuffed in a barrel near the station's cash register. The I-can't-believe-I-forgot-her-birthday bouquets.

"Roses. Real ones." Candy had read my mind. "She showed them to me. A whole dozen."

Now I was impressed. "I'll bet Jill was happy."

Candy stared at me with an odd expression on her face. Just as I was starting to wonder what I had to do to lure Candy to my chair, she took a hesitant step closer.

"Can you do that to me?"

Have I mentioned in the past five minutes that I want to kill Alex Scott? Because—I'm sorry, God—but I really do. "Why don't you sit down and tell me what you're thinking."

Candy sat down. But her hands were anchored to both sides of her cap like she was holding on to the hatch of a submarine and water was coming in. "Don't laugh."

I was actually afraid of what I was going to see. Was she prematurely bald? Had she tried one of those home kits and ended up with hair the color of an eggplant?

"I'm not going to laugh. Candy, let go of the hat."

With one last miserable glance at me in the mirror, she lowered her hands and twisted them together in her lap.

I tugged off the cap. And tried not to laugh.

"Candy…" I gasped. I couldn't believe what I was seeing. "You have *beautiful* hair."

And it was. Thick and glossy with a natural wave—and the pale ash-blond only found in nature. There were no chemicals invented that could duplicate the color.

"I know." She looked even more miserable.

"Why do you keep it covered up all the time?"

"It's a nuisance."

"So you want me to cut it?"

"No!" Candy rose halfway out of the chair and I pressed her back down.

"Look, no scissors." I waved the comb in her face. "Comb." She slumped back down. "I have to keep it long for Robby."

I tried to place the name and came up blank. "Robby?"

"My baby brother. Every year he buys me hair ribbons for

Christmas, so I have to have hair to put them in, right?" Her expression dared me to disagree.

"Right." It looked safer to agree with her, even if I didn't have a clue what she was talking about.

"He lives in a group home in Milwaukee." Her voice softened. She didn't sound like Candy-the-mayor or Candy-the-feed-store-owner. She sounded like a woman who wished that sometimes life worked out a little bit differently. "He has Down syndrome. I think he'd cry if I cut my hair because he always tells me that it reminds him of Mom's."

I exhaled slowly. "Oh."

"So that's why you can't cut it."

I heard the edge come back into her voice but I was distracted by the difference in Candy now that she was holding the cap instead of wearing it.

"I need to trim it a little. You've got some split ends."

"I usually do that myself."

With your pocketknife? I tamped down the question and snapped the cape around her neck. Candy's feet tapped out an uneven beat against the legs of the chair.

"If you don't want me to cut it, what do you want me to do?"

"I don't know." Her voice was irritable but her eyes were terrified. "Do something. Like you did to Jill."

Her voice lowered. "I have a…date."

"A date?"

"Shh. Not so loud."

Maybe she thought Mindy Lewis had bugged the Main Street businesses. Maybe she knew something that I didn't.

"First things first. Let's get you over to the shampoo chair." I'd found that the combination of warm water and a shampoo massage worked better than truth serum for obtaining information. Of course, I'd taken the secret hairstylist's oath never to repeat what I heard.

At the first spray of warm water, Candy's eyes closed and a blissful smile came over her face. She obviously didn't pamper herself. No makeup, not even foundation. Judging by the condition of her skin, she didn't believe in sunscreen, either. I plucked a piece of hay out of her hair and watched it swirl around the bottom of the sink and disappear.

"Anyone I know? Your date?"

Candy tensed. "No. He's not from Prichett. I've never met him before."

"He's not someone you met on the Internet, is he?" I couldn't help it. My protective streak kicked in. The same one that had had Candy threatening Alex instead of giving him a bag of birdseed. We women—the kind who had once stood shoulder to shoulder and held up the wall of the gymnasium during high school events—stuck together.

"It's a blind date. A friend of mine set us up. He's picking me up at six o'clock tonight. If I go. I was thinking that maybe I should just cancel. You know."

I did know.

"It won't hurt to go out for dinner." I squeezed the excess water from her hair, wrapped a fluffy towel around her head and shepherded her back to my chair.

"I didn't want to do this but she talked me into it. The guy is her first cousin and he just moved to Munroe a few months ago. He's a lawyer."

"Then you'll have a lot to talk about."

"We will?"

"You're the mayor, Candy," I reminded her, my heart cracking a bit under the weight of the doubt I saw in her eyes. "Plus you own a business."

Why did these things not matter when compared to the ar-rangement of a person's facial features and body parts?

"He's going to be disappointed when he sees me. I've gone

through this before. I'm shaped like a freezer, Bernice. I'm thirty-two but I look ten years older. Maybe a steak dinner isn't worth all this. I thought, after I saw Jill last night, that maybe you could…"

Make her beautiful. Like replacing the siding on a house, she wanted me to put a fresh coat on her exterior. But I knew that nothing I did to the outside could make her feel beautiful on the inside. I'd been there.

I wished that Annie or Elise or Esther were here to tell her how things really were. I didn't know how to talk to someone about God. It seemed to come so easily for Annie. Elise was quieter about her faith, but she'd still know what to say. And Esther…she always knew what to say. I wanted to be her when I grew up.

"I know how you feel." Our eyes met in the mirror. "I don't know what people said to you. I know what they said to *me*. You pick a feature and someone made fun of it when I was in junior high. But now…I don't care. Because someone thinks I'm beautiful and His is the only opinion that matters to me now."

"Alex Scott?"

I laughed but my fingers were shaking when I ran the comb through Candy's hair. "No. God."

"God?" Candy blinked, then her eyes narrowed. "Did you get religious, Bernice?"

"No. I just met Him. And decided to stay with Him." It was a relationship, Esther had explained to me. It was God's heart and my heart knit together forever. *He loves you, utterly and completely, Bernice,* she'd said. "I remember those comments people made but I decided I'm not going to listen to them anymore. I'm only going to listen to what He says."

"What does He say?"

"He says I'm worth fighting for."

"Worth fighting for." A small smile crept out and Candy's eyes lightened. But only for a second. "I only agreed to this date because I'm so tired of being alone."

I understood that, too, although I hadn't been tempted to date for a long time. "Just be yourself."

"Did that work for you?"

Her words cut deep but because the question was honest, I could answer the same way. "No. For some reason I kept sabotaging my life. When things would start going well, I'd tell myself that I didn't deserve to be happy and then I'd do something to make sure I wasn't. Very stupid. I don't recommend it. I want you to make me a promise. If I do my part to fix up your outside, think about letting God do His work on the inside, okay?"

"I'll think about it."

This was Candy. I knew if she said it, she'd do it.

"Bernice, I really should cancel this date. The two of us, total strangers, staring at each other in a dark corner of some restaurant. Not knowing what to say. I hate that."

The fear in her eyes was real.

"Where are you going?"

"He said we could decide when he picked me up."

"Do you like chili?"

Chapter Nine

"We're going to *church?*"

"I promised Annie."

Alex had appeared at five minutes to six and I'd had to spritz cold water in my last customer's face to bring her back to consciousness. By this time I was sure that everyone knew Alex Scott was hanging around town but hearing about him and seeing him were two different things.

"I thought maybe we could go somewhere more private."

"You don't have to go along," I said, keeping my voice casual. "We can always reschedule."

By the look on his face, I knew he saw right through my pathetic attempt to delay the inevitable.

"I'll go with you."

"Give me five minutes to run upstairs and change my clothes. I'm running late today because none of my customers seem satisfied with their usual hairstyles anymore."

Alex hadn't touched me since he'd shown up in Prichett, but suddenly he reached out and his fingers brushed a path down my jawline. "You're welcome."

"*You're* impossible." I stepped away from him so quickly that I almost tripped over my own feet.

I locked up the salon and stepped into the shadow of Alex's mammoth pickup truck. "I'll be right down."

"Mind if I come up? I need a drink of water."

I looked at him suspiciously. He could have asked for a drink five seconds ago. The truth was I was having a difficult time keeping a safe distance between us. "I suppose."

Alex chuckled but when we walked through the narrow alley to the back of the building, he suddenly frowned. "Is this the only entrance you have? Isn't that against fire codes?"

"I have an alternate escape plan if the stairway is blocked."

"Really? Let's hear it."

"I jump out the window onto the awning above the Cut and Curl and slide gracefully to the sidewalk."

He didn't laugh.

"Alex, there's an enclosed entrance on the other side of the building that I could use, but don't." I pushed the door open, bracing myself to be humbled when he saw my apartment.

"Are you selling furniture on the side?"

"We're going to be late if I have to explain everything." I huffed. "It's a hobby, okay?"

"Collecting chairs and benches?"

"They're antiques."

"I hate to say this, but I'm pretty sure they're just *old*."

"I'll be right back." I left him to save up more insults while I got dressed. I didn't have many "church" clothes so I put on the brown suede skirt that had carried me through the past few Sundays and threw on a crocheted jacket over a long-sleeved cotton T-shirt. I kicked a pair of leather sandals out of the way and rummaged around for the pair of low-heeled boots that I knew were hiding in a shoe box somewhere. The temperature had warmed up into the forties, teasing us before winter struck, but it was officially November now and so I officially switched to my fall and winter wardrobe. And no one had to know that underneath my boots were white socks printed with rows of smiling green frogs.

In record time, I reapplied my makeup, ran a brush through my hair and hurried back into the living room to see what Alex was getting into. Thank goodness I kept my copies of all the movies he'd starred in tucked away in a special case instead of openly displaying them with the rest of my collection. No reason to give him that kind of ammunition.

"Are you the one who's been teaching Murphy all those Bible verses?" He waved a three-by-five card at me.

"No, but I've been tempted to ask *him* for help."

Alex just looked at me, an unreadable expression on his face. I wasn't sure what to say. In all the conversations Alex and I'd had when we were seeing each other, God had never been mentioned in a single one. I had no idea if he even believed in God.

"This is really strange." Alex shook his head slightly and studied the card in his hand.

I moved closer, trying to see what I'd written on the card. I was reading the Psalms out of the Bible that Annie had given me. She told me when something that I read touched my heart that I should write it down, not to memorize, but to *remember.* The trouble was, everything was so new that everything touched my heart! I'd gone through an entire package of cards and was working on a second one.

"Nothing." He put the card on the coffee table. "Are you ready to go?"

Alex was quiet on the way to the church and I wondered if he was worried that he'd be the main course at the chili supper.

"So, what did you do all day?" I cast a line out, fishing for something that would give me a clue to his sudden shift in moods.

He rubbed the back of his neck and shot me a rueful look. "You don't want to know."

"What could possibly top buying a truck and a house and telling everyone in town that I've been holding out on them all these years?"

"I babysat Murphy while Charity was out with some of her friends."

"You babysat Murphy?" I repeated.

"According to Charity, if she leaves him alone all day he does, and I quote, 'naughty things.' She wasn't going to go but I told her that I didn't have anything to do, so I'd be happy to keep him company for a few hours."

"You lied through your teeth."

"Basically." Alex sighed. "After three hours of listening to him recite Bible verses, mimic the doorbell, a train whistle and a dog barking and *then* sing the choruses from several Broadway show tunes, I decided that he needed some downtime. So I tried to put him in his cage."

Why did I have the feeling, judging from the tone in Alex's voice, that the word "tried" was significant?

"After chasing me through the house, he finally cornered me in the parlor and walked toward me like he was reenacting Jimmy Stewart's big scene in *High Noon*."

I couldn't help it. By this time, I had my head in my lap, trying not to laugh as tears leaked out of my eyes.

"And then Charity came home and rescued me before I was just another body, lying there in the dust."

"Take a right up here and it's at the end of the block," I said, coming up for air and realizing we were almost to Faith Community.

Faith Community was one of three churches in Prichett. Businesses hadn't been the only things affected over the years. The town had lost several churches, too. One had merged with its sister congregation in Munroe and the others had simply closed their doors because they couldn't stay afloat financially. Annie had mentioned that Faith Community was bursting at the seams but so far everyone still fit.

I'd picked up on some of the murmurings that maybe there should be an addition, or even a brand-new building on some land that had been donated a few years ago, but I got the impression that no one really wanted to make such a drastic change. I was glad. Made out of brick with a row of narrow stained-glass windows that glowed in shades of ruby, emerald and blue, Faith Community looked like the front of a Christmas card.

As welcoming as it looked on the outside, though, the truth is I was scared to death the first time I went to a service there. I'd seen people coming and going through those wide double doors for years but had never pictured myself among them. When Heather had come to visit me, I'd taken her there with Elise and her family. I didn't know what to expect but there were no flashes of lightning when I walked in and no one pointed at me and asked me what I was doing there.

Sam had been right. He told me that church was a lot like supper on the front porch. Welcoming. Satisfying. A place where you were surrounded by people who were taking time out of their lives to be together.

"Bernice!"

Annie was the first person I saw when Alex and I made our way down to the basement. I opened my arms expectantly and Annie moved into them. There was no escaping Annie's hugs. I'd learned that right away.

"Hi, Mr. Scott."

He got one, too. His eyes, wide with shock, locked on mine over Annie's shoulder.

"I just know these are boys because they're already playing tackle football," she said, releasing Alex and curving an arm around her middle. "I couldn't sleep last night because they were practicing for the play-offs."

"Hey, time out, guys," I said to Annie's bulging abdomen. "Give your mom a break."

"If that works, you're going to move in with us until spring."

We followed Annie into the fellowship hall and she ushered us right into line. "I scoped out the dessert table at the end," she said in a low voice. "Carolee's coconut cake, Sally's pecan pie, two kinds of brownies—frosted or plain—and chocolate-chip cookies."

My mouth started to water. "Coconut cake. Definitely."

"Mr. Scott?"

"Um…"

"I'll just get you one of everything, like I do for Stephen." Annie darted away.

"She's a friend of yours, isn't she? I met her in the park."

"She's married to the youth pastor."

"So you go to church here?" Alex looked confused, as though he were reading directions that didn't make sense.

"I do now."

"Hi, Bernice. It's nice to see you." Jeanne Charles, the minister's wife, was standing behind the table, ladling chili into cardboard bowls. She was wearing a plastic apron over her navy-blue dress. "Crackers?"

"Just a few."

She carefully counted out four and dropped them into my chili.

"For you?" She smiled warmly at Alex.

And I could tell she didn't have a clue who he was.

"Sure." Alex stared at her intently.

Annie glided back. She gave us a discreet wink that told me our desserts were safely stashed away. "Need some help, Jeanne?"

"You can pour coffee. I had a few of the teens helping but I think they're hiding out in the nursery, eating pizza. It's a conspiracy."

Annie met us at the end of the row. Now she was wearing a plastic apron, too, and she plucked happily at the hem. "I know, don't say it, I look like a basketball covered in shrink wrap. Coffee or lemonade?"

She had to raise her voice because by this time, the buzz of conversation was louder and a group of kids was playing a noisy game of catch with an empty milk carton on the other side of the room. Someone must have thought that we needed music, so in the speakers on the ceiling a loud crackle fought for dominance against the soft strains of Handel's "Messiah."

There was no way Alex and I were going to be able to talk.

Thank You, God!

"You're a movie star, aren't you?"

Since the question came from a place somewhere by our feet, Alex and I both looked down.

Seven-year-old Becky Frith was standing not quite a foot away from us. Her mother had six children and did a *Seven Brides for Seven Brothers* thing by naming her children alphabetically. Austin, Becky, Cody, David, Ethan and Francis. I knew them all, not only because they all had heads as red as a pileated woodpecker and an explosion of matching freckles, but because I'd given each and every one of them their first haircut and every one since.

"Yes, I am." There was relief in Alex's eyes and I almost laughed. He'd probably been wondering if he still looked the same.

No, Alex, you're not in Kansas anymore.

"Mom won't let us watch your movies. She says there are bad words in them."

"Oh." Alex frowned.

"And blood."

Alex glanced at me. The relief was gone, replaced with something that looked like panic. Obviously he wasn't used to dealing with pint-size movie critics. "There isn't *that much* blood."

"Austin went on a birthday sleepover and when Mom found out he watched your movie, she grounded him for two weeks. He couldn't go bowling with us." The look in Becky's eyes promised Alex that somehow, somewhere, he would get what was coming to him for wrecking the Frith family's bowling day.

"How old is your brother?"

"Twelve and a half. I like princess stories."

Alex looked desperate now to make things right. "Like *Cinderella?*"

"You could be in one of those, and then my mom would let us watch it."

"I'll keep that in mind."

Becky grinned, showing a ridge of rosy-pink gums where there should have been teeth. "Don't be the bad guy." Her voice dropped to a whisper. "He always gets killed in the end."

"Thanks for the heads-up."

Becky nodded and skipped away.

"Let's go sit down before another one of your devoted fans finds you," I suggested.

"There really isn't that much blood."

"If you say so."

"You haven't seen my movies?"

"You mean those testosterone-driven sweat-fests with the thirty-minute car chases that double as a plot?"

"Just for the record, there's never been a car chase that lasts longer than fifteen minutes. And I have a stunt double for the sweating part."

What came out of my mouth next can only be described as

a giggle. And everyone at the table heard it, too, because they stopped talking. Sam. Elise. Jim Briggs. *Jim Briggs?* Stephen.

"Sit down. Annie saved you a seat…seats." Stephen waved us closer and Jim pulled out one of the metal folding chairs.

"Careful, Bernice, you know how dangerous these things can be." He winked at me.

Alex's eyes settled on Jim and he must have decided that if the chair was potentially dangerous, then he should be the one to guide me safely into it. He chivalrously put his hand on the small of my back. Which I reacted to exactly like I would have if I'd been singed with a branding iron. I jumped several inches off the floor. Two touches from Alex in the space of an hour. Inwardly, I started to pack my suitcases. I had to leave town. It wasn't big enough for the both of us!

Elise, bless her heart, accurately read my expression like only true friends can do and took the pressure off me by introducing Alex to everyone at the table.

Jim gave him a short nod but Sam stood up and reached across the table to shake his hand, in the universal way men weigh and measure each other. Alex must have tipped the scale on the right side because when Sam sat back down, the first words out of his mouth were, "Hope you can come for dinner while you're here."

Now I took note of Elise's expression. Was her pot roast really up to par with what Alex was used to eating?

I picked up my cardboard cup of chili and wiggled it at her, just so she could get her perspective back again, then I came up with a question guaranteed to take her mind completely off cooking for a Hollywood celebrity.

"Have you heard from Bree lately?"

"She's coming home for Thanksgiving," Elise said, a smile glowing in her eyes. "What are your plans? Are you coming for dinner?"

I couldn't talk about plans without mentioning Heather. And I couldn't mention Heather with Alex just inches away, using the tip of his spoon to carefully and precisely pile all the kidney beans into a tiny, kidney bean mountain on one side of his bowl.

"I'm not sure yet."

She understood. Sam, however, wasn't completely tuned into our station.

"Alex, you're welcome to come along. It would be nice to even things up a little. Have someone to watch football with while the women watch *It's a Wonderful Life* and sob into their hankies."

"Thanks for the invite," Alex said, then arched an eyebrow at me. "I just may take you up on it."

No, no, no, I wailed silently. Heather had mentioned that she wanted to see me during her break from school, too, and I hadn't planned on Alex being in Prichett. But now that he'd bought my house, anything was possible.

"Bernice, have you come up with an evening we can get together to talk about the grant?" Jim interjected.

"How about next Monday? Right after work?"

"It's a date." Another wink.

Sam wanted to know about the grant and the second I mentioned Lester Lee's addition to the agenda, Elise was on the verge of a conniption fit.

"Not Junebug," she groaned. "She's got a big head already from the calendar and the parade. No one will be able to live with her if she's the model for a statue in the park."

"No one will be able to live with Lester, either," Sam said under his breath.

"Who's Junebug?" Alex asked.

"Lester's cow," Jim said. "She's a local novelty."

He put the smallest amount of emphasis on the word "local." I fought the urge to kick him under the table.

"Lester Lee?" Alex made the connection sooner than I hoped he would. "Isn't he the guy who just sold me that little house outside of town?"

Silence suddenly ballooned into the air space around our table.

"You bought the old church house?" Elise squeaked.

She knew about my futile attempts over the past ten years to convince Lester to sell.

"It's falling apart," Jim said helpfully.

"I noticed that." Alex leaned closer to me and tipped his bowl in my direction. "Do you like these?"

Everything was gone except for the mountain of kidney beans. "Uh-huh."

"Here." He scraped them into my bowl before I could protest.

"I can't believe Lester decided to sell," Sam ventured, flicking a cautious glance at me. "It's been in his family for years."

"Must have made him an offer he couldn't refuse," Jim snorted.

"I think it was a fair price," Alex said mildly.

Only I recognized that the glint in his eyes had nothing to do with the fact that he'd gotten a fair price.

"I'm missing my wife again." Stephen sighed suddenly.

"She was drafted to the beverage table." *Thank you, Stephen!* Every good pastor must be trained to defuse a tense situation. Kind of like those guys who work with bomb squads.

"She needs to take it easy," Stephen said, and his eyes were shadowed with worry. "She's only in her fifth month and she was having some pretty strong contractions yesterday. I'm afraid Dr. Meyer is going to put her on bed rest if she doesn't slow down."

Now I was worried. Annie is one of those people who bubbles and fizzes like a successful chemistry experiment, so it's hard to imagine that her energy isn't inexhaustible. "What can she cut back on?"

"Right now what's going to take most of her time is organizing the teens for the live nativity the church has every year."

I suddenly saw an opportunity to help Annie and get myself out of the Main Street Christmas open house. "I'll do it."

Stephen stared at me with an expression of gratitude and…fear? No, it couldn't be fear. That didn't make sense. How hard could it be to dress up some teenagers like Mary and Joseph, wind some garland into halos for the angels and snag a sheep or two from one of the farmers?

"Are you sure, Bernice? I already found out last Sunday that the Jensens, who usually let us use their barn for the nativity, are going to the Caribbean this year and don't want us on their property because of liability. I've still got a few people I can call but even when we decide on a place, there's a ton of work to do."

"You could use our place but it's a little farther out than what you like, isn't it?" Sam said.

Stephen nodded. "We like to keep it as close to town as possible."

"You could have it at my house," Jim offered. "I don't have a barn or anything, but maybe some of the guys could build a stable."

Alex raised his hand, like he was back in third-grade reading class.

"I have a barn."

Chapter Ten

No one said a word. Maybe they were all choking on a mouthful of kidney beans, just like I was.

"That's...great," Stephen finally said. "We'll have to see if anyone else..."

"It's perfect." Annie had left her post, armed with two plates piled high with cake, and gracefully maneuvered herself, belly included, into the chair next to Stephen. "Thank you, Mr. Scott."

"Please, call me Alex. This Mr. Scott stuff makes me feel old."

"Good thing there's plastic surgery so you'll never have to *look* old though, right?" Jim gave him a friendly cuff on the shoulder.

Just as I was about to stuff a spoonful of kidney beans into Jim's mouth, rescue came in an unlikely form.

"Is that *Candy?*" Sam asked.

We all turned toward the doorway and saw Candy standing next to a—no one was quite prepared for this, I could tell—man. Her blind date. Her entrance couldn't have been timed more perfectly because in another minute, Jim might have been the one needing plastic surgery.

I saw her eyes desperately scanning the crowd and decided that since bringing her date to the chili supper had been my suggestion—not that I thought for a second they'd actually show up—I was the one who had to save her. I stood up and waved.

"She looks different," Elise murmured.

"She has hair," Sam said in awe.

Elise elbowed him lightly in the ribs and rolled her eyes.

Alex leaned back, crossed his arms over his chest and looked smug, as if he knew exactly why Candy looked different.

As they crossed the room toward us, I was amazed to see that Candy had shed her overalls, flannel shirt and boots for a black pantsuit with a stylish cut. It was the perfect contrast for her hair and silently I applauded her choice. With only a few precious seconds to stare before they reached the table, I concentrated on the blind date.

He was exactly Candy's height and he was definitely over-dressed for a chili supper in the church basement. If Candy hadn't been so nervous about being alone with him, it was obvious she would have gotten her steak dinner. He was wearing a shirt and tie, paired with pants that had pleats sharp enough to draw blood. He had a studious look about him—distinguished wings of gray hair at his temples and narrow, gold-framed glasses perched on his nose. I couldn't resist a smile. They looked like a cute pair of matching salt and pepper shakers.

"Hi, you guys." Candy plowed ahead of her date and almost leaped into the empty chair that Sam had pushed away from the table.

Everyone casually said hello, like it wasn't as rare as a solar eclipse to see the mayor of Prichett at a church function…and without her baseball cap.

"This is Mark Fielding," Candy said, silently daring us to say a word about her hair.

None of us was stupid—we all knew Candy. All of us except Alex. Just to be safe, I stepped on his foot as a warning.

We went around the table and dutifully said our first names like we were part of a support group, which, if you think about it, we are.

"I'll get you both a bowl of chili," Annie said.

Stephen put his hand on her shoulder and pressed gently. "I'll do it."

Silence. Painful silence. Why was it up to me to yank the cord that would get the conversation flowing? Probably because I was the reason Candy and Mark Fielding were getting a cardboard cup of chili instead of a porterhouse and a baked potato.

"Candy said you're new to the area." First pull.

Mark Fielding glanced at Candy, obviously wondering just how much she'd told me about him and why I'd been the chosen victim. "That's correct."

Sputter. No good. I tried again.

"And you're a lawyer?"

"That's correct."

"If you get another one right, do you win a prize?" Alex breathed in my ear.

Just as I was about to find out, everyone realized that Candy was on a real-live date with someone she didn't know. And suddenly poor Mark Fielding was pelted with questions from every side.

"What do you think of the area?"

"Where are you originally from?"

"What do you like to do in your spare time?"

Mark Fielding cleared his throat and straightened his tie. I imagined him doing the exact same thing in front of a jury.

"I love the area. I grew up around Eau Claire but I went to law school out east. In my spare time I do some fishing. A lot of reading. And I help out with Special Olympics."

Candy's eyes, which had been riveted on a red juice stain on the tablecloth, lifted. "Special Olympics?"

Mark nodded, looking a bit startled that she could talk. Obviously, Candy had *not* taken my advice and acted like herself.

Stephen delivered two bowls of chili with the panache of a waiter at an award-winning restaurant and Candy's posture relaxed. And I relaxed. I hadn't realized I'd been holding my breath practically the whole time until white spots began to dance in front of my eyes and I felt a little dizzy.

People began to approach our table. They smiled politely, almost shyly, at Alex and then proceeded to make a huge fuss over Candy. Welcoming her. Patting her shoulder. Bringing her extra crackers. There wasn't anything fake or insincere about the attention she was getting. I could tell that after the initial shock wore off, she was actually starting to enjoy it. She even bravely introduced Mark Fielding as her date when Pastor Charles paused to say hello.

Finally, when the stream of people began to dwindle to a trickle, Sam, never one for sitting still very long, stood up and stretched.

"Well, honey, think we should call it a night?" He turned to Elise and she nodded happily, with just the faintest hint of pink stealing into her cheeks.

It was hard not to be around Sam and Elise, and even Annie and Stephen, and not feel a bit envious. There was so much love and electricity in the air that you felt like you were watching the Northern Lights. Annie and Stephen hadn't been married very long, so they still had the newlywed sparkle but Sam and Elise had been married nineteen years. Time had polished that sparkle into a deep, warm patina that was just as mesmerizing. It was a gift to see what love was supposed to look like, covered in years.

"Ditto for us," Stephen said, looping one arm around Annie's slim shoulders.

"I've got a long day tomorrow, too." Jim stood up and shook Mark's hand but ignored Alex. "Nice meeting you, Mark."

As if on cue, the entire room began to clear out. Leaving me and Alex and Candy and Mark sitting at the table. Just the four of us, while a boisterous group of teens turned up the music and started their own karaoke club in the kitchen.

"You don't have to leave yet, do you, Bernice?" Candy asked.

I glanced at Alex. His lips quirked into the crooked smile that had won hearts across the country. Including mine. I shook the pesky thought away.

"Mark, how do you feel about Monopoly?" He practically sighed the question.

Mark's eyebrows drew together over his nose and he shrugged. "It's up to Candy."

"That's a great idea." Candy tucked a long strand of blond hair behind her ear. "If Alex and Bernice want to," she added quickly.

I held back a smile.

"Are you up for a game, Miss Strum?" Alex asked me.

I wanted to hug him. I could see in his eyes how much he wanted to talk to me—alone—but he was willing to put that aside to help out Candy, who he didn't even know. Who had threatened him with ordinance B31, section eighteen.

Candy and I cleaned up the napkins and empty bowls while the guys went over to see what was left on the dessert table.

"So, Alex, what do you do?" I heard Mark ask.

The cold air ran into me as soon as I opened the door to go to work the next morning. I decided to go to Sally's and pick up a few Danishes. Several of the clients I had lined up for the day had a sweet tooth and it had gotten to the point now that they expected *something* chock-full of calories and sugar to be waiting for them by the coffeepot when they came in.

The café was quiet when I walked in, the entire row of

farmers shoulder to shoulder, hunched over their first cup of coffee. I skirted around them and headed straight for the cash register when I noticed that one of the stools was empty. Lester Lee's stool. Then I saw him sitting alone in a booth in the far corner, morosely stirring his coffee with a straw. Uh-oh. It was obvious that a certain someone had been sent to the café's equivalent of Siberia.

Sally gave me a meaningful glance.

"He's still here, isn't he?"

I had no doubt who *he* was.

"It looks that way."

"He still at Charity's?"

"For now." I wasn't sure if everyone knew yet that Lester had sold Alex the house.

"So it is true." Sally frowned. They knew. Her words carried and a low grumble of discontent made its way down the row of farmers.

Alex's arrival in Prichett had obviously added a new layer of weirdness to my beloved town. I glanced over at Lester Lee, who wouldn't meet my eyes.

"Here you go." Sally bagged up six pastries without my having to even tell her what I wanted. Just as I reached out to take them, she put her hand on mine. "You have a nice day, Bernice."

"Um, sure." I needed to get back to my salon, where things were in their rightful place.

God, stick really close today, okay? I got out of talking to Alex last night, but I know it's only a matter of time and I have no idea what to say to him. And I'm afraid of the reason he's here. And by the way, why is he here?

It's too bad God didn't have some sort of cloaking device for hiding His children.

When I got to the Cut and Curl, there was a note taped to

my door. This in itself wasn't strange because sometimes people did tape notes to the door, asking me to call so-and-so or asking me to cancel an appointment. I peeled it off, then licked my index finger and tried to scrub off the sticky residue that the tape had left on the glass. The words had been typed in a font so tiny I had to squint to read them.

Don't worry. We'll take care of him.

I could only assume the mysterious reference to *him* meant Alex. And what exactly did it mean? Did it mean that someone was going to make sure he had a warm coat and plenty of food to eat or was it something more ominous? I blew out an exasperated breath. Honestly, Prichett loved to create its own little dramas. It was no wonder that Alex had settled right in. He was probably taking notes. I shoved the paper in my pocket and opened the shop, mentally running through the inventory of my day and trying to find little gaps of time that I could use to call Heather. And my mother. And Annie. Especially Annie. I knew if I didn't get busy and start forming a plan for the live nativity, she'd position herself at the epicenter and not take the time she needed to rest.

"Hi, Bernice."

It was the Candy we all knew and loved. Heavy brown canvas coat over her bibs and her hair once again tucked under a cap.

"Hi." I waved her inside but she shook her head.

"Can't chitchat right now. I've got a truck scheduled for eight. I just wanted to say thanks."

"Don't thank me." *I should be thanking you. Alex and I didn't have a minute alone.* "It was fun."

Candy hesitated. "He said he's going to call me."

My heart ached at how quickly the light was extinguished. Swamped by fear. I knew that that was the reason I hadn't dated. I'd had enough of feeling that way while Alex and I were seeing each other. The constant roller coaster of my insecurity. Always feeling nauseous. Better to just submerge myself in my work and watch the seasons change outside the window.

"You know, Alex isn't such a bad guy."

Oh, no. He was winning people over left and right. I was sure that was his strategy. I had to put things back into perspective.

"Not so bad? Did you notice the way he kept buying up the last property I needed so I couldn't get three of the same color?"

"I noticed he slipped you his Get Out of Jail Free card when you couldn't roll doubles."

"Don't let that fool you."

"Right. Have a cup of coffee, Bernice." She backed out the door and bumped into Greta Lewis, who was on her way in.

I'd asked God several times to forgive me for initially judging Greta by the way she looked. If you would have dropped the girl in Madison or Milwaukee, no one would have given her a second look, but this was Prichett. There was practically a dress code and even though I didn't exactly adhere to it, ninety-nine point nine percent of the teenagers that walked past the shop's plate-glass windows or sat in my chair were all wearing a slight variation of the same outfit. Blue jeans and T-shirts. If it was hot, they had short sleeves. If it was cold, they had long sleeves. Either way, their clothes made a statement: blend in.

Greta, having a more artistic bent, used her clothes to make a statement, too: stand out. And she did. Like the one colorful sock that accidentally gets thrown into a load of whites. Although most of the time she wore black. Her hair was black, too, compliments of one of those home kits that are the bane of my existence. I'm forever fixing the havoc that those kits create when placed in the hands of the innocent. Today she was wearing black but had added a spark of color to the dreary ensemble by wrapping a vibrant purple wool scarf around her neck.

"Hi, Bernice."

It was eight-fifteen. School started at eight-ten. Greta was a senior, which meant she knew what time school started, so I decided not to point it out. "I just bought some Danishes from Sally's. Help yourself."

"Thanks." She rustled around in the bag and zeroed in on the raspberry. Rats. My favorite. "Aunt Mindy said she made an appointment for me to get my hair fixed for the Senior Tea."

"Is it too early?" I started flipping pages in my appointment book. "I can try to squeeze you in somewhere else, although my day is pretty much booked."

"I want you to cancel it." Her voice was flat. Harsh. "I'm not going."

Okay... "Mind if I ask why?"

"It's just not my thing."

I didn't believe her for a second. Not when I could hear the tears, all loose and gravelly, in the background of the words.

"Greta, what's going on?"

"Melissa Turner."

I knew Melissa well. Head cheerleader. Lead in the school play. She had a group of devoted followers that had been known to take up every one of my chairs in front of the window while they waited for her to get her hair cut. They ate all the sugar cubes out of the sugar bowl and quietly ripped pages out of my celebrity hair magazines when I wasn't looking.

It was now eight-twenty. The second bell had buzzed. Greta was officially late for school, which meant an official check mark on her record. I took an apricot Danish and sat down next to her.

"I take it the two of you don't get along."

"Mom always says that it takes two people to have an argument, but I don't think anyone ever told Melissa that. She seems to manage one all by herself."

I poured us both a cup of coffee. And suddenly wondered if Heather had ever gone through this kind of stuff in high school. Her entire life was an unknown. All I knew was the beautiful, confident twenty-year-old I'd met just a few months ago. No one managed to get through high school unscathed, so she must have had days like this. There was no getting over the fact that I hadn't been there. But there had been two good people who were. *Thank You, God, for her wonderful adoptive parents.*

"She told some kids I'm into voodoo, whatever that means. Annie and Stephen have been picking me up for youth group and it made me feel even worse that she'd say that about me. And everyone probably believes it." She looked at me with haunted eyes. "I feel new, Bernice, but they won't let me be new. Then I start to feel...old again. Does that make any sense?"

It did. But I didn't know what to say because there'd been times recently that I felt the same way. "Have you talked to Annie about it?"

"I have her phone number in my speed dial," Greta said. "She gave me this."

The three-by-five card. More of Annie's grace graffiti.

I skimmed through the verse and saw that on the top of the card, Annie had written, "Just a reminder that people will let you down but God never will."

The reminder was as much for me as it was for Greta. I smiled and gave her back the card.

"All I know is that a lot of things are coming at us and telling us what to think about ourselves. But what we have to hold on to is what God thinks of us."

"Even you?"

I almost laughed at the question. "Even me. You can talk to God about Melissa. He understands. I think He had a lot of people in His life that accused Him of things that weren't true. And I've been reading the Psalms, and it looks like David had a lot of trouble with people who were out to get him."

Greta smiled, just the slightest softening of her lips. "Don't cancel the appointment yet. I'll…think about going."

I had an idea.

"I could use a little help if you have any free time."

"Doing what?"

"I need someone to play the part of Mary in the live nativity."

Greta's eyes widened. "Really? I can be Mary?"

I couldn't think of any reason why she couldn't. Black eyeliner and pierced nostril aside, she had an appealing serenity about her. "I may even need some help with costumes. If you're interested."

"I'm interested. And I'm late." Greta took another Danish and jumped up. "Thanks, Bernice." She smiled. "Mary. Wow."

And then she was gone.

Chapter Eleven

❧

"…and she didn't believe that you have to let the turkey *rest* for fifteen minutes after it comes out of the oven. So she called the turkey hotline. Can you imagine that? Right in front of me. And I could tell the second that hotline lady told her that you *did* have to let the turkey rest for fifteen minutes because her face got as red as the cranberry sauce." Marjorie Duncan crossed her arms under the cape, her expression smug.

It never changed. The entire month of November I learned everything a person needed—and wanted—to know about Thanksgiving. How much nutmeg to put in the pumpkin pie. How much sage to put in the stuffing. Trying to stay neutral while listening to the constant war that raged between the women who put sausage in their stuffing and the ones who used the turkey's, uh, more *natural* parts. To be honest, I was firmly on the sausage-stuffing side. And, of course, the secret to roasting the perfect turkey. I had so much information that I knew if I was at a loose end on Thanksgiving Day, I could probably moonlight as a turkey hotline lady myself.

But no chance of that. I could already taste Elise's mashed potatoes and gravy. She only held me responsible for the dinner rolls and she didn't mind that I bought them from the grocery store, either.

Somehow, over the years, I'd fallen into the trap that probably ensnared a multitude of single working women. I was simply too tired to create a fabulous meal...for one. The times when I shamed myself into making an attempt, I somehow ended up with something that didn't even faintly resemble the picture in the cookbook. I had decided to turn my culinary efforts over to the woman who produced the food in these pictures. Namely, Betty Crocker.

"That's the second truck I've seen this morning," Marjorie said. Her hands fumbled under the cape for her glasses, which she wore around her neck, suspended by two fragile gold chains.

I didn't have to look out the window to know exactly what she was talking about. The first truck had been as big as a commercial airliner and had barreled down Main Street like it was its private runway. I barely caught the words painted on the side: Montague's Furniture. I'd never heard of Montague's Furniture before but I had a pretty good guess as to who had.

"It's in a big hurry, that's for sure," Marjorie said.

"Okay, under the dryer for twenty minutes," I said, not wanting to think about the trucks. It was hard enough to picture my sweet country house being permanently maimed by the contents of a truckload of chrome and glass without thinking about *who* was doing the maiming.

Marjorie made her way agreeably over to the dryer, with only a slight detour to the coffeepot, where a lonely Danish waited. The last raspberry. I didn't mind. Marjorie was the first person all week who hadn't repeated those fateful words, "fix my hair the way you see it." She'd stuck to her usual shampoo and set.

Strangely enough, I hardly saw Alex the rest of the week. I did see more trucks. Another one from Montague's Furniture. One from a place called Kibling, Verone and Kibling, which sounded like the name of a law firm but claimed to *know kitchens*. Big deal. I knew my kitchen. It took up an eighth of my apartment and probably assumed it was semi-retired, which was another reason I didn't like to put too much strain on it.

On Friday afternoon, a van with the words Custom Interiors and Design cruised past.

My curiosity was killing me.

I was sure that after our board game marathon, Alex would have been anxious to have dinner alone with me. Now he seemed to have forgotten that I, too, lived in Prichett.

I tried to tell myself that being forgotten was a good thing. That I wasn't in a hurry to take a walk with him down Memory Lane.

A flash of red bobbed past the window and Annie came in.

"Hi, Bernice," she said breathlessly, pressing one hand against the twins to steady them in much the same way she might have steadied a tippy Jell-O mold. "I'm glad you're still here."

Pregnancy looked good on Annie. Her willowy figure had suddenly gone to curves that even her loose denim jacket couldn't disguise. Her eyes always seemed to be lit from within but now they practically glowed.

I glanced at my watch and realized it was already five o'clock. Who knew that watching for mysterious trucks would make the day go by so fast? It could be a new sport. Too bad it didn't burn any calories, though.

"I'm still here," I echoed. *But where was Alex?* I silently shook the traitorous thought away. I knew where he was. He was in my house, turning it into some sort of overblown, custom-color-coordinated nightmare. Painting the walls an anemic shade of cream called Eggshell. That's where he was.

"I just wanted to stop in and tell you that Stephen put two

boxes of clothes for the nativity costumes outside your door. Just weed out the ones that aren't in good shape. Or anything that has *words* on it. We get some strange donations sometimes. And I mentioned at youth group that we should have a quick meeting after church on Sunday to choose the main parts. Everyone argues over who's going to be Mary and Joseph, just so you know. I've already been told that Melissa has been Mary since her freshman year—"

My heart took a sudden dive. "Melissa Turner?"

"Yup. Does Sunday work for you? I know I should have checked with you first."

"It's fine."

"You don't look fine."

Confession time. "I already told Greta that she could be Mary."

"Oh." Annie's mind appeared to be working on that as carefully as if she were handling a live grenade. And maybe she was! "Greta. You're a genius, Bernice. I've been trying to think of ways to help her feel special."

While Annie had been trying to build Greta up, Melissa Turner's gossip had been busy tunneling beneath the surface, searching for vulnerable spots. And now I had inadvertently done something else to set them at odds.

Lord, maybe I'm not cut out for this.

After all, I was still letting God do some repairs on *my* vulnerable spots. And I'd been a lot like Greta in high school. I hadn't fit, either.

I was just about to suggest that maybe Annie and Stephen would rather have someone else take over the nativity when Annie hugged me.

"I'm so glad you volunteered to do this," she whispered. "You remember how I found out I was pregnant with the twins…"

I had. And I shuddered at the reminder. Annie had started to bleed. And we all thought she was having a miscarriage, until an ultrasound showed two little hearts beating inside of her.

"I had an appointment with Dr. Meyer this morning and he told me if I didn't cut my activities in half, he was going to put me on complete bed rest until my delivery date."

"You have to listen to him." I forced the words out, terrified of something happening to them.

"I know—the little bookends need me to take care of them."

"Little bookends?"

"That's what Stephen calls them," Annie said. "Because everything that happens in our lives from now on—our story—is going to happen *between* them. One on either side."

I knew what she meant. Even though Bree had been eight when I'd moved to Prichett, I'd watched Elise and Sam raise her for the past ten years. Every decision—no, every breath—was in the context of *family*.

"Don't worry about the nativity," I said bravely. "In fact, consider yourself working on a consultant-only basis from now on."

"Just remember if you need help, ask. Everyone works together," Annie said simply, as if that was just the way things were supposed to work. Obviously she'd never been at a PAC meeting, but I wasn't going to be the one to disillusion her.

I need help.

Just kidding.

No, really, Lord, I need help!

"I'll remember," I promised.

"We'll see you Sunday." How Annie could still manage to walk with such a spring in her step was beyond me.

"I'm going to make sure you follow the doctor's orders," I called after her.

Annie gave me a salute and almost twirled out the door.

I closed up the salon, hurried up the back steps and dragged in the boxes that Stephen had left. I riffled quickly through the contents, immediately pulling out a ratty green-and-yellow bathrobe with the Packers football insignia appliquéd across the back. And although some die-hard Packers maniacs might disagree, I seriously doubted that the shepherds camped outside of Bethlehem were football fans.

Mary's long blue robe was still intact but the hem had come unstitched. There were three white satin graduation gowns, as thin as parchment, that were going to turn the angels into ice sculptures if they wore them. Another purple robe that looked suspiciously like the one I'd donated to the church rummage sale a few weeks before. It had a piece of paper pinned to it that said "Wise Man."

Pitiful. We definitely needed an expert. I knew that the nativity drew people from all over the area and there was only one thing I could do: turn the entire contents over to Greta and pray that the shepherds wouldn't come to Bethlehem dressed like a bunch of guys headed to a rock concert.

I took a break to call my parents, just so I could check it off my list. No answer. I'd been trying twice a day now for the past three days and not once had they picked up the phone. I'd even left messages. Okay, one message. A brief one. But still.

Daughterly duty done, I decided to follow the natural order of things and have supper. Halfway through my rice pilaf, I dropped my fork. This was crazy. I had to see what Alex was doing to my house. He couldn't just send a convoy of trucks past my window all week and not expect me to be obsessed. No, curious. That was the word I was looking for.

Before I could change my mind, I pulled my coat back on and drove over to the house, assuming that there had been a bed in one of those trucks and Alex had moved out of the

Lightning Strike. The whole place was lit up, inside and out, but when I knocked on the door, no one answered.

Bump. Thud. Curse. Thud.

I winced and made my way cautiously around the side of the house, following the repeating pattern. Bump. Thud. Curse. Thud. Until I ended up in the barn. As far as barns went, it was very cute. A stone foundation, a hip-shaped roof and faded red paint—but it was half the size of a regular barn. Almost in miniature. I hated to admit it, but it was the perfect place to have the live nativity. I'm surprised no one had thought of it before.

"Alex?"

Thud. Fortunately, no curse.

"Bernice?"

"Yes…" I still couldn't see him, even though I could hear his muffled voice somewhere in the shadows.

"It's about time."

I decided to ignore that. "What are you doing?"

"Looking for Colonel Mustard. If he doesn't have dinner by seven…well, it's hard for him to make it through the night, if you know what I mean."

I didn't. But I did suddenly feel like I was being watched. I slowly turned around and saw a pair of mournful brown eyes staring up at me. On a dog that had legs much too short for his body.

"Is Colonel Mustard a basset hound?" I asked cautiously. I dropped to one knee and held out my hand. The dog shuffled closer and searched my palm for treats. Then eyed my empty hand reproachfully.

"He's a dog." Alex emerged, covered in dust and cobwebs. "Yeah. That's him."

"Where did he come from?"

"Someone dropped him off a few days ago," Alex said.

"You mean they just *left* him here?"

"Not exactly. It was a farmer up the road. He said he couldn't take care of him anymore. Told me he figured I needed a watchdog."

I laughed. "A watchdog?"

"He never barks," Alex said with a disgusted shake of his head. "Maybe if someone tries to break in, he knows tae kwon do or something."

"Look at this sad face," I crooned, scratching the silky ears. "Maybe he just guilts them into giving up their life of crime."

"Maybe." Alex scooped up the dog in his arms. "Come on. Suppertime. Or else we're going to have a case of Colonel Mustard—in the front hall—with…"

"Alex!"

"Sorry."

There was a movement to my left and I suddenly realized that there was something on the other side of the fence. And it looked a lot like…

"Is that *Junebug?*"

I stopped short and found myself almost eyeball to eyeball with the most infamous Holstein in the county.

"That's her." Alex was still moving, obviously extremely motivated to get Colonel Mustard his supper by seven, and I reluctantly followed.

"But what is she doing here?"

"Lester brought her over yesterday. He said that for some reason, she's been…"

"She's been what?"

"Depressed."

Junebug kept up with us along the fence. She didn't look to me like she was suffering from…*depression?*

"But what is she doing *here?*" I asked again.

"Lester thinks that… This is going to sound crazy, Bernice."

"Please. You forget I've lived in Prichett for ten years. Nothing sounds crazy to me anymore."

"He thinks she's upset because he just got some new cows in and there's one who's prettier than her."

Mmm. Where did I attach the label of crazy? To Lester, who thinks that cows actually know when another cow is prettier than they are? Or to Alex, for believing him?

How about a two-for-one special?

"You don't believe him, do you?" I had to ask.

Alex set Colonel Mustard down and pushed open the back door. "No. But what could I say? Lester showed up, reminded me that I have an empty barn and he's convinced that Junebug needs some time away from Ruby."

Ruby, the prettier cow.

In the last ten minutes I hadn't even had time to think about what Alex had done to my house. And without adequate preparation, I found myself stepping into the kitchen. The kitchen that introduced itself as the home of a gourmet chef. A gourmet *country* chef. He'd actually remained loyal to the quaint charm of the place. The old tin-punched ceiling hadn't been covered up with recessed lighting and the small but impractical leaded-glass window above the sink remained untouched.

"I know I already started doing some renovating, but I still need your advice on some things," Alex said, pouring kibble into a state-of-the-art, gold-trimmed ceramic dog dish that must have come off a truck I'd missed called Pathetically Spoiled Pets.

I looked around the rest of the room in awe. I'd only peeked in the windows on occasion but I know there hadn't been hickory cabinets or a marble countertop.

"Some renovating," I repeated. "What I want to know is where you're hiding the team from one of those home makeover shows."

"It's a small room. It didn't take long."

"You did this yourself?"

"I'm not completely useless, you know." Alex kicked off his leather shoes. "Stephen helped me last night with the cabinets. Esther put up the curtains."

"Wait a second. Esther was here?"

"And John. I stopped by the nursing home the other day and he said he wanted to see the place." Again, that slightly confused look in response to John's sense of humor.

"He can still see. I mean, he's blind, but he wasn't always blind. If you describe things to him, he can see them in his imagination."

"I figured that out when he beat me at chess the other day," Alex said wryly.

I wandered through to the tiny breakfast room and was happy to see chaos in the form of unpacked boxes and paint cans stacked against the wall. I couldn't prevent the words, even though I hadn't studied for the heart-to-heart that I knew Alex and I needed to have.

"Why are you here?"

Chapter Twelve

Alex motioned for me to sit down on the sofa. It was as soft as a cloud and I sank into the spicy scent of new leather. Just as I was about to close my eyes in a state of comfortable bliss, Alex sat on the matching leather ottoman, about a foot away from me.

"I needed to get away for a while."

"And you don't have a private island somewhere?"

Alex didn't smile. "That's beside the point. When Phoebe told me you'd called, I really needed to know why."

I tried not to think too hard about what he'd meant by a private island being *beside the point.*

"I started to think about the way I walked out on you," I said cautiously. "Without even telling you why. And I realized it was wrong."

"It took you twenty years to figure that out?"

"You didn't try to find me."

We stared at each other and I wanted to grab the words back and stuff them inside.

"Was that some kind of test, Bern?" Alex's eyes narrowed. "Because when I saw you in Chicago, *briefly,* I might add, you acted like you were mad at *me.* That I'd done something terrible. That's it. I failed the test, didn't I? When you left, you were waiting to see if I'd come after you."

I wanted to deny it but it was the truth. And it made me realize how immature I'd been. How I'd desperately wanted Alex to show me that I was worth fighting for. And instead, his rejection had acted as a highlighter, boldly emphasizing what I'd believed to be the truth. That I wasn't worthy of someone's love.

And when I'd seen him again in Chicago, I'd blamed him for not coming after me. For not knowing about our daughter, even though it wasn't fair to blame him for that since I'd never told him about her.

"Why didn't you?"

"Find you?" He read my thoughts. "Pride, I guess. But mostly resignation. I had the feeling that no matter what I did, no matter how much I tried to convince you, it would never be enough. You'd always doubt me. And yourself."

"You were right." Alex alone wouldn't have been able to carry all the stuff I was dragging around with me. It took God to take my hand and steer me away from the baggage claim. I was starting a new life. I had a new wardrobe. I didn't need to hang on to that old junk anymore. "You couldn't have. I wanted you to, but all I could think about was that someday, you'd see the real me and it wouldn't be enough."

Alex blew out a quiet breath. "When I was a kid, my mom took me to the circus and I was fascinated by those guys who walked on the high wire. One of them didn't even have a net underneath to catch him if he fell—all he had was a pole to help him keep his balance. When I met you, Bern, I knew that no matter how crazy life got, you could be that for me. The thing that kept me from falling."

I wasn't going to cry. The truth ignited a clear picture in my mind. I realized that even though we'd claimed to love each other, our relationship would have never lasted. Because we'd both wanted each other to do something that only God could do. Rescue us. Steady us. The truth was, neither of us would have had the strength to carry each other's expectations.

But I didn't know how to tell Alex that. It was so easy to talk about God with Elise and Annie. To soak in Esther's wisdom, knowing that she never took my questions and turned them into an argument or a sermon. I had no idea what Alex even thought about God and I was afraid that any attempt to explain it would reveal my ignorance about all that I *should* know. My faith was still so new. Even though I was walking God's path, I still left baby footprints.

People can argue about religion until they're blue in the face, Esther had told me one day. But the thing they can't argue with is what God's done in *your* life. How can they? Not when the proof is right in front of them—you!

"I didn't plan on staying more than a few days," Alex said, stealing the moment away from me. "I thought we'd have a cup of coffee. You'd tell me all about your husband and show me pictures of your kids. And your Labrador retriever and your house with the picket fence. But the truth is I need some more time. You aren't the only one who's been doing some thinking. You wanted to explain to me why you left. I think I knew, but I guess I needed to hear it to be sure. You know what the shrinks say about closure." Alex shook his head. "But I *need* this. It feels good to have some privacy. Hey, it even feels good to be *ignored.*"

When he mentioned photos of children, I knew that now was the time to tell him about Heather. But just as I opened my mouth, his next words slammed the lid on my own.

"I try to keep a low profile in public but there are the paparazzi, even the occasional obsessed fan. I hate that part of it, but that's the way it is now. Fortunately, there are younger and more interesting celebrities out there who get most of the attention and I can usually fly under the radar."

Usually. But what if word leaked out that Alex Scott had a daughter? And what would it do to that daughter to see her face on those magazines at the grocery store checkout? There was no pretending that Alex had a normal life. He didn't. And neither would Heather if the truth came out.

I couldn't do that to her. She was the one I needed to talk to first. She needed to know about Alex before he knew about her. I knew she was curious about her birth father but in the times we'd talked, she'd never come right out and asked about him. And I hadn't volunteered any information. But now I needed to. She was the vulnerable one. The one who would have the most to lose.

"Are you okay, Bernice?"

"Yeah. I think…it's getting late." I needed to take refuge in God. My strong tower.

"Truth? All I was hoping for this evening was some help picking out the tile for the bathroom."

I managed a shaky laugh to match Alex's. We stood up, which meant that the space between us shrunk to inches.

I held my breath when Alex's fingers grazed a path down my arm.

"What do you think would have happened if we'd stayed together, Bernice? Do you think we would be like Esther and John…married forever? Still holding hands?"

"They've only been married a few months." It was safer to nitpick details than to answer Alex's pensive question.

"What?"

I nodded. "Didn't they mention that? They met in the nursing home. Esther had been married to someone else most of her life. He died and she met John when he moved into Golden Oaks. She says John is her new beginning."

"How old are they?"

"In their late eighties."

"Most people think that's the end."

"Not Esther and John."

Now his hand had drifted down to mine and he traced my ringless fingers.

"So what do you think about new beginnings?"

God, this is too much for me right now. What am I supposed to say?

And no kidding. It was almost as if God whispered the answer in my ear.

"New beginnings are good," I managed to say, because I truly believed it. Terrifying, but good. "Let's try friendship this time."

"Friendship." Alex repeated the word. Tested it almost suspiciously. The way he might have looked at a carton of cottage cheese a few days after its expiration date.

Don't disappoint me, I begged silently. *Don't show me how far you've fallen off that wire.*

"Can I ask why?"

Did he really think I was going to cheerfully hand him my heart again, knowing he was only in Prichett on a temporary whim? That any day he could get a phone call from his agent that would whisk him back to the surreal world?

"Our relationship went...way too fast the first time." The understatement of the year.

Alex's hand released mine and my skin suddenly felt cold. And my hand felt very empty.

"Does this *friendship* thing have anything to do with the fact that one of your best friends is married to a minister and that your idea of a night out is eating in a church basement?"

"Maybe." I couldn't stop a smile. "Definitely."

"I was wrong. You have changed." He blew out a quiet

breath. "Does *friends* mean you're going to help me paint this weekend?"

Sweet relief poured through me. *Thank You, God.* "I work on Saturday but I can help Sunday after church."

"You should hire a part-timer. I don't know how you can manage all by yourself."

"I usually do…except for some reason, business has been picking up lately."

"Still ticked off about that, huh?" Alex grinned.

I'll bet you have that smile insured by Lloyd's of London.

There was a sudden mournful howl from Colonel Mustard, who was standing by the front door. A puddle expanded beneath him on the hardwood floor.

I wished I had a camera. I could have sold a photo of Alex's expression to the tabloids for a million dollars.

"Bernice?"

"Not a chance."

"I'll give you a thousand dollars."

"You have way too much money."

"Five thousand."

"Look at the bright side."

"There's a bright side?" Alex began to stalk around, searching for a roll of paper towels.

"Junebug lives outside."

"Bernice, as your friend I feel the need to point out something." Elise and Sam had squeezed beside me into the church pew on Sunday morning and Elise had let a whole two seconds lapse before she leveled the truth-in-friendship gun at me.

"What?"

"This is the fourth Sunday in a row that you've worn that…how shall I say it…extremely ugly skirt to church."

"Ouch." I scowled at her.

Sam had heard and I could tell he was trying not to laugh. "It's not ugly."

She raised her eyebrows.

"Okay, it's ugly, but it's the only churchy skirt I have."

"What exactly is a *churchy* skirt?"

"You know…" I glanced around and for some reason there wasn't another woman in the sanctuary wearing anything remotely resembling an ankle-length burlap bag.

"You have a closet full of nice clothes."

"But those are so…me." Like Greta Lewis, I didn't exactly follow the Prichett dress code. I liked bold colors and odd fabric combinations. Nothing immodest, just a little on the dramatic side. I had a pair of turquoise cowboy boots that were as comfortable as bedroom slippers and I still had a closet full of gauzy peasant blouses and broomstick skirts, even though I knew they were hopelessly out of style. I was confident that if I waited long enough, they'd soon be riding the crest of the next fashion wave.

"There is nothing wrong with coming to church looking like you." Elise whispered the words, because Gina Mullins had taken her place at the organ. She had to be close to ninety and yet she was wearing a snazzy red wool skirt and blazer. And her skirt was a scandalous inch above her nearly-ninety-year-old knees.

"I think that God happened to give Bernice Strum a snappy style to match her snappy personality." Elise squeezed my hand. "Now please give that outfit the decent burial it requires."

"I just wanted to look like everyone else." I tried to defend my decision.

"God doesn't want you to look like everyone else. He had a chance to do that and He decided He liked variety."

Pastor Charles took his place at the front of the church and Elise sat back, a satisfied smile on her face.

"You should be up there," I mumbled. "You give a pretty mean sermon, Elise Penny."

In response, Elise winked and dropped a hymnal in my lap.

Annie found me after the service and told me that Stephen had successfully corralled the youth into one of the Sunday school rooms for the meeting about the live nativity.

My stomach took a few loops on the way there so I tried to focus on Annie's cheerful commentary about her and Stephen's Thanksgiving plans for the following week, which centered on Stephen's parents, who lived in Illinois.

"Are you going to Elise and Sam's house?" In typical Annie fashion, she wanted to make sure that I was taken care of.

"If I don't, there won't be any dinner rolls." Well, at least not from the grocery store.

"Elise is so excited that Bree is coming home."

"So is Riley." I'd seen him float past my window several times during the week.

"What about Heather?"

"She doesn't have enough time off from school to come for Thanksgiving, but she mentioned visiting over her Christmas break."

We'd exchanged some newsy e-mails over the past week but I had a difficult time pretending everything was normal—well, as normal as possible—in the small town of Prichett.

Ordinarily, Christmas was the one holiday I suffered through every year. I could deal with Thanksgiving because it meant a day off from work and a lot of pumpkin pie with whipped cream. But Christmas... I'd always been a silent Scrooge in the truest sense of the word. I only decorated the salon because people expected it but I didn't so much as light a cranberry-scented votive in my apartment. I opened the gift from my parents as soon as it arrived the week before Christmas so that it wouldn't feel like I was opening a Christmas gift. And since it was always the same thing every year—a cheese box—it wasn't exactly the kind of thing you wanted sitting under a tree. Not that I had one of those, either.

Instead of a time to rejoice, like the taped songs that Candy pumped down Main Street claimed, it had become several long, silent days. Perfect for licking one's wounds. Because Christmas was Heather's birthday. As part of my penance, I refused to accept Elise's invitation to join her and Sam for eggnog and cookies after the Christmas Eve service and I wouldn't let myself be warmed by their hospitality the next day. Not even for a few hours. After the first few years, Elise seemed to realize that I wasn't going to budge on this and she stopped asking.

I didn't think it was fair that I took part in someone else's Christmas traditions because I had my own. Which included a box of tissues and a journal. The first year after I'd given Heather up for adoption, I started writing letters to her. I'm not much of a writer, but I had to pour my thoughts and feelings into something or go crazy trying to keep them stuffed inside.

I'd tell her what I'd done during the year, which I could condense into half a page, and then I'd ramble on for another page about what I imagined she had done. I used my pint-size customers as a gauge as to what Heather might be like. What she might be doing. Walking the first year. Tying her shoes at four. Losing her first tooth at six. Starting piano at seven.

Until we met recently, I hadn't even known her name. We hadn't had enough conversations yet to fill in all the gaps over the past twenty years because I didn't want her to think she was under interrogation, but slowly I was piecing together a picture of her life. She did play the piano but she hated ballet. She'd gone on a youth mission trip to Mexico in high school and gave away half her clothes when she got back. Her favorite foods were seafood fettuccini and all desserts.

"I'm sorry," Annie said, her voice snapping me back to attention. "I mentioned Heather and you completely disappeared."

"You can pray for me," I told her. "Alex is going to stay for a while and I decided that I need to talk to Heather before I tell him. I can't just turn her life upside down with something like this." I paused just outside the Sunday school room, where the closed door couldn't contain the laughter and excited buzz of conversation inside. It sounded like everyone was having fun.

"How are you doing? Knowing he's going to stay?"

"We're going to be friends."

"Is that possible?" Annie asked candidly.

"I don't know what he wants from me. He talked about closure and new beginnings practically in the same sentence."

Annie opened her mouth to say something, then obviously changed her mind. "You should talk to Esther."

I'd been thinking the same thing.

Annie and I walked into the room and the first person I saw was Melissa Turner, surrounded by her fan club and a few love-struck boys. She wasn't paying any attention to them, though. She was in a standoff with Greta, trying to wrestle something away from her.

I took one look and saw that what they were wrestling over was a doll.

I could only assume it was baby Jesus.

Chapter Thirteen

By the time I left the church, a dull throbbing pain had burrowed its way into the back of my head.

Baby Jesus had barely made it through the tug-of-war match. If Annie hadn't been there as peacekeeper, my group of wise men would have been reduced to one painfully shy boy stricken with acne. As it was, my shepherds all disbanded early to watch the football game and my angels fled to the girls' bathroom with Melissa. And I practically had to sit on Greta to convince her to stay.

Annie had looked a little pale, which scared me. So I pretended that I was used to teenage angst, told her everything would be fine and sent her home. Then, in the interest of world peace, I made sure Greta and Melissa were in separate corners of the room, told everyone that we'd have another meeting next week and shooed them out.

If I skipped lunch, I knew I'd have a few minutes to spend with the one person guaranteed to adjust my perspective. And hopefully quench the raging terror that I felt about supervising the nativity.

I drove to the Golden Oaks.

Esther was alone and she smiled at me when I peeked in.

"Bernice. I was just thinking about you." Esther jumped out of the chair with the energy of a woman half her age and met me at the door.

After their marriage, John and Esther had moved into a suite. It was larger than most of the rooms, complete with a tiny sitting area and a private bathroom. They had their own television set but I knew that John liked to spend time with the other residents, too, which made him extremely popular not only with them but with the nursing staff.

"Sit down. Sit down. John is listening to a symphony on The Learning Channel with a few of his friends."

I slumped into a chair and pulled off my gloves. And ignored the burning sensation behind my eyes.

"How have you been?" I mustered up the polite question but Esther gave me a shrewd glance that told me I wasn't fooling her a bit.

"Never mind about me," Esther said. "Don't feel the need to make small talk, Bernice. You look like you could use a heart-to-heart. Is it Alex?"

I'd thought it was a pack of hostile teenagers but the second I heard the word "Alex," tears leaked out of my eyes. He was doing it again.

"No. Yes." I did an Eliza Doolittle and swiped at my face with my sleeve. "He's staying. Things are going well. We're...friends." I tried to smile. "That's a nice change."

Esther didn't smile back.

Come to think of it, Annie hadn't looked so confident, either, when I told her that Alex and I were going to be friends. Okay, maybe it sounded too high school...but what was I supposed to do? He was in Prichett. He was going to stay awhile. He'd offered the church the use of his barn so now we were involved in the live nativity together...

"Whose idea was that? To be friends?"

"Mine."

"Oh." Esther looked thoughtful. And concerned.

I felt my face start to burn, right along with my eyes. If it got any hotter I was going to spontaneously combust.

"He's been spending a lot of time here," Esther said, surprising me. "John likes him…and from a woman's point of view, I think he would be an easy man to love."

"I didn't expect to still have…feelings…for him," I said. "But things are different now."

Esther nodded. "Now you aren't free to love him."

"I'm not free to love him? Why can't I love him?" That wasn't what I'd meant, but Esther's quiet words stunned me. My questions rushed out from some deep place I thought the years had filled in.

"Oh, Bernice." Esther bowed her head. When she looked up again, I saw tears in *her* eyes. "One of those most precious things that John and I share is our faith. There are things that John can't see, but he always sees the path that God wants him to walk. When I heard him singing 'Amazing Grace,' I knew he was a man who had *experienced* it. The Bible says that two people who love God and love each other are equally yoked. That means that they're going in the same direction, dedicated to the same purpose. It's what *works*."

I couldn't argue with that. I could see that Elise and Sam worked. Even when they'd hit a bumpy spot in their marriage not too long ago. And Annie's life hadn't been the rosy one that most people assumed she'd had…but Stephen had seen more than a lonely, abused runaway. And Esther and John…it was their wedding that had opened my heart to new possibilities. New beginnings.

"It's not enough for one of the people in the relationship to simply tolerate the other's faith. Or to go through the motions, just to please them. Life is too full of unknowns. Both the man and the woman need to know God and know Him deeply. *He's* the yoke that keeps them together and moving in the right direction."

I realized I had much more to worry about than the live nativity now. I had seen the look in Alex's eyes. He had willingly agreed to friendship. I was afraid to consider what that meant. Maybe he was having some kind of midlife crisis that had brought him to Prichett, looking for a way to connect to the past. And I'd just happened to be part of that past, so hey, why not? It was nostalgia. That had to be it. He couldn't possibly be in love with me.

Because if he was, and if what Esther said was true, I couldn't love him back.

It was close to two and I knew I could call Alex and back out of helping him paint. But I didn't. At the moment I was feeling only slightly put back together because Esther and I had prayed together before I left. The weighted down feeling had lifted but I still felt fragile. And I hated feeling fragile.

I'm just like one of Charity's teacups, God. If You drop me now, I'm going to shatter into a thousand pieces.

A thought swept in right on the heels of my prayer as I pulled into Alex's driveway. It wasn't an audible voice that I heard, but one that spoke to my heart and one I instantly recognized.

I won't drop you, Bernice. Trust me.

"Maybe Alex does believe in You. He's just waiting for the right time to tell me. Maybe if You find a place for me to bring it into the conversation…"

It was just a suggestion. Just a little one. Maybe we were equally yoked and didn't even know it. Hope and fear collided and the result was a light-headed, nauseous feeling similar to the one that made me collapse on the sofa with a box of crackers and a bottle of ginger ale twenty years ago.

The first thing I saw when I got out of my car was Junebug. Only now she had company. A thin black horse with a short broomstick tail stood at a safe distance away from her. I could tell he was old because the years had scooped out his back so deeply that a heavy rain would have created its own pond.

Junebug looked at me and then made a point of aiming a kick at her pasture mate. Depressed. Right.

Okay, Lord, we're going into this together. Just like Esther said before I left. You're going to protect my heart.

"Pegasus," Alex said as I walked in. He was clutching a handful of paper towel.

I took one look at Colonel Mustard's guilty expression and made a pretty good guess as to why.

"Someone Lester knows dropped it off this morning. He said cows don't like to be alone."

"That's horses." I looked out the window, just in time to see Junebug lower her head and bellow at the poor old horse. "I think you're going to have to put up some more fencing. That horse is no match for Junebug."

"I'll just add that to my list," Alex muttered.

"Something smells good." My stomach growled in agreement.

"Chicken dumpling soup."

I followed the aroma straight to the pot on top of the stove. "Did you make this?"

"Cooking is kind of a hobby, but if you tell anyone, I'll deny it."

"Lots of men cook." I couldn't resist lifting the lid for a peek and steam rolled out, giving me an instant facial. "It looks great."

"I take it you didn't have lunch yet?"

"I had a meeting after church about the nativity. It went a little later than I expected." I decided not to mention my conversation with Esther and the fact that baby Jesus was now safe in the backseat of my car, swaddled in the blanket I kept under the seat for emergency breakdowns.

"Stephen called. He's bringing some guys out later to take a look at the barn."

"You're really going to have the live nativity here? It's four evenings, you know. For two hours every evening. People are going to be traipsing through your yard."

"I might as well. I've got half the animals already." He pulled a bowl out of the cupboard and began to ladle soup into it.

"Is that one of Marissa's?"

"Yup."

Marissa Maribeau had a small studio and shop just off Main Street, the only artsy person who had ever stayed in Prichett. She sold most of her pottery through an exclusive shop in Madison and somehow those vases and bowls mysteriously generated enough income to support her.

I loved her work because it was chunky and solid and she used earthy glazes. The whole effect was rather rustic. If any of her pieces had flaws, she priced them exactly as she would have for the ones that didn't, as if she'd purposefully added them for character. And maybe she had. She had several designs that she used for dishes and though my budget didn't allow me to indulge myself, I did have a tiny candy dish with my favorite pattern—which happened to be identical to the one Alex was pouring my soup into. The one with fluffy white dandelion seeds blowing like tiny parachutes across the surface of a sky-blue glaze.

"The designer from Creative Interiors said that it's best to buy from the local artists if you can. It helps the house stay true to its origins."

"Wow. Did you have to write that down somewhere to remember it?"

"You're not the only one with three-by-five cards." He winked at me.

He'd remembered that my apartment was practically wall-papered with them. Was this a good thing or a bad thing?

"So how was church?"

"Great."

"You sound like you mean that."

The first dumpling I zeroed in on practically melted in my mouth—which distracted me from the surprised look on Alex's face. But only for a second.

"I do mean it. I haven't been going to Faith Community for very long, but it's like…family."

"That explains it then."

I was suddenly wary of the expression on his face. "Explains what?"

"You. Church. You always wanted to settle into something solid. You found your small town. And your small-town, Midwestern faith."

Small-town faith? I could tell that Alex wasn't trying to be insulting but the skin on the back of my neck began to prickle. Yes, I had just prayed that God would give us an opportunity to talk about Him, but this wasn't quite how I'd imagined the conversation going.

"There is nothing Midwestern about my faith," I said slowly. "In fact, it just happens to have its roots in the Middle East."

"So why did you pick Christianity then?"

Okay. Was I missing something? Because even though Alex and I were sitting at the same table, we were suddenly in different galaxies. Or maybe at opposite ends of the field. No yoke in sight.

"I didn't exactly *pick* Christianity."

"You researched everything, though, right? And decided that it was the best fit?"

Like picking out a new shirt? What style did I want? What color? What kind of fabric? Just as long as it's comfortable and I can do the things that I want to in it? Is that what he was saying?

I remembered the day that I'd been on Elise's front porch, agonizing over whether to call Heather back after she'd made that first attempt to contact me. Her tentative phone call had sucked me in like quicksand, almost drowning me in the guilt that I'd barely been keeping my head above for years. I decided not to return the call and went to Elise's for backup. I needed someone to agree that I was making the right decision.

And then Annie had shown up, with a plate of cinnamon rolls and some simple words. *God loves with you with an everlasting love.* I didn't hear it in church. I didn't hear it on the radio or a special television broadcast. But right after she said the words, I'd heard the echo in my heart.

She's right, Bernice. That's how I love you.

And while Elise prayed, I knew He was there. And I knew if I grabbed on to Him, He'd be there forever. All I had to do was ask. So I asked. There were still a lot of things I didn't know. Things I didn't understand. Even things I questioned. But no one could tell me that God hadn't rescued me that day.

But how to explain it to Alex?

"No, I didn't research all the world religions and pick the one that lined up the most with what I already believed," I said, trying to keep my voice steady. If I showed too much emotion, Alex would assume that I was some kind of weirdo. One of *those* kinds of Christians. "It didn't happen very long ago, so I can't even tell you much about the faith, but I can tell you what happened to me."

I glanced up at Alex, afraid of what I'd see, but he looked interested. The polite interest that someone might show if you were about to explain how you picked out the dressy black boots over the casual black boots.

"Never mind." Something inside me curled and died. I'd asked God for an opportunity to find out if Alex was a believer—and I'd just discovered that he was. It was just that he believed in something else.

"Tell me," Alex said. "I'm curious what made someone like you turn to religion."

"This has nothing to do with religion. And what do you mean, someone like *me?*"

"You aren't the type of person who needs anyone. I guess you proved that when you left."

Okay. Someone needed a reality check and it wasn't me.

But did I really want to bare my soul to Alex and show him just how big a phony I'd been?

How can someone argue with the proof that's in front of them? A changed life. You.

Esther's words came back to me and I nodded, as if someone had just asked me a question. I dropped the spoon into the bowl because my fingers were beginning to tremble and I would have ended up with the contents down the front of my sweater.

"It's like my entire life, from the time I was young until now, I'd never seen my reflection in a mirror. I just listened to the way other people described me. Homely. Too harsh, not cuddly or sweet like other girls. Always lacking something. That's me, I thought. No way to change it. Just have to live with it. But then, He gave me a mirror—His mirror—and I realized that in His mirror I was a beauty. Someone He loved. Someone He would fight for. Someone He *died* for. Someone He came back for. And all that junk that I'd hidden while I was pretending to be confident and strong, it spilled out and He cleaned it up and got rid of it. We could argue religion all day, but I *know* what was inside of me before I gave my life to Jesus… I know what He took away. And what He gave back to me. We can't argue that. It's real. It's truth."

"I don't understand it, but I'm glad you found that in your life, Bern. Whatever gets you through."

No, no, no, I wanted to shout at him. It's the *only* thing that gets you through.

Defeat tackled me and left me gasping for air.

There isn't anything more I can say to convince him, is there, God?

"You want to hear something strange?" Alex gave a short laugh that seemed to be directed at himself.

Please!

"When I was in your apartment that day and I picked up that note card…it said something about treasures in heaven. I can't remember all the words, but anyway, while Digger and I were on our way here, he wanted to hear the local weather and we couldn't get any radio station to come in but some religious one. And the guy said that exact same verse. I recognized it."

The religious radio station he was talking about was WSON and the music it played was as conservative as a pair of brown loafers. And its tower was child-size in comparison to others in the county, so it was extremely unlikely that they couldn't tune into another station.

In a state of wonder, I tried to figure out what that meant. And why Alex had brought it up now.

You did your part, God seemed to say. *Now let me do mine.*

And right after that there wasn't time to think, because I glanced out the window just in time to see Pegasus live up to his name. The two animals raced across the length of the small pasture, the horse in the lead with Junebug in hot pursuit. I held my breath as Pegasus reached the fence.

And then I watched him sail right over the top.

Chapter Fourteen

"Heard you had some excitement out on the county road yesterday." Jim sauntered in, a leather briefcase in one hand and a white paper sack from Sally's in the other.

There was no pretending ignorance. Not when Junebug and Pegasus had become, in the space of two hours, as famous as Butch Cassidy and the Sundance Kid. It had taken four farmers, two sheriff's deputies, a volunteer fireman, a youth minister and an actor to round up the two escapees. And let's not forget the hairstylist, who, along with the basset hound, were the ones who actually made the final arrest.

And I still had the bruises to prove it. Not that they were anywhere I would willingly *show* people as proof.

"You know how those farmers exaggerate."

"Really? So yesterday's barnyard version of *The Great Escape* didn't happen?"

"Cows get loose all the time."

"But this was Junebug." Jim's voice dropped to a teasing whisper. "Are you sure she didn't get the horse to cooperate? You know, plan a diversion so she could jump over the moon?"

I couldn't help it. I laughed. "Maybe it was."

Jim grinned. "I doubt it, but if it gets you to laugh…"

Something in his eyes stole the lightness out of the moment. For the first time I noticed that he was freshly shaven and smelled…really good. Since it was just the two of us meeting to talk about the grant, I figured it didn't make much sense to ask Candy to keep one of the conference rooms open for us. I'd asked Jim to meet me at the salon. I had a small office in the back and I kept the temperature at a toasty seventy, unlike Mayor Candy, who was as fiscally responsible with the thermostat as she was with the rest of the town budget. Her building was like a refrigerator.

"We better get started. We've got a ton of work to do. What's in the bag?"

"Two chicken dinners from Sally's." Jim opened the bag and the aroma that wafted out made my knees weak. "You worked all day. It's a five-thirty meeting. I figured you wouldn't have time to eat supper."

I watched, mouth watering, as he began to pull out an assortment of containers. Coleslaw, Sally's crispy-fried chicken and fluffy dinner rolls. There had to be dessert. Sally always added dessert.

"What else is in there?" Like a kid, I tried to peek into the bag.

Jim pulled it away. "What if you don't like it?"

"I'll take it. No matter what it is."

"Darlin', I wish I'd tied an engagement ring to that chicken leg, then."

He said the words in a terrible backwoods accent but I could only stare at him.

"Jim…"

"I was kidding, Bernice."

I was afraid to think that maybe he wasn't.

"It's banana-cream pie." He shook open a tablecloth-size

napkin, leaned over and tucked it into the top of my sweater like a bib. "Should I ask a blessing or do you want to?"

"You can." I kept my eyes open a second longer than I should have. Long enough to watch Jim bow his head. Instead of folding his hands, though, he lifted them up, his palms open and empty. As if he was waiting for God to fill them. There was something so humbling in the gesture that I felt a prickle of tears in my eyes.

You're turning me into a softie, God.

"Heavenly Father, thank You for Your blessings. Thank You for this food and the hands that prepared it. Amen."

Simple and sweet. Like one piece of dark chocolate.

"Amen," I echoed.

"Now, I'll talk and you eat, then we'll switch."

"I like the sound of that." I tried to reclaim some of the laughter we'd shared but now Jim was the one who was all business.

"I talked to Marissa this morning because she's the only person I know who might actually have a clue about how we go about finding an artist to commission for this sculpture."

"What did she say?"

"Between fits of laughter when I told her the size of the grant? That we'd have to have the fifth-grade class make it out of modeling clay. And then I'd have to hold an umbrella over it every time it rained."

I didn't know Marissa had a sense of humor.

"So now what?"

"She did come up with a pretty good suggestion. We could hire a graduate student to do the sculpture. It would give them some exposure and it would keep us within the budget. Candy was hoping that some of the businesses would match the state grant dollar for dollar, but I'm not going to hold my breath. Not when they won't spring for new Christmas decorations for Main Street."

He had a point. And we had the construction-cone bells to prove it.

"An art student." It was a good plan. "Let's do it."

"A bronze cow?"

I sighed. "A bronze cow."

"Junebug?"

"Or Ruby."

"Who is Ruby?"

"She's the *prettier* cow."

"No more coleslaw. It's affecting your sanity." He grabbed the container away from me and gave me a sidelong glance. "It's too bad we don't have more money. Then we could have a whole bunch of statues in the park. Junebug. A horse. A police car. A basset hound…"

"That does it. I want the coleslaw back *and* the banana-cream pie."

"And if we wait long enough, there might even be a llama."

A llama?

"What are you talking about?"

"Nothing." Jim's ears turned pink.

"You're a terrible liar and, I hate to remind you, it's a sin."

"Ouch." Jim winced. "It's just that…you know, a llama. Wouldn't that be funny?" He tried to laugh. And failed miserably.

The only person I knew with a llama was Lester's cousin, Phil, a farmer a few miles out who was known for the acres of pumpkins he grew. The elementary school kids always took a field trip out to his place in the fall so he'd created a petting zoo of sorts to make the day more exciting. And he could justify the extra dollar he tacked onto the cost of the pumpkin they chose.

Wait a second. I began to connect the feed caps. And suddenly it all began to make sense.

"This is a plot, isn't it?" I plucked a dinner roll out of Jim's hand before he could stuff it into his mouth and stall. "That's why Alex's place has suddenly become the county animal shelter. That's what the note was about."

"I have no knowledge of a note."

"But you know about the plot."

"I don't know anything."

I gave him a meaningful look. Remember? *Lying? Sin?*

"Okay, I may know a little. But I'm not involved. It was Kevin's idea."

Kevin, the local veterinarian. Who was Bree's former boss. And one of Riley Cabott's best friends. Who would know all about Heather. And therefore, have the proverbial ax to grind against Alex. I wanted to howl.

"So they put their heads together to make a brain and decided that by dumping off a sorry bunch of animals, they could get Alex to leave?"

"Apparently, Alex told Lester that the reason he wanted to buy the house was because Charity's bird was driving him crazy. So, Kevin figured that if one bird got him to do something as drastic as buying a house, then a few other animals…" He shrugged.

"Would get him to leave town," I finished. "That's just…" Twisted? Diabolical? *Ingenious?*

"How many more is he going to get?"

"I can't tell you."

"If you ever want to get your hair cut in this town again, you'll tell me."

"A litter of kittens tomorrow. Irv Howard offered his goat, as long as he gets it back, and Phil's llama. The llama is only a last resort if the rest don't work. Actually, they were hoping that Colonel Mustard would take care of him."

"Colonel Mustard with his bladder control problems." And of course the local vet would know every animal in the county that had an ailment.

Jim's lips twitched. "I guess."

"You guys are something else."

"Hey, I just happened to be at the café while they were planning it. I was an innocent bystander. Phil and some of the other farmers got mad that Lester sold to an outsider, so Lester figured that if Alex left, he'd turn around and sell the place back to him."

Poor Lester. That was why he'd been banished to the corner booth at Sally's.

"They didn't have to go to so much trouble," I said, trying to iron the crankiness out of my voice. "If they just leave well enough alone, I can get rid of him all by myself."

"How can you?" Now Jim wouldn't look at me. "When you're the reason he came here in the first place?"

In the interest of self-preservation, I let several days go by, delaying the inevitable. Alex.

How can I avoid thee? Let me count the ways.

I didn't have the heart to tell him the reason why he was suddenly playing the part of Dr. Doolittle. I couldn't sleep because a little recording in my head kept replaying our conversation in his kitchen on Sunday afternoon. I was even having a hard time praying but I had the hunch the reason I was still in one piece was because the prayers of my friends were holding me together.

But worst of all was that I had the feeling that even after I'd explained the change in my life, Alex still didn't understand.

Whatever gets you through.

Did he still feel that way? Even after I'd told him what had happened to me? Those unanswered questions and my own cowardice had me scheduling extra appointments into the evenings, although I tried to tell myself that it was because of Thanksgiving. Women who were going to put on a huge dinner needed the added boost of making sure they pulled it off looking their very best.

I knew I was going to see Alex at Elise and Sam's but at least we wouldn't be alone. I was beginning to realize that *alone* with Alex was not a wise thing. Esther had been right. He was an easy man to love. I wished I wasn't beginning to remember that. Twenty years ago, if I'd met him in the alley and he'd been the guy emptying my soda cans into a truck every week, I still would have fallen in love with him. In fact, it may have been easier if that's what he had done for a living.

When I ran to the grocery store during my lunch break, it was obvious that half the town was tied with me for a first-place ribbon in procrastination. The lines were long and even the manager was stationed at a cash register, looking stressed.

I knew I should have picked up the dinner rolls at the beginning of the week and tucked them into my freezer but they didn't taste as fresh that way. I'd tried it. So, even though it was a trivial request, I sent up a prayer as I dashed to the bakery department that they'd still have Sam's favorite—the little potato rolls with a dusting of flour on top.

They were gone. I frantically searched through packages of cloverleaf, tea rolls and knots.

"Bernice!"

I could barely see Julia, the cake decorator, waving to me over the wall of people pressed against the deli case. I gave her a halfhearted wave and plunged back into the sub buns.

"Bernice, here you go. I saved you a package." Her voice cut a clear path through the deli.

Okay, God, so maybe You don't mind being bothered with trivial things, I thought. And this was another reason why I loved small towns. Because there were people who paid attention to *other* people—like people who bought the same kind of dinner rolls ten years in a row and always at noon on the day before Thanksgiving.

I was still basking in the glow of the potato rolls on my way back to the salon.

And that's when I saw it.

An RV the size of a school bus, parked right in front of my salon. *Blocking* my salon from view.

Hopefully whoever was driving it wouldn't be there very long. I tried to remember from conversations during the week who was expecting out-of-town company. Or maybe it was someone who'd stopped at Sally's for a cup of coffee and a slice of pie.

As I crossed the street and walked past the front of the RV, I happened to glance over and saw a man sitting in the driver's seat, reading the newspaper.

And he looked a lot like my father. I froze.

It was my father.

And if my father was here, that meant…

"Bernice!"

My mother was with him.

"Where have you been? I thought you worked!"

She was standing in the doorway of the salon, her muffled voice coming from the depths of a down coat that made her look three sizes bigger than she was. It was canary-yellow and she'd wound a coordinating scarf around her neck several times so all I could see was her tiny, wire-framed glasses peering out at me.

"Mom." That's all I could say. Because I didn't know my mother owned a yellow parka. Or a scarf. Or an RV.

"Your father wouldn't get out until you showed up," she said. She maneuvered around me and rapped sharply on the window. "Bernice is here. She walked right past you! Didn't you see her?" Then she turned back to me. "If he leaves the engine running any longer, it'll be cheaper to buy our own oil well than to put more gas in this thing."

My vocal cords were frozen. A hundred questions knotted together but only one squeezed out.

"When did you buy an RV?"

"We decided to buy it after I officially retired," Mom said. "And two weeks ago, I officially retired. You'd know that if you ever answered your phone. So, we decided to take our first trip."

That sounded temporary. *Please, God,* I begged. *Let it be temporary. I'm serious. This is more important than potato rolls!*

Dad lumbered over, tucking the tails of his short-sleeved seersucker shirt into his pants. He looked older somehow. Maybe a week trapped in an RV with my mother had caused it.

The thought sprayed out of the anger that sizzled inside. I felt the familiar churning in my stomach but now I couldn't just hang up the phone and go back to life as usual. Not when they were standing right in front of me.

"Bernice." He ducked his head shyly and even though one of his arms lifted, like he wanted to hug me, he didn't. "You picked a cold state."

They'd never been to Wisconsin. If you wanted to get picky, they'd never been *out* of California. And now they were here. Cruising the country in an RV so old, they probably wouldn't be able to get parts for it if it broke down.

Lord, please don't let it break down!

"You sure did," Mom said, her voice clearly communicating that I'd picked a cold state on purpose. Just on the off chance they'd show up out of the blue for a visit once in, say, ten years, and I could arrange the temperatures to drop to twenty degrees.

"Come into the salon. Or would you rather go up to my apartment for a while?"

"Of course we want to see the beauty shop," Mom said. Her

eyes squinted up at the striped awning. "It's smaller than I thought it would be."

Of course it was.

"Can you stay a few hours before you have to get on the road again?"

They both turned to stare at me like I'd just shouted a four-letter word.

"What are you talking about?" Mom said irritably. "We're here."

"Here?" I pushed the word out.

"We're not driving across the country. We took a trip. To see you. We're *here.*"

"We should have called," Dad muttered.

"We tried. It's not our fault she never calls us back."

It didn't pay to argue that particular point. I had called back—several times—and talked to an answering machine. Remaining blissfully ignorant that the reason I couldn't reach them was because they were on their way to Prichett.

I needed to sit down. The phone rang and I eased over to the counter to answer it.

"What do you know about kittens?"

I'd totally forgotten that this was the day Alex would become acquainted with a little thing called sleep deprivation. Bree had taken in a litter of orphaned kittens once and it had been round-the-clock feedings until they were able to drink milk from a dish. I remembered that Elise had taken a few shifts and had had the dark circles under her eyes to prove it.

"Um…" I glanced at my parents. Dad was studying a hairstyle magazine like it was *Consumer Reports* and Mom was inspecting the shampoo sink. "How old are they?"

"Old enough to terrorize the Colonel and sharpen their claws on my leather sofa."

They were older than I thought. I felt a grudging respect for Kevin and his secret ops. They chose their weapons wisely.

"How many are there?"

"At least a hundred."

"Alex." I choked on a laugh and saw my mother turn into an ice sculpture right in front of my very eyes. She knew I was talking to a man and had obviously drawn a conclusion similar to the one she had years ago. When I refused to tell her who my baby's father was, she thought it was because I didn't know. It's one thing to have your mother think that you're single because you have ridiculously high standards, entirely another to have her assume you're as easy as a box of Bisquick.

"Okay, there are four of the furry little beasts."

"Alex, I can't help you right now," I murmured. "My parents surprised me with a visit."

Silence. I wondered how good his memory was.

"Are you okay?"

The simple question drove the air out of my lungs. Apparently there was nothing wrong with his memory.

"Uh-huh."

Mom had sidled closer, pretending that she wasn't eavesdropping.

"They'll be here tomorrow? That means you won't be going over to Elise and Sam's."

Alex's brain was working better than mine because it had continued down a path that mine had stalled on the minute I heard my mother's voice. "I don't think so. No."

My thoughts began to lurch forward. Thanksgiving. What on earth did I have in my freezer? I'd be lucky if I could find a package of chicken wings at the grocery store now. I would have to give up a warm, cozy day with my best friend, turkey with all the fixings, curled up in a lavender-scented quilt while we watched *It's a Wonderful Life* and giggled like teenagers.

Grief swamped me.

"I'm sure if you told Elise, she'd invite them over, too."

He was right but there was no way I was going to do that to my friends. "No. But you go ahead. They'll still want you."

"Bern...I'll trade you four kittens for a turkey dinner."

"It's a deal."

Chapter Fifteen

As soon as I could sneak away, I called Elise and told her that I wouldn't be able to come over for Thanksgiving dinner. And she did just what Alex thought she would do—she tried to convince me to bring them along.

"Trust me, El, you don't know my mother. She could single-handedly suck the joy out of the Halleluiah choir."

"But you're all right, aren't you? She can't do that to you anymore."

"No." I knew I didn't sound too sure. And I knew why. Anger. The truth was, I could barely look at Mom without gritting my teeth and I didn't know why. And being gifted in denial like I was, I didn't want to examine the reason too closely.

Yes, it took at least ten Tootsie Rolls to calm me down after I talked to her on the phone once a week, but I could go on with my life, safe in the knowledge that my parents were in a galaxy far, far away. California.

But now…

"I hate feeling like this. Every time she gives me one of her disapproving looks, the clock goes backward. Right now, I'm twelve years old again."

"How long are they staying?"

"They prefer the slow torture of not sharing that information with me."

"You can change your mind about coming over, even if it's the last minute. We *want* you here. And I'll be praying for you. I know it's hard sometimes to forgive."

Forgive? I wanted to ask Elise what she meant but Mom found me, hunched in a corner of my little office. I pointed at the phone but Mom ignored it.

"Your customer is here," she announced. Loudly. "I'm going to make your dad a cup of instant coffee. We can't drink that stuff you have out there."

"Call me tomorrow," Elise said, her voice heavy with sympathy.

"Save me a piece of pie."

I finished up a cut in record time and took advantage of the extra twenty minutes to slink up to my apartment and do some power cleaning. The campground was closed for the year and with the temperatures the way they were, I knew I would offer my parents my bedroom while I camped out in the living room. Honestly, did anyone travel cross-country in an RV in *November?*

I swept a finger across the coffee table and winced at the path I created in the dust. I kept my apartment fairly tidy but not close to my mother's standards, which I knew would hold up under a surprise inspection by the state.

Another phone call. This one on my cell. Which I found under the stack of bathrobes destined for the nativity.

"Hi, Mama B." Heather. As usual, her cheerful voice rose like a buoy in the midst of any storm I happened to be in.

"Hi, yourself." I closed my eyes to savor the moment. "How are you?"

"I'm great. I just wanted to call you before we leave for

my grandma's tomorrow. We won't get back until after ten and I thought that might be too late to call."

Grandma's. Of course. Heather not only had her adoptive parents, she had an adoptive *family*. A whole network of loving people who were as familiar to her as her own reflection.

Take me with you, I wanted to say.

I picked up the photo that Heather had sent me soon after we'd met for the first time. It was her senior picture and she was sitting on a huge rock, her arms wrapped around her knees, with a waterfall shimmering in the background.

"Bree e-mailed a few days ago and said you're spending Thanksgiving with them."

"I was, but my parents showed up this afternoon."

"That's great! I'll bet you were excited to see them."

Excited wasn't quite the word I would have chosen. I was suddenly relieved that Heather hadn't been able to come to Prichett for Thanksgiving. I tried to imagine Heather meeting my parents. Her grandparents. The grandparents who refused to come to the hospital nursery to see her. Who hadn't even asked me if I'd had a boy or girl.

The memory hit me like a breaking wave and anger sprayed up again. I pushed it back down, choosing to concentrate on what Heather was saying.

We spent the next few minutes exchanging stories and I had to leave huge Alex-shaped gaps in mine. I told her about Candy's blind date, but not about the board game we'd played afterward. I mentioned the live nativity but left out that it was going to be held in Alex's barn. She in turn told me she'd gone to a movie with a boy named Andy who fell asleep halfway through the show. She'd left him there and taken a cab home. She'd gotten an A on her first perm but cut the bangs crooked on a four-year-old girl who wouldn't sit still.

There was a loud rap on my door that even Heather heard. I could only assume that my parents had finished their coffee and found me. Again.

"I'll let you go but I'll call back soon and tell you when I can come for a visit," Heather said. "I have exams the second week of December but then I'll be on break for a few weeks."

"That's fine. I'll be swamped the first weekend in December, anyway, making all the high school girls beautiful for the Senior Tea."

The doorknob was rattling now and I said a hasty goodbye to her while I went to answer it.

Dad stood at the top of the stairs, his cheeks rubbed red from the cold. He had hauled an enormous suitcase up the stairs that looked like it would hold enough clothes for a month. Or a year. Which sparked a sense of panic. Maybe they'd sold their *house* to buy the RV. Maybe they planned to retire in the parking space in front of the Cut and Curl.

"Let me help you, Dad." I reached for the case and was surprised when he let me take it without a struggle.

"I get winded when I walk up a flight of stairs," he said, shaking his head. "I love retirement, it's the getting old part that goes along with it I don't care for."

These had to be the most profound words I'd ever heard my dad speak. My dad had always been a man of few words but the ones he spoke tended to be practical. Like, "Pass the potatoes and gravy."

He'd been a silent figure most of my life. The person who came home from work at the end of the day and disappeared behind a newspaper in the den, emerging only for meals and to fulfill certain obligations—like taking out the trash.

When I came home one weekend, uncertain about my future but certain that it was going to involve me *and* a baby, he hadn't said a word to me. Just looked at my mother. Who, not surprisingly, had had plenty to say.

"My fingers get sore sometimes when I'm cutting hair."

Scrambling to find some common ground, it was the best I could offer given the shock of hearing Dad say something that had come from his heart.

"Arthritis." He glanced at my hands. "I have it. My mother had it. You'll get it, too."

And on that cheerful note...

"Where's Mom?"

"In the RV. Taking a nap."

"Oh."

"She's tired." A slow smile crept out, sinking into the creases that bracketed his mouth. "Takes a lot out of a person to criticize their way through seven states."

My mouth fell open.

Dad shuffled past me and I put the suitcase in my bedroom. When I came back, he was examining my ragtag collection of furniture.

"I'm going to refinish those." He didn't have to know that I'd had some of them for over two years, now did he?

"I refinished a dresser once—the one in your bedroom. Bought it at an estate sale on my way home from work one night."

"Mom said that was part of a set." And that was her excuse for not letting me take it with me when I moved out, even though I'd always loved it. It had tiny birds carved into the top and clear glass knobs on each drawer. I'd had no idea my dad had picked it out and refinished it.

I walked over to him, collecting three-by-five cards as I went. I didn't want them to see the verses I had written down. *My grace graffiti.*

I knew if I tried to explain to them what had happened to

me—how I'd become a Christian—they'd immediately assume I had joined some kind of weird cult. My new faith—and Heather—weren't available for critiquing. Not right now.

"Make yourself at home, Dad. I'm just going to straighten up a little."

"No need." Dad looked around. "It looks fine to me."

"Are you hungry? I suppose I should start supper."

"We ate on the way here. I told your mother it wasn't fair to expect you to feed us when you didn't know we were coming."

My throat closed. I was struck with a sudden urge to hug him.

"Who is this?"

My mother, recharged from her nap, had appeared just as I was making Dad another cup of coffee. She'd started an inch-by-inch inspection of my apartment, questioning the authenticity of my antique chairs, frowning over my collection of snow globes and clicking her tongue at the black-and-white posters of old movie stars on my living room walls.

When I dared to glance over, she was holding Heather's picture.

I didn't know what to say. Without thinking, I'd put the picture back on the coffee table after I'd finished talking to her instead of finding a safe hiding place for it. Like Switzerland. I resisted the urge to leap across the room and grab it out of Mom's hand.

"Heather Lowell." *My daughter. Your granddaughter.*

"She's a pretty girl." Mom put the frame down, angled it just so and moved on to the kitchen.

Dad picked up the frame and studied it, but I wasn't worried. Heather was a beauty—the only thing we shared was eye color...

"She looks like you."

As I was recovering from this, Mom opened the refrigerator. "Bernice! Where on earth is the turkey?"

* * *

You can't possibly take care of a baby, Bernice! What is there to think about? You can't even keep a plant alive.

It was a cactus, Mom, and I was eight years old. I didn't know it needed water. You can't compare the two!

My fists clenched under the comforter as the conversation I'd had with my mother all those years ago seeped into my thoughts. What was it about that thin bridge between waking and sleeping that leaves a person vulnerable to the past? During the day I could keep my mind focused on work but the minute my head hit the pillow at night, that's when it always snuck in—when I was too tired to fight. I tried to do what Esther said and wedge Scripture into the weak zones to shore them up, but there was a bitter voice inside me that didn't want to be silenced.

She doesn't deserve to know about Heather.

Sometimes it's hard to forgive.

Elise's words sprang back to me and I sucked in a breath.

God, what's this about forgiveness? It's not like I'm holding a grudge. You know Mom and I have never been close. I've always been a disappointment to her, so why even try?

I twisted onto my side and stared at Heather's picture a few feet away on the coffee table, but I couldn't see her face because of the shadows.

You blame her.

No, I don't. That's the way she is. There isn't a compassionate bone in her body...

Even as I silently argued my case, the truth began to shine in the shadowy parts of my soul. I'd always wondered if Mom hadn't been so cold that day when I'd told her I was pregnant—if she had offered to let me stay with them until I got back on my feet—maybe I wouldn't have put Heather up for adoption. Maybe I would have been the one to watch her grow up into the beautiful, confident young woman she'd become. There would have been laughter in my house instead of silence.

I buried my face in the pillow and squeezed my eyes shut. Maybe I did blame her. For being cold. For being critical. But worst of all, for being indifferent.

The kind of woman I had slowly been becoming. Until I asked God to give me a permanent makeover. Not the outside, but on the inside.

"I would never have ended up like her. Bitter. Cold."

I whispered the words, as if saying them out loud would make them true. But I knew it wouldn't. Mom and I had had more in common than I thought. I was different now, and just to prove it…

Okay, I'll love her, God.

I waited patiently but didn't feel a warm rush of fuzzy feelings. It was scary. The anger stubbornly remained, a cold lump that had settled in my chest and wouldn't move even when I pushed against it with prayer.

And it was still there when I woke up in the morning.

When the phone rang at seven o'clock, I expected to hear Alex's voice. Instead, it was Esther.

"Happy Thanksgiving," I said automatically. Feebly.

She chuckled. "Is it? I heard your parents are visiting."

"Elise told you."

"No, Alex did," Esther said, shocking me down to my red chenille slippers. "He stopped by last night for a visit. He's never met your parents but he thought you might be having a hard time."

"It's complicated." I still wasn't comfortable pouring out my troubles and felt guilty when I did. "I told God last night that I would love her and it didn't happen."

"Mmm." Esther let a few seconds slide by. "Maybe you're starting in the wrong place. Think of it like a woman who's going to run in a marathon. She doesn't just hit the ground running the minute she steps out her front door. The beginning isn't when the whistle blows. The beginning of the race is stretching first, getting her muscles ready to go."

I wasn't sure I liked this exercise analogy. "So where do I start?"

"Start by praying that God would give you the *desire* to love her."

"I don't know if I want to love her." The words slipped out before I could stop them and immediately I felt terrible—like I just wasn't getting this faith stuff right. To love her—to forgive her—seemed unfair. *To me.* Like she was getting completely off the hook somehow.

"That's why you start there. God gets you ready for a *journey* of faith, sweetie. It isn't one jump and we're there. From what Alex said, there's been a lifetime of pain in your relationship with your mom. One step at a time, you're going to have to let God warm up your heart—condition it—so the loving will be easier."

"How did you get to be so smart?"

"I've got a few years on you." Esther laughed.

"I wish God would just hit the fast-forward button on my faith so I could get this stuff right away."

"Oh, you don't want to miss the race and just end up at the finish line. The race is the fun part."

"I'll have to take your word for that," I muttered, watching Mom as she marched out of the bedroom, her hair replaced by a pink cap of tiny plastic rollers. She aimed straight for the coffeepot.

"While you have your coffee, read the middle of Romans 8," Esther said. "And stop by when you can."

"I will." I hung up the phone and imagined that God was standing behind me, rubbing my shoulders like a personal trainer would. Taking a deep breath, I forced a smile. "Good morning, Mom. How did you sleep?"

"Your mattress feels like a concrete block."

Nothing like the bed of nails you're probably used to.
Sorry, Lord!

The minute I heard the shower start, I ran for my Bible and looked up Romans 8. As soon as I skimmed through it, I knew exactly what verses Esther was talking about.

"For you did not receive a spirit that makes you slave again to fear, but you received the spirit of sonship. And by him we cry, 'Abba,' Father. The Spirit himself testifies with our spirit that we are God's children."

I was God's child. I closed my eyes. No matter how hard it was to deal with Mom, she didn't have the power to tell me who I was—or wasn't—anymore. I was listening to God now and figured out that anger had temporarily dulled my hearing. I had to get rid of it.

I didn't like the way I'd felt the day before. The feelings I'd experienced when I'd unexpectedly come face-to-face with my mother had left me with an icky, discouraged residue that I couldn't seem to scrape away. Not on my own.

Lord, I don't want to be a grave-tender, poking around in the ashes of the past, stirring things up so I can't see clearly. Help me want to love her.

Chapter Sixteen

"Good morning, Bernie."

My eyes flicked open and Dad was standing several feet away. He hadn't called me Bernie since I was a kid.

"Hi, Dad. How did you sleep?" I was almost afraid to ask.

"Fair enough. Never like your own bed." He sighed and settled in the chair opposite me. I watched his eyes stray to Heather's picture.

No. I'm not going to share Heather with them, only to have them tear her apart…

"You've met her?" His eyes swung in my direction and I was shocked by the sadness in them.

"Just a few months ago. She found me." I added the last words, wincing at the defensiveness that sprang in.

Dad nodded. "She doing okay?"

"Better than okay." My voice thinned out. "She's just the best, Dad. The best."

"Good." Dad cleared his throat and drummed his palms against his knees. "I always wondered."

"What are you two whispering about?" Mom said, sweeping out of the bathroom, dressed to kill in a houndstooth jacket and black slacks. She always dressed up for a holiday, even if she was spending the entire day in the kitchen. The pink rollers were only a minor distraction.

Dad looked away and didn't say anything, so I leaped into the gap.

"I have a confession to make."

Mom's eyes narrowed.

"I don't cook. I was planning to have Thanksgiving dinner with some friends today, that's why I don't have a turkey thawing out in the refrigerator. In twenty minutes, another friend is going to bring a turkey over, although I have no idea what to do with it. So maybe you could help me."

"Honestly, Bernice…" I braced myself as Mom gathered enough internal steam to scorch me.

"We've got potatoes in the RV," Dad interrupted. "And some of those little chocolate cupcakes in the glove compartment. I'll go get them."

Mom glanced at him almost uncertainly.

There was a knock on the door. Alex. I felt a sudden surge of panic. How was I going to explain Alex Scott, turkey delivery man?

"Hi." It wasn't Alex standing on the landing, it was Riley Cabott. He gave me a little salute. "Reporting for duty."

"Alex sent you?"

"Yup." Riley's feet were surrounded by brown paper grocery bags. "A turkey. Cranberry sauce. Green beans." He lowered his voice. "Everything I could sneak out of Mom's pantry without her noticing. I'm going to be in deep trouble for the apple pie, though."

I glanced in one of the bags and saw a turkey. But this one wasn't in government-inspected, safety-sealed plastic. I swallowed.

"And the turkey?"

"Oh, that came from the backyard last night," Riley said cheerfully.

I felt a little nauseous. Which was silly. I knew that turkeys strutted around the farmyard before they ended up on the Thanksgiving table. I just wasn't expecting…this!

"How did you get involved in this?"

"Pegasus. I'm the one who donated…um, asked Mr. Scott if he'd take him for a while," Riley said, scowling. "It must be payback time because he stopped by last night and said if I didn't deliver Thanksgiving dinner to you this morning, he was going to give Bree's phone number to Hunter Davis."

Hunter Davis had co-starred in Alex's last movie and if I remembered correctly, he was in his early twenties and one of Hollywood's newest rising stars. And naturally had stop-traffic good looks.

"Thank you." Now was not the time to tell Riley that Alex might be on to their little scheme. I started to collect the bags.

"One more thing."

"What is it?"

"I've got four psycho kittens scratching up the upholstery in my truck. Where do you want them?"

"Can you just—"

"Mom would kill me."

I wanted to remind him that he was part of the conspiracy, which meant that he should have to pay the penalty. Not innocent bystanders like me.

"Bring them up."

I hauled the grocery bags into the kitchen. Mom was folding the blankets that I'd used during the night, her movements quick and sharp.

When Dad clumped back in with a bag of potatoes, he also had a cardboard box tucked under his arm. A cardboard box that was vibrating.

"That kid outside told me these are yours."

"What on earth…" Mom surged across the room and took the box away before I could react.

"Mom, don't open it!"

Like tiny calico twisters, four kittens hurtled out of the box and spun in every direction. North, south, east and west.

"I told a friend I'd take care of them for a few days. Until he can find them a good home."

While Mom stared at me like I'd officially lost my mind, Dad took his car keys out of his pocket, knelt down on the floor and started to jingle them softly.

"Oh, honestly, Harris, that isn't going to work!" Mom rolled her eyes and stomped into the kitchen. "Let's get started, Bernice, or we won't be eating until noon tomorrow."

I abandoned Dad and followed Mom into the kitchen, trying to remember everything my customers had told me about creating a memorable Thanksgiving meal. Except that I had a strong hunch I would *never* forget this day.

"This looks like a nice fresh bird."

"You couldn't get one fresher." *Trust me on this, Mom.*

"You make the stuffing and I'll get the bird ready."

I remembered that Mom was a giblet-free stuffing maker all the way. I decided to thank every one of the women who had unknowingly given me knowledge into the secrets and mysteries of the perfect stuffing. I didn't even need to follow a recipe.

"Four hours." Mom slid the bird into the oven and looked at her watch.

Four hours. And even though I'd never relied on Dad to shield me from my mother's barbs, his gentle comments about Heather had ignited a strange hope inside of me. When I made a quick scan of the living room, I saw him dozing in the armchair, decorated with drowsy kittens. No help there.

"Would you like to look at a magazine?"

"I read my way through four states." She had brought her own apron, which she untied and folded with the precision of a soldier with the American flag.

Okay, I'll take that as a no. What to do? For four hours? With my mother. When I visited them every Mother's Day weekend, all three of us maneuvered into our own spots—Mom in the kitchen, Dad in the den and me wandering the perimeter of my old bedroom—which had been converted into a sewing room— counting the seconds until my return flight. It worked for us. But my apartment simply wasn't big enough to hide three people.

Mom reached out and straightened the dish towel that I'd looped over the handle on the oven door. I hadn't done that right, either! Anger began to lap at the edges of my heart again.

I just can't do this, Lord. Shouldn't You save tough tests like this for the people who've studied for them? Not for the people who just walked into class and sat down!

"We're leaving tomorrow afternoon," Mom said abruptly. "Your father wants to visit an old friend in Illinois since we're just a few hours away. They've got some kind of plan cooked up. We're going to leave the RV with his friend until spring and fly back to California. Then his friend is going to drive it back to us in June."

"Sounds like a good idea."

"Of course it is. We don't get caught in some freak blizzard and the Hermeisters get a free vacation."

Of course. Now that we exhausted our list of conversation topics, I was tempted to rummage through the cupboards for a deck of cards so Mom could play solitaire while I hid in the bathroom. I was beginning to understand why Thanksgiving involved such a huge dinner. When you had seven different things piled on your plate, it made it difficult to talk to the people sitting next to you at the table.

Bernice, you're such a cynic. You're supposed to be looking at the world through new eyes, aren't you? I scolded myself even as a sassy voice replied, *New eyes, yes, but it's still the same scenery they're looking at!*

My eyes shifted toward Dad, who had begun to snore softly, the kitten curled up on his chest rising and falling with the rhythm of his breathing. I couldn't help it. I smiled. When I glanced back at Mom, I caught the almost *wounded* look in her eyes. It wasn't possible. Not from the woman who'd handed me her blueprints on how to build a wall around myself and then had given me enough bricks to start one of my own.

"I better get these curlers out," Mom said, touching the pink plastic tubes stacked on her head like cordwood. They were the same ones she'd had when I lived at home. "If I didn't have your father to stop me, I'd walk out the door with them."

I couldn't remember Mom forgetting anything.

Four hours. I almost *felt* the nudge that God gave me.

"Do you want me to give you a perm?" I blurted the words and immediately wished I could yank them back.

Mom stared at me and I waited. Not just for her to say no, but to tick off every reason why she was saying no.

"Can you color it, too? I've got some gray that keeps sneaking through."

Exactly an hour after my parents left the next day—with leftover turkey, half a pumpkin pie and a milk-bloated kitten Dad had named Charlie—Alex called the salon.

"This is creepy. Do you have spies on the roof?"

"I'll never tell."

It was good to hear his voice. It reminded me of one of those little marble fountains in the bank, soothing but with an undercurrent of laughter.

"Are you all right or do I need to come over and check for bruises?"

I ignored the comment. "It wasn't so bad. They left a little while ago, as your spies probably told you."

"Give me the highlights."

"Mom and I cooked the turkey Riley brought over—thank you very much—and I made the stuffing. It was a little soggy but it tasted good. Dad spent most of the afternoon entertaining the psycho kittens you dumped on me and took one home with him. I'm going to let him figure out how to get it home on the plane. I gave Mom a perm and she actually liked it. Not one complaint." That was the surprise of the century. "Last night we played a board game. They went to bed at nine o'clock and packed up this morning."

"What dedication, to drive half way across the country to torment you for twenty-four hours and then leave."

"It wasn't torment." For some reason, starting at the point Esther had suggested—to pray for the desire to love Mom—had given me a curious sense of freedom. Which gave me room to breathe. Which gave me room to want to *love*. Which made me realize even more that God was patient. Which made me love *Him* more. I was constantly amazed at the domino effects of grace.

But the real surprise didn't happen with Mom at all. It happened with Dad. He'd waited until Mom was in the RV before he gave me a loose, one-armed hug and whispered in my ear, "You're doing okay, Bernie."

"Thanks, Dad."

"Can I tell your mother?"

He was talking about Heather. I hesitated.

"I'll wait until we're flying over the mountains," he'd promised.

"Harris!" Mom had rolled down the window. "We're wasting gasoline."

"Okay. Mountains." I took a risk and brushed a kiss across

his cheek while he was still within reach. He stepped away but gave my cheek an awkward pat.

My heart took a hesitant step toward Mom but my feet didn't want to move. I opened my mouth to say something to her—what?—but the window was already gliding up. Just before it closed, I found some words before the window sealed between us.

"See you over Mother's Day?"

"Of course. I'm going to need another perm by then."

One step at a time, I reminded myself. It was nice that God didn't expect me to instantly be perfect...just willing.

"Bern, are you still there? You're pretty quiet all of a sudden." Alex's voice pushed through.

"I'm here. I hope you had Elise save me a piece of pie."

"I didn't go over there."

"Why not?"

"Their daughter was home from college and without you there, I would have felt out of place. Sam and Elise are great but they're your friends, Bern."

"So what did you do?"

"I helped serve dinner at the Golden Oaks, ate turkey with Esther and John until I couldn't move and then spent the afternoon in the lounge watching a Devon Ross movie marathon."

"You didn't," I sputtered. Alex never watched his own movies. Humble but kind of quirky.

"And one of the ladies told me that if I was ten years younger, I'd look just like him."

I laughed, and then looked up as the bells jingled. A teenage boy was standing just inside the door.

"I have to go, Alex."

"Stephen is coming over with some kids this weekend to put up lights. Are you going to be here, too?"

"I could stop by after work. I do have three kittens to

deliver." I hung up the phone before he could protest. He told me I had to take the kittens—he didn't specify for how long. As far as I was concerned, the statute of limitations on kitten-sitting was officially over.

"Hi, Miss Strum."

Thank you for reminding me I'm an old maid, kid. Maybe I'll just keep one of those kittens and start giving piano lessons in my spare time.

"Do you want to make an appointment?"

"No." He shook his head and inched forward.

I knew I should recognize him. Tall and muscular, his blond hair razored close to his head. Wearing a Panthers letter jacket…

"Kyle." Star quarterback. Varsity. He was probably doing some fund-raiser for the team. Pizzas, no, chocolate, yes! "What brings you here?"

"I was gone last weekend when you picked parts for the live nativity." He ducked his head self-consciously. "I heard that Greta is going to be Mary."

Any goodwill I'd had toward the kid vaporized.

"That's right."

"I was wondering, uh, if I could be Joseph?"

I could see right where this was going. His big, innocent blue eyes couldn't conceal the fact that there was a major practical joke in the works. I'd been the brunt of some of those jokes myself when I was in high school and still had the scars to prove it.

"Not a chance. And I don't know what you're planning but maybe I should remind you that this is a *church youth group?* You of all people should be a little more accepting of differences, especially because the church is supposed to be a *family.* You just sealed your fate because I'm going to make you a great big donkey costume and plant you right in the pasture next to Junebug. And if you even look sideways at Greta Lewis I'll…"

The boy's eyes bulged and he started to gurgle. "We're not planning anything like that… I want to be Joseph because…I kind of *like* her. Greta. She's cute. But she never lets me get close enough to her so I can ask her out so I figured if I was Joseph…"

"Melissa didn't put you up to this?" He sounded sincere but I wasn't going to risk Greta's tender new heart.

"Mel? No. Honest."

The way his voice cracked in a way it probably hadn't since seventh grade convinced me. I caved in. A softie for romance every time and my collection of Cary Grant movies proved it. "You can be Joseph."

"Thanks, Miss Strum."

"Call me…Bernice." I sighed as my name was lost in the jingle of the bells. He'd spun around and disappeared out the door in a maneuver so fast it was probably in the playbook.

Chapter Seventeen

I woke up Saturday morning to an eerie silence. When I looked outside, I saw why. The clouds that swept through during the night had dumped six inches of *light flurries* on the ground, creating a meringue of peaks and drifts along Main Street, and it showed no sign of stopping.

I wrapped myself in a blanket and perched on the edge of the chair, watching the wind lift up the snow and swirl it around in an energetic dance.

I loved it. After growing up in California, snow was one of those things that would keep me in Prichett forever.

Which brought back the wisp of a memory. I resisted it for a few seconds and then let it in. The beginning of my snow globe collection. Alex and I had been out on a date and we'd ducked into one of those cheesy, touristy kinds of shops after a day on the beach. I'd been complaining about the heat and mentioned that I would love to live in another state—where the weather wasn't always so beautifully predictable. He'd told me I was crazy but then surprised me later with a snow globe. There was a tiny house inside that looked more like a castle than the ski chalet it was supposed to be.

It scared me to death. Not the snow globe but the fact that Alex listened. And instead of taking advantage of the moment and giving me some worn-out line like, "Hey, baby, if you really want to see some snow we could head to the mountains this weekend," he'd given me something that would guarantee I'd think of him every time I saw it.

Moving around a lot those first few years after I'd left California, I bought a snow globe in every city I wandered through. I hadn't added to my collection now for ten years and that was fine with me. I had the real thing right outside my window.

The phone rang and I knew exactly who it was.

"You can't possibly still like this stuff."

I tucked the phone between my ear and my shoulder and perched on the arm of the chair again. The plows weren't even out yet and no one was on Main Street. "Isn't it great?"

"Not if you have to go out and feed animals."

Lester would have been hopeful if he'd heard the words, except that Alex was laughing.

"You should have kept the kittens and given Colonel Mustard to me. The kittens use a litter box."

"So I suppose the entire county shuts down during something like this."

"Just about."

"That means you can't come over."

I closed my eyes. *Alex, please go back to California. I don't know how much longer I can do this.*

"Tomorrow. When Stephen and the kids are there."

"Are you implying we need a chaperone?"

"Don't be silly." *Of course we do.*

"I admit—it's been hard not to kiss you."

"What?" The word came out in a squeak.

"You heard me." Alex was quiet for a moment. Then, "Don't you feel the connection we still have, Bern?"

My heart picked up speed so fast that I wondered if an ambulance could make it through all the snow on Main Street.

I felt the connection, no doubt about it. But Alex? The man who'd been escorting beautiful *young* women around for the past twenty years? Women who had personal trainers and enough money to slow down the aging process?

"That doesn't make any sense." I was irritated with him for not being honest with me. "I'm not spring or even summer anymore, Alex. I'm…autumn. Not even the beginning of autumn. The middle of autumn. You know, when the pretty colors start to fade and the leaves are falling and they're dry and crunchy."

"Whoa…" There was a sudden commotion and Alex gasped over the line. "I can't get the front door open and Colonel Mustard needs to go out."

Click. I was suddenly holding a phone with no one on the other end. And realized I wasn't alone.

Three pairs of bright eyes were staring up at me. The kittens always started out the day strung together like a fifty-cent pack of firecrackers but I quickly learned that within minutes they'd separate and create individual explosions around the apartment. That's why I'd named them Snap, Crackle and Pop.

"Go easy on him when I take you home tomorrow, okay?"

One yawned in boredom. The other two just laughed.

My celebration of the first big snowfall had become a tradition. I made pancakes, slathered them with peanut butter and ate them while I sat in the chair overlooking Main Street.

The first plow didn't come through until almost noon and that's when I heard a scraping sound on the back steps.

When I went to investigate, accompanied by a small contingent of kittens that padded cautiously behind me, Riley was almost to the top of the back staircase, shovel in hand.

"Why are you shoveling my steps?"

He pushed a few strands of dark hair off his forehead. "Being neighborly?"

"Riley."

"All right, *he* called and *asked* me to."

I bit back a smile. "Why?"

"How should I know?" Riley growled. "I'll shovel the sidewalk in front of the salon, too, since I'm here."

From the look on his face, I had a hunch that the name *Hunter Davis* had figured heavily in his discussion with Alex.

An hour later there was a knock on the door. I expected Riley but instead it was a windburned teenage boy, holding an enormous plastic bag.

"Delivery from Applegate Floral." He glared at me as if I'd sent myself something from Applegate Floral just to make him come out in a blizzard.

"There must be a mistake…" I said, but he had already started to pick his way carefully down the stairs.

The kittens, who had scattered at the sound of his voice, crept out of hiding. I pulled the plastic bag off and reached a shroud of tissue paper. Carefully peeling away the layers, I unearthed a treasure. A huge bouquet of exotic tiger lilies, creamy miniature carnations and yellow roses. Interspersed among the flowers were slender, velvet brown cattails and glossy ferns.

I read the card.

"Autumn is my favorite season."

I hugged the bouquet, buried my face in the cushion and cried hot sticky tears while the kittens brushed against me and purred in stereo.

By Sunday morning the snow had stopped, the streets were plowed and I had no excuse not to go to Alex's after church. In fact, I was thoroughly *expected* to go because Stephen was bringing the youth group over to string lights along the driveway.

"Guess who?" Hands covered my eyes as I hung up my coat in the church foyer.

"Bree!" I twisted around and hugged her. "Let me look at you."

She gave me a saucy pirouette and curtsy.

"You look great. College agrees with you." I hugged her again because I couldn't help myself.

I'd fallen in love with Bree Penny the first time Elise had brought her in for a haircut, when she'd solemnly told me not to make her look "too girlie." She'd been eight years old, with skinned knees and wide, smoke-blue eyes. I'd begged for opportunities to babysit but they were few and far between simply because Elise and Sam never left the farm. Still, Bree and I had forged a relationship based on a shared love of pistachio ice cream and Nancy Drew mysteries. I'd become her adopted auntie.

"Feel good to be home?"

Bree nodded. "But I have to go back this afternoon already. I get a longer break in December after finals."

"Heather is coming over for Christmas, too."

"She told me." Bree squeezed my hand. They'd met and become instant friends. "I'll bet you can't wait to see her."

I thought of Alex and what I was going to have to tell Heather, and it definitely cast a shadow on my excitement. I wanted to see her but had no idea how she would take the news. Maybe she would pull back...

"I know you haven't told her about Alex," Bree said softly. "And I want you to know that Mom and I are praying for you. This has to be tough."

I felt tears sting my eyes. Here was an eighteen-year-old giving me some much-needed encouragement. And I soaked it up like a sponge. Did that make me pathetically needy? I didn't care anymore. Because it certainly made me feel loved!

Elise came up to us, glowing. Her chick had returned temporarily to the nest.

"I saved you a piece of pie but you have to come out to the house to get it," Elise told me.

"It's a deal."

The soft strains of the prelude drifted over us and we found an empty pew. Just as I started to scan my program, a shadow fell across me.

"Move over, will you?"

Candy. I blinked several times to keep my eyeballs from falling out of my head. She was wearing a black wool coat and her hair spilled over the collar in an eye-catching blond waterfall. I saw several people twisting around to get a better look at her, their eyes wide with surprise.

Had she told me she was going to be here? I doubted it. Even though I was within shouting distance of menopause and was constantly forgetting things, I don't think I would have forgotten if Candy had mentioned she was coming to church.

Dutifully, I bumped my hip against Elise's, pushing her closer to Sam. Who smiled and tucked his arm around her shoulders.

The worship team in the front began to sing "Amazing Grace." I pressed a hymnal into Candy's hands. By the time we got to the last verse, she was belting out the words in a clear, beautiful soprano. Several people around us had stopped singing and closed their eyes, soaking in the sound of her voice. I was one of them.

At the end of the service, Candy didn't move.

"Thanks."

"For?" I frowned.

"For fixing my hair," Candy responded. The way her eyes lifted toward the ceiling told me she was being sarcastic. "For telling me about God, Bernice."

She was here because of me? I was overwhelmed and scared and grateful all at the same time.

"There's something different about you," Candy said. "You can't fake that."

The waterworks were threatening to go on again. I thought I'd cried every tear my eyes could possibly produce the day I'd read Alex's note. Apparently not.

"I need your help with something else." Candy lowered her voice. "I bought some makeup but I had a little trouble putting on the mascara this morning. Maybe you could give me some pointers."

I studied her face and hid a smile. The blush she'd applied was two stripes of cherry-red, racing up her cheekbones. And she had enough mascara on her eyelashes to block bullets.

"Stop by the salon tomorrow."

Candy looked relieved. "Mark is taking me out to a fancy place for dinner tomorrow night. The God stuff I can accept but this froufrou girlie thing takes some getting used to."

When I got to Alex's, the youth van—painted in a garish array of colors with the words Jesus Rocks emblazoned on the side—was already parked by the barn. I could see Stephen standing on a snowbank, issuing orders to a group of teenage boys. The girls were nowhere to be seen. Uh-oh.

I slipped into the house through the back door and found Alex's kitchen had been taken over. Melissa wasn't there but the rest of her entourage was seated around the table. Completely silent.

"Hi…" I began but was instantly shushed.

Alex walked in, waggling his cell phone. "Who's first?"

Six hands shot up in the air. He handed the phone to the girl who was closest to him. She bit her lip, looked at her friends and then said a cautious hello. Then collapsed against the back of the chair. If she hadn't had such a goofy smile on her face, I would've thought she'd fainted.

"What's going on?" I asked.

Alex grabbed my elbow and pulled me into the living room. "Hunter Davis is on the phone."

"You called him?"

"They've been here for ten minutes and I was going to gag if I heard his name one more time," Alex said. "'Did you hang out with him? What's he like? Does he have a girlfriend?' Finally, I just told them if they were quiet for one minute, I'd call him and they could ask him any question they wanted to."

"You're brilliant."

Alex shrugged modestly. "So I've been told."

"So it didn't bother you that instead of hanging on *your* every word, they wanted to know about Hunter?"

"Please, Bernice. Those girls could be my daughters. And for your information, I have quite a fan club of eighty-year-old women at the nursing home who *do* hang on my every word."

"If they have their hearing aids turned up." I couldn't resist.

Another peal of laughter pierced the room and Alex cringed. "I think I'll go out and see what the guys are doing to my barn."

"I think I'll come with you."

We ducked out the front door, with Colonel Mustard trotting along behind us.

"Who plowed you out yesterday?" I asked curiously.

"Riley." An evil smile surfaced.

"You need to give that poor kid a break," I said, elbowing him in the side.

"Break?" Alex looked confused but he wasn't fooling me for a minute. "I don't know what you're talking about."

"Right."

Stephen waved when he saw me. "Annie says hello. We

just got back a few hours ago from my parents' and she's taking a nap."

Annie, Elise and I needed some serious, uninterrupted friendship time. Just the three of us. Even though Sam took down the porch swing in the winter, there had to be a place the three of us could hide for a few hours. I decided that before life got too busy with Christmas activities, I was going to plan something special.

"Anything I can do?" Alex asked.

Stephen looked around. "We're going to need to wrap the fence posts with lights so people can follow them to the barn. Go ahead and grab these boxes and a few teenagers to help you. Bernice, will you get some of the girls to help you sweep out the barn and clean up some of the loose junk lying around?"

In ten seconds, he'd neatly separated Alex and me. I felt nothing but relief. I'd wanted to thank Alex for the flowers. Knew I *had* to thank him for the flowers. But I was scared down to my bones.

I trudged back to the house and shooed a reluctant gaggle of girls outside. They were off the phone with Hunter Davis but were replaying the conversations, giggling their way through every word he'd said. Just as we reached the barn, Greta's little car pulled up. I was glad that I'd brought the boxes with the nativity costumes along.

"Where's Melissa today?" I asked casually.

"She called me last night and said she wasn't feeling the best," one of the girls told me.

I frowned. The cold and flu season was probably starting early this year. I hoped I wasn't going to be one of its first victims. I didn't have time to get sick.

"According to Stephen, all this junk needs to be put away in that back room," I instructed, shaking the pesky thought away. If I wasn't careful, I'd wind up like Mindy.

"What about this?" One of the girls held up a metal rake.

"Let me clarify. Anything that a ten-year-old boy can turn into a weapon or a grandma could trip over needs to be put away."

They got busy, their giddiness over Hunter giving them loads of excess energy.

I saw Greta peek in and went to intercept her before she ran back to her car.

"Hi." I gave her a lumpy hug, all I could manage in my heavy wool peacoat. I gave hugs sparingly but Annie's influence was definitely winning me over.

"Did you bring the costumes?" she asked.

"They're in my car."

"Maybe I could start sorting through them. It looks like you've got enough help in here."

I could read her mind. Even with Melissa gone, she still wasn't comfortable with the girls in the youth group.

"Alex won't mind if you go in the house," I said. "You may as well be warm while you sort. When we're finished here, I want to finish assigning everyone a part and we'll have a quick practice."

"Do you still want me to be Mary?"

"Don't be silly. I can't think of anyone better."

Greta smiled and for the first time I realized that she'd added two bright spots of color to her usual black: a multi-colored striped scarf and matching hat.

"Cute scarf."

"Annie gave it to me a few days ago." Greta fingered the silky fringe on the hem. "She said that I needed some wild-flowers in my wardrobe."

Wildflowers?

"Okay…"

Greta laughed and dug in the bag slung over her shoulder. When she pulled out a three-by-five card, I laughed, too.

"Grace graffiti."

Greta nodded and looked down at the card. "It says that God ripped off my mourning band and decked me with wild-flowers. I think Annie was trying to tell me to stop dressing like I'm going to a funeral."

"That's…" I was about to say *beautiful* but there was a movement by the door and Kyle was standing there, staring at Greta, his eyes wide with longing.

"Did you need something, Kyle?"

As soon as Greta heard the name, her shoulders set rigidly and she refused to look at him.

"I…" His mouth worked several times, like he was pumping the handle of a well that had suddenly gone dry.

Then I heard the shouting.

"What's going on?"

"The cow and the horse…" He couldn't take his eyes off Greta, which seemed to be robbing him of the ability to speak. And think.

"What *about* the cow and the horse?"

"They…got out. Of the fence."

The sound of the yelling grew closer. And so did the flat thud of hooves against the hard-packed snow outside.

That's when I realized that we were standing right in front of the grain box.

Chapter Eighteen

It was a good thing that Kyle was the quarterback of the football team because he was used to thinking on his feet in high-pressure circumstances. He pulled Greta up to the top of the stack of hay bales first, then stretched out his hand to me. Seconds later, Junebug charged through the door with Pegasus right behind her.

"She's rabid," Kyle muttered, peering down.

I peeked over the hay bale and saw that Junebug must have recently taken a huge drink of water. It had frozen in the cold temperatures so it looked like she was foaming at the mouth.

"That's frost." Okay, I was ninety-nine percent sure it was.

The animals were studying the grain box as though it were the Franklin Mint when Stephen and the rest of the boys burst in. They looked up and saw us. And started laughing.

"Wish I had a camera, Gibson," one of the boys chortled. "Your picture would be on the front of the yearbook."

"If we weren't up here, we'd be squashed down there," Greta pointed out.

Kyle shot her a grateful look, which Greta ignored.

"It was weird, man," one of the boys said, grabbing

Pegasus' halter. "That goat opened the gate and let them out. No kidding."

"What goat?" I hadn't noticed a goat.

"Houdini," Alex said.

I tilted my head, waiting for him to make the connection between the name and the crime. Suddenly his eyes narrowed.

"What's next?" He laughed softly.

Mmm, I don't know. A llama?

The boys formed a human gate to keep Junebug and Pegasus from leaving the barn while Stephen, Alex and I went out to examine the fence. There *was* a goat. Instead of having taken the opportunity to escape, he was still in the pasture, nibbling snow. While I held the frayed ends of the fencing together, he wandered over and tasted the glove that was hanging out of my pocket.

"You're trouble with a capital T," I muttered. "You even *look* like trouble." It was true. He was white with a ragged patch of black over one eye that gave him a jaunty, piratical look. If goats could look jaunty and piratical.

Within twenty minutes we'd fixed the fence and herded the felons back to the pasture. Then Stephen gathered everyone into a tight group.

"Mr. Scott and I are going to keep working on the lights but Bernice is going to take over now," he said. "I just wanted to say again how much I appreciate you guys volunteering to help out with the nativity. Let's start by dedicating this time to the Lord." He bowed his head and I felt, rather than saw, Alex's jolt of surprise. "God, we give this time to You. We thank You for the gift of Your son Jesus and ask that as we draw closer to the celebration of His birth, let this nativity draw people here so they can quiet their hearts and remember Your overwhelming love and grace. Amen."

When I opened my eyes, I had a sudden case of the jitters because everyone's attention was on me now.

"I have everyone's parts written down here." I fumbled in my purse for the scrap of paper I'd jotted some notes on after the first meeting we'd had. "Don, Craig and Mitchell are the three wise men. The shepherds are Luke, Travis and Jonathan. The girls are the angels. Melissa is the angel of the Lord. Greta is Mary and Kyle Gibson is Joseph."

"Better luck next time, Gibson," I heard one of the guys whisper.

"I know you've done this before but this is a new barn so we'll have to figure out where everyone is going to be placed."

I felt a tug on my coat sleeve. Greta. I could see the panic in her eyes.

"I changed my mind. I want to be the angel of the Lord. Melissa can be Mary."

"This doesn't have anything to do with *Joseph,* does it?" I deliberately kept my voice low because Kyle was pacing the perimeter of our conversation, casting anxious glances at Greta.

"Maybe." Greta looked miserable.

"You don't even have to talk to him," I said. "You don't even have to *look* at him. All you have to do is stare serenely down at baby Jesus for a few hours."

Greta fiddled with her scarf. "All right."

Working out the logistics of the nativity took longer than I thought. The daylight began to fade and Stephen turned on the hundreds of miniature white lights that lined the driveway. They didn't provide much in the way of light but that didn't matter. They were beautiful.

Just as I was explaining to the wise men—for the third time—why we couldn't rent real camels, something whistled past my head.

A snowball.

There was a feminine shriek followed by another white missile being launched several feet away. I took cover behind my car and watched the war begin.

"Lost control, huh?"

Stephen leaned against the hood and I could see the flash of his grin.

"I'm amazed you and Annie can do this all the time. I'm completely exhausted."

"That's from scrambling up a mountain of hay bales to get away from Junebug," Alex reminded me.

"I'll round them all up and take them home," Stephen said. "Annie has hot chocolate and cookies waiting."

"You can stuff all those kids in your apartment?"

"They kind of spill out over the edges, but it works." Stephen wrapped an arm around my shoulders. "Thanks, Bernice. This has taken a load off Annie, for sure. You're a good friend."

I felt the warmth of his words kindle inside me even as I moved restlessly under his arm, uncomfortable with the praise. "Tell her I'm going to call her tomorrow."

"She said Elise promised to help her make fudge for the fellowship time after the nativity. I'm sure they could use an extra set of hands. Or maybe a taste tester."

"I'm in."

A snowball suddenly came hurtling in our direction and we instinctively ducked.

"What do you say, Alex?" Stephen bent down and plowed his gloved hand through the snow. "Ready to show those kids that even though we're outnumbered, *they're* hopelessly outsmarted?"

"I'm in."

They looked at me.

"Come on, Bern, you love the snow." Alex was already molding a huge paw full of snow into a ball.

"Not down my back."

"If you're not with us, then you're against us," Stephen pointed out.

As if on cue, they tossed the snowballs in the air and caught them again, leering at me.

I squeaked and took off, heading toward the girls, who were huddled behind a snowbank by the barn. I collapsed beside them just as another snowball was launched and clipped the side of my hat.

"Where's Greta?" I looked around, wondering if she'd taken sanctuary in the house.

"Kyle took her captive," one of the girls murmured. "Spoils of war, he called her. We offered to trade her for Jonathan but so far he's refusing to cooperate."

Of course he was. I smiled.

By the time the boys surrendered an hour later, I was soaking wet, my socks had slipped into the toes of my boots and I couldn't feel my fingertips. Still, the girls and I managed a decent victory dance on the top of the largest snowbank.

Stephen reached into the van and honked the horn to get everyone's attention. "Hot chocolate at our place. Let's go."

The kids piled in, wet and laughing, and the vehicle rumbled down the driveway. Greta's car puttered along after it, filled with the girls who had, in the space of the snowball fight, become her friends.

Thank You, God.

"I've got a fire going," Alex said, moving to stand beside me. "Do you want to come in and warm up a bit?"

It's a good thing my silent prayer was still lingering in the air.

"I need more than a fire. I need a whole new wardrobe. A dry one." I started walking toward my car and Alex fell into step beside me. I tensed, wondering if he was going to push the issue. Wondering if I'd be strong enough to drive away if he did.

"Feeling like this. It's strange."

For a split second I thought he was talking about me, but then he took a deep breath, tipped his head back and looked at the stars that were peeking through bits of clouds.

My heart gave a sudden, hopeful thump.

"Feeling…"

"Normal. I don't know." He laughed softly. "Is this what normal feels like?"

"I'm not sure. Maybe normal is what you're used to."

"Then this definitely isn't normal." He pushed his hands into his coat pockets.

I took refuge in the front seat of my car and pulled the door shut between us before I launched myself into his arms. I rolled the window down a crack.

"Thank you for the flowers." It was safe to say it now.

"You're welcome." He was distracted, still staring at the stars.

"Just to warn you, we'll all be over again later this week."

"I'll make sure I have some soda and chips this time. I didn't realize a guy could get lynched for not providing junk food. It must be written somewhere in the fine print of the teen handbook."

"Can I borrow a copy of that?"

"Sorry, I never got one." Alex smiled but I couldn't. I'd never gotten one, either. Regret began to edge in and suddenly Heather's face was superimposed over Alex's. Their smiles perfectly matched.

"I'll see you later." *Exit stage left.*

Alex shot me a bemused look. "You know something?"

I was afraid to ask. The only thing I could manage was a short jerk of my head, like someone had yanked on my earlobe.

"I like *friends*. And I like *normal*."

And he obviously liked inflicting pain. Because that's what he was doing, whether he knew it or not.

* * *

I stopped by Annie's after work the next day, ready to spend the evening making fudge. She met me at the door, adorable in a sunny-yellow sweatshirt under denim overalls that stretched across her tummy.

"Did you bring them?"

"Right here." I pulled a box of frozen waffles out of my purse and Annie practically pounced on them. I followed her to the tiny kitchen.

"Do you want one?" She shook the box. There were only four left. If I'd had more time, I would have stopped at the store and bought her a new box but she'd sounded a little desperate, so I'd just brought the ones from my freezer.

I could tell how much it was costing her to be polite. "Go ahead. I had a bowl of soup before I came over."

"Did you have weird cravings like this?" Annie asked, pulling a container of cottage cheese and peaches out of the fridge. Then she stared into the toaster and tapped her foot impatiently.

"I don't remember." I wouldn't let myself remember.

Annie waited. I wiggled in the silence. Then gave in.

"Bananas. I ate about ten of them a day and all of a sudden I couldn't look at a banana without getting nauseous."

There was a light tap on the door and Elise came in, holding a grocery bag.

"Frozen waffles?" I guessed.

"Did you bring some, too?" Elise's eyebrows rose.

We both looked at Annie, who didn't look a bit guilty.

"I had to cover my bases," she said. "Just in case one of you forgot."

Elise put the bag down and studied me. Then, she pulled out three aprons. Not the cute little ones that tied around your waist but the old-fashioned kind that covered everything you could possibly spill on. Or sit in.

"Here are the rules," she announced.

"There are fudge-making rules?" I glanced at Annie and she shrugged, still distracted by what was happening inside the toaster.

Elise tapped one finger against another. "No talking about the weather, no talking about work. No talking about husbands…or parents…or Alex Scott. Tonight is all about fun, friendship and fudge."

Pure, undiluted relief poured through me. I hadn't realized how much I needed a break from reality. And who better to provide it than my two best friends?

Annie raised her hand.

"Um, can we talk about babies?"

Elise smiled. "That's the *only* thing we're going to talk about."

The next morning when I was unlocking the salon, I saw Denise across the street, wrapping one of the light poles in front of the variety shop with a length of evergreen. Now that Thanksgiving was officially over, she could pull out all the stops. She was even wearing a cardinal-red sweater with a gigantic snowman face embroidered on it.

"Bernice! Christmas open house!" she called, waving a scarlet ribbon at me.

"Can't," I shouted back. "I'll be working at the live nativity."

Even from where I was standing, I saw her deflate like a happy red balloon that'd just been poked with a Scrooge pin.

"Bernice!"

The wail heard around the world.

"I'll talk to you later." I ducked into the salon and closed the door, tempted to lock it behind me. But that wouldn't work. I had customers coming in.

Not five minutes after I hung up my coat, the phone started ringing off the hook with women who had canceled because of the storm and were now fighting a battle in which dark roots were beginning to win. I squeezed them in the best I could and added two more cuts after five o'clock, when I normally closed up, just so I wouldn't have a mutiny on my hands.

When I slunk over to the coffeepot, I saw Denise talking to Candy and then she pointed in my direction. Great. That was all I needed...

The bells jingled.

"Hi, Candy."

"Denise says you're not going to take part in the Main Street Christmas open house."

The way she said it made it sound as serious as if the president of the United States had suddenly refused to attend the inaugural ball.

"I'm already busy with the live nativity at Faith," I said, wishing I'd stopped by Sally's for some Danish. Sally's Danish alone could qualify for a peacekeeping mission.

"Can you at least decorate your front window with something other than dust and hair magazines?"

"There isn't any dust..." Okay, there was a little dust. But not enough to write your name in. "People expect to see hair magazines. This is a beauty salon." She couldn't argue with that.

"I'll let you off the hook for the open house," Candy said. "But you have to decorate your front window so when people walk by, to go into the businesses that *will* be open for the open house, they'll at least know that Bernice Strum is a team player."

Yes, but I'd been drafted.

"Fine."

"Now, do you have a few minutes to show me how to put this stuff on or do you want me to come back later?"

I'd forgotten I'd promised her some makeup pointers.

"My nine o'clock is always ten minutes late, so we have time. Take a seat."

"You'd think people assumed I was bald the way they keep going on about my hair," Candy mumbled.

"I knew it was just a nasty rumor." I'd noticed she wasn't wearing her hat again.

Jackpot. I found a cache of makeup in the drawer that a new cosmetics company had sent me recently. For a second I'd been afraid I'd thrown it away. If I hadn't liked doing hair better, someone had told me once that I could have been a success as a makeup artist, too. Even though I didn't bother with it much for myself, everything I'd learned suddenly came flooding back.

"You need mascara. Your eyelashes are so light, they practically disappear, but you want to use brown, not black, okay?" I came at her with the mascara wand and she stared right into my eyes.

"You don't like Christmas, do you?"

The mascara wand dropped out of my fingers and bounced across the floor, giving me time to recover from the question as I chased it.

"What makes you say that?" I wiped off the wand and wondered how I was going to manage putting it on Candy's lashes now that my hand had begun to shake.

"You never have a tree in your window upstairs," Candy said. "Ever. And when people talk about Christmas, you get this look on your face like they're talking about this year's flu strain."

My first inclination was to deny it, but there was something in Candy's expression that called for honesty.

"Something...happened at Christmas. A long time ago." Why hadn't the image of putting my newborn baby into a nurse's arms faded over the years? It was just as sharp and clear as if it had happened the day before. Loss. Self-imposed exile and a letter to someone I knew I'd never see again. That's all Christmas had come to mean.

"But now that you know something good happened, you're okay. Is that stuff supposed to smell like licorice?" Candy's nose wrinkled.

"You mean Heather?" I blinked. How did Candy know Heather's birthday was Christmas Day?

"Heather?" Candy leaned away from the wand and eyed me suspiciously. "No, I'm talking about Jesus. Now that you're a Christian, Christmas will be different."

I suddenly got it. With two-by-four force. I could celebrate Christmas this year. I didn't have to cringe away from it. Or avoid it. God was in it. The reason for it. And that tiny girl I'd placed in someone else's arms had somehow—amazingly— found her way back to me twenty years later. And I knew God had done that for me, to put my fears and guilt to rest. To know that even though I couldn't see her all those years, He could. And He'd been taking care of her. And He'd been watching over me, too. And when He'd chosen the time for us to meet, He'd made sure that I had friends like Elise and Annie to lean on if I started to sway.

"You're right." I felt the smile form on the inside before Candy saw it on my face.

"Sure I am." Candy leaned forward to peer at herself in the mirror. "I can't see a difference."

"The trick with makeup is to look natural."

"Natural?"

"Like you aren't wearing any."

"Then what's the point?"

"That's a good question."

"It's a good thing you don't do this for a living," Candy said. "You wouldn't sell much of this stuff."

I didn't respond.

"Are you listening to me?"

"I was thinking about the best spot in my apartment to put a tree," I confessed.

"Right in front of the big window overlooking Main Street." Candy looked way too pleased with herself.

"I knew you were going to say that."

Chapter Nineteen

When Greta stopped in after school, I took one look at her white face and figured I'd been wrong about that Gibson kid.

"What happened?"

"Melissa..."

Was it possible to *fire* the angel of the Lord?

"Is she bothering you again?"

Greta shook her head. "She's... The principal made an announcement today. She's going to be out of school for a few weeks. She has cancer."

I sagged against the counter and stared at Greta. "Are they sure?"

"It's one of the bad kinds," Greta said, her voice barely above a whisper. "I can't even remember what he called it, but it's in her arm. Her mom thought she was achy because of the flu but when she didn't feel better, they took her in to see a doctor."

Not knowing what else to do, I hugged Greta while the tears spilled over.

"Do you think she'd mind if I called her and told her I was praying for her?"

I shook my head. "I'm sure she'd appreciate it."

Greta looked uncertain. "I don't know."

"She needs her friends right now." I squeezed her shoulder. "And she needs them to pray for her."

When Greta left, I called Annie.

"I heard about Melissa. Greta just stopped in and told me."

Annie sighed heavily. "Osteosarcoma. It's not good, Bernice. Stephen is with the family right now. They're going to do surgery and start chemo treatments but this is an aggressive cancer and the doctors have already warned them that if the chemo doesn't do its job, they're going to have to amputate her arm."

I exhaled raggedly. "How is she doing?"

"Devastated," Annie said. "Stephen told me she's in shock and all she can focus on is that if they have to amputate, she won't be able to cheer anymore or get her volleyball scholarship."

Those seemed like trivial things to me but I bit my tongue. Who would be thinking clearly in a situation like this?

I jotted down the name of the hospital, murmured a distracted goodbye to Annie and hung up the phone.

Cancer, God? She's only seventeen years old.

The phone rang and I debated whether to answer it, still trying to absorb what Annie had told me. When I picked it up, Carolee Lee's perky voice came through the line, telling me that she needed a trim again. When I turned the page, I saw the list of names of teenage girls scheduled to have their hair done for the Senior Tea.

And Melissa's name jumped out at me. In two weeks, after several rounds of chemotherapy, the reality was that she would be losing her hair, not getting it swept into an elaborate updo.

I penciled Carolee in and took a deep breath as the doorbell jingled, exhaling silently in prayer.

My next three clients had already heard about Melissa and I tamped my emotions down while I listened to them sort through the medical history of their families and friends and their own personal experiences with cancer.

By the time I was ready to close up, I didn't ever want to hear the word again. Instead of going up to my apartment, where there was way too much silence, I got in my car and drove.

Alex opened the door before I reached it. Almost as if he'd been expecting me.

"Come on in."

I shook my head. "Too dangerous," I managed weakly, wishing that my car had gone to Elise's house. Or the Golden Oaks to see Esther. What was I doing here?

"Then I'll come out."

Did he have to be so understanding? Why didn't he get offended? Or tired of what he probably thought was the silliest game of a woman playing hard-to-get he'd ever experienced?

I waited in the cold while my nose began to run and my fingertips turned numb and the wind burned through the fabric of my slacks.

Finally, Alex came out, wearing a heavy coat and a black cashmere scarf. And a leather mad bomber's hat complete with earflaps trimmed in rabbit fur.

"Where did you get that?"

"Charity. I had tea with her at the Lightning Strike this afternoon. She said it was her husband's but she didn't think he'd care because my ears looked cold."

I turned away and impatiently brushed a tear off my cheek, hoping Alex wouldn't notice. He did. He pulled me against his chest and pressed my face into his coat.

"Bern? What do you need?"

"A Christmas tree."

"Let's go find one."

* * *

"No peeking." I led Elise into my apartment and made sure her eyes were still closed. "Okay, now you can look."

"Wow. There are…"

"Three of them. I know. I couldn't decide which one I liked the best."

The trees were only three feet tall and Alex and I had discovered them growing in the shadow of an ancient tangle of cedar. I'd strung a different set of colored lights on each tree. My favorite was the strand of white ones that looked like frosted pinecones. Denise had talked me into buying them the day before, thrilled when I went into the variety store to actually *shop*.

"They look prettier at night. I didn't have many ornaments but Carolee told me that she covers baby's breath with gold spray paint and tucks it in between the branches, so I tried it. What do you think?"

"They're beautiful."

"Heather is going to be here for a few days around Christmas. And this year, I wanted to really *celebrate* the day. You know what I mean?"

Elise nodded. I was glad there were some things you just didn't have to explain to a friend. She took a step toward the window and was attacked as she passed the sofa.

"You still have those kittens?"

I looked down and saw Snap hanging by a claw to the hem of her coat.

"Just this one. The other two are in Alex's barn, living the high life. He bought one of those ridiculous carpet castles for them to sleep in, put in a heated water dish and an automatic feeder."

Elise chuckled. "And this one has to suffer."

"That's right." When the time came, I just found I couldn't part with Snap. Not after I discovered she was a kindred Cary

Grant fan. When I put a movie in before bed, she wound herself around my neck like a feather boa and purred, her lime-green eyes riveted on the TV screen.

"You're ahead of us as far as decorating goes," Elise told me. "We decided to wait until Bree comes home to cut down the tree. It just wouldn't be right to do it without her. Traditions—they take on a life of their own."

"Well, I'm ending my traditions and starting new ones this year."

"That's okay, too." Elise bent down and set Snap free. She looked around the rest of the apartment, her gaze pausing on the hand-carved nativity set I hadn't been able to say no to, either. Then she noticed the empty buffet. "What happened to all your snow globes?"

I felt my face get warm. "They're downstairs."

"In the salon?"

"I took all the shampoos and conditioners out of the glass case and put them in there." It had taken me three hours the evening before to transport them all. All but one, which I'd put on the coffee table next to Heather's picture.

"Bernice…" Words obviously failed her but the look in her eyes said it all.

"I know." I groaned. "I'm a jelly doughnut. I'm marshmallow fluff. I'm *slush.*"

"You're changing," Elise said, sighing. But there was laughter in her eyes. "Welcome to my world."

"Did Annie tell you about Melissa?"

Elise sobered instantly. "Yes."

"The youth group is meeting at Alex's again tonight and Stephen said they're going to have a special time of prayer after we're done setting up for the nativity."

"According to Annie, Greta is taking it pretty hard."

I'd been afraid of that. "They haven't gotten along since

seventh grade. I think Greta wants to be friends but Melissa hasn't exactly been receptive."

"God paves the way for things like that," Elise said.

I thought about Thanksgiving with my parents. If they'd shown up so unexpectedly a year ago, before I'd moved over to let God in, the day would have turned out completely different. One more reason to celebrate. Now if He'd only clear a path for Alex to take back to California, maybe I'd be able to sleep again at night.

When I got to Alex's, he was shoulder to shoulder with Stephen, hammering the manger in place. A group of kids were kneeling on the floor of the barn, painting letters on a large welcome sign.

"Is Greta here?" I was worried she wouldn't show up.

"Inside working on costumes," Alex said, surprising me that he knew who she was. "And could you scrounge up a Band-Aid while you're in there?"

"Where did you cut yourself?" I demanded, looking for blood.

Alex looked offended and Stephen laughed.

"It's for me." He held up a hand and I saw the half-inch gash next to his thumbnail. "No hurry, Bernice. It's not like I faint at the sight of a little blood."

When I slipped into the house moments later, the first thing I heard was Greta's voice coming from the living room. I peeked in and saw Kyle Gibson standing in the center of the room—a desperate look on his face—decked out in a long, filmy gown and a pair of wings.

"Hi, Bernice," Greta said through the pins she'd stuck in her mouth.

Kyle nodded in my direction. Miserable but polite.

"It's beautiful," I teased. "But I pictured Joseph in something a little more…" Did I dare say *masculine?* Probably not. *"Plain."*

"This is Melissa's costume," Greta said. "I needed to finish the hem and Kyle happened to come in and offer to help."

Melissa's costume? I didn't want to point out that Melissa might not be feeling well enough to take part in the nativity this year. I could tell by Kyle's expression that he was thinking the same thing, but neither of us wanted to be the one to crush the hope in Greta's voice. My respect for him went up another notch.

"All done." Greta sat back on her heels. "You can slip this off before your friends see you wearing gold sequins."

"And wings." Kyle smiled, and Greta's face got pink. And it matched the oversize sweater she was wearing.

"You're wearing pink." The words slipped past before I could stop them.

"Yeah, well, the wildflowers kind of took over today," she said with a shrug. "That's been happening a lot lately."

Kyle cleared his throat. "You look good in pink."

Greta began to gather her supplies together.

"You look good in black, too, though. You look good in everything…" He was rambling and I felt sorry for him because Greta was already walking toward the door.

"Heads up, Gibson!" a voice yelled from the kitchen just as a toy football flew past me.

Greta jumped up and snagged it, then lobbed it to Kyle, who caught it in the chest.

"Nice throw," he gasped.

"Four brothers." Greta disappeared.

Kyle looked at me pleadingly. "What do I do?"

I laughed. "Throw it back to her."

Stephen had gathered everyone in the kitchen and the mood instantly became somber. The kids knew why they were here. I glanced at Alex and realized from the confused look on his face that he didn't. As far as he knew, we were going to use his microwave to make popcorn and pass around the sodas he'd bought.

"I talked to Melissa's mom this afternoon. She said that Melissa is pretty down right now. I wanted to be sure to pray for her before we leave tonight."

There were nods of agreement. I bowed my head but didn't close my eyes. Greta was standing next to me and she slipped her hand into mine.

"Lord, this cancer didn't take You by surprise," Stephen said. "We don't understand how these kinds of things can happen to the people we care about, but we know that through everything, You're right there with us. We're confident that as Your children, we never have to walk through hard times alone. Show us how we can encourage and comfort Melissa and her family. We know from Your word that You're faithful and we trust You with the things we can't see."

There was a quiet ripple of amens around the kitchen and I squeezed Greta's hand before releasing it.

"Meet back here next week for rehearsal," I told everyone as they started to grab their gloves and hats from the pile by the door.

Stephen thumped Alex on the back. "We'll be out of your hair in a few weeks. I promise."

"No problem."

I could tell that Alex meant it. It didn't make sense. Why was he still here? Because he liked *normal?* As far as I was concerned, Prichett wasn't exactly the picture displayed next to that word in the dictionary.

"See you, Bernice," Stephen said, pausing at the door. "I'd hang around for a few minutes but I have to stop at the store and pick up something for Annie."

"Waffles?"

Stephen nodded. "You got it."

"She'll move on to something else. I told her that I ate ten bananas a day—" I broke off, horrified at what I'd been about to say. I couldn't even look at Alex.

"Ten bananas a day?" Alex said. "I can't believe you went on that crazy diet."

There was actually a banana diet? I was able to pull my foot out of my mouth and mutter, "Bananas are good for you."

"Whatever." Alex rolled his eyes.

My heart was still pounding at what I'd let slip out so I grabbed my coat before I could incriminate myself again.

"See you later." I shut Alex's goodbye in the door.

Stephen's car was already turning out of the driveway when I stepped outside. Mine was parked by the barn and just before I got in, I changed direction. I wanted to see the manger now that it was finished.

It was quiet inside except for the soft movements coming from the stall the animals had crowded in for the night. I walked over to the manger and ran my hand along the edge, trying to imagine what it must have been like to give birth under such primitive conditions and to have to put your child to sleep in a feeding trough. To have that sense that this child really didn't belong to you at all—that he was a gift you were going to have to share. Just like Heather had been.

I sniffed and brushed at the tears that were leaking out of my eyes. I really was getting soft. But even pain was better than the numbness I'd been encased in for years.

"I thought maybe your car wouldn't start," Alex said behind me.

I looked away, not knowing how to begin to explain to him why I was crying.

"I just wanted to see what you and Stephen did." My voice was too raspy.

"It doesn't make sense."

"What?"

"If God really wanted to get people's attention, why not just do something really big? Get in everyone's face so there's no doubt He's here?"

"I think that it's pretty big that He came to earth as a baby. But you know the really miraculous thing? It's that He *chose* to."

Chapter Twenty

Every one of my customers who trudged in during the course of the week commented on the snow globes I'd put in the case. But I'd discovered something. It wasn't enough to just stare at them through the glass. No. They had to *shake* them.

It started with Denise, who came into the salon to let me know she'd gotten a new shipment of artificial greens in. She noticed that one of the globes had tiny gold snowflakes in it instead of the usual white confetti, and she had to see what it looked like. I gave in. After Denise was one of the Frith boys, who's competitive spirit urged him to see how many globes he could get *snowing* at once. We found out that it was six, if he used both his hands and chose the biggest ones with the most snow inside.

Even Jim, who stopped in to give me a list of colleges we could contact in our search for Junebug's sculptor, couldn't resist opening the case and messing with them.

I finally gave up and left the case open. By Wednesday, I knew I'd have to dump every one of them in a Windex bath to get the fingerprints off.

"Bern, can you take some time out for lunch? I'll meet you at Sally's."

I jumped a half a foot in the air and fortunately Amy Reznik's bangs weren't in my scissors at the time. I'd just finished her cut and even though she was only four years old she'd sat like a statue, her eyes trained on her reward—the jar of suckers next to the cash register.

"Alex." I greeted him through clenched teeth.

"Sorry. I didn't mean to scare you."

Sure he didn't.

"Your bells are gone." He pointed to the top of the door.

"Just for December."

There was mistletoe in their place. Cute but silent. Denise's idea. She'd figured out quickly that I was more than willing to go overboard this year to make up for all the Christmases I'd turned my back on.

"I'll be there in five minutes," I said, just to get rid of him. "All done, Amy. Go pick out a sucker." I helped her down from the elephant chair and waved at her mom, who was sitting by the window, nose-deep in the latest *Reader's Digest*.

"Here, B'nice." Amy handed me a sucker, too.

"My favorite." I winked at her and unwrapped it.

"Thanks, Bernice." Amy's mom searched through her purse and wrote out a check. I shifted impatiently. And was suddenly terrified. Because I wanted to get to Sally's. Why? Because I'd missed *him*. In the past month, Alex had somehow become woven into my life again. I was getting used to hearing his voice on the phone. Getting used to seeing his smile. Hearing him laugh. I was in serious trouble.

"Are you okay, Bernice?"

Mrs. Reznik was looking at me, concerned. I managed to nod.

"Fine," I croaked.

Amy stared up at me. "Don't chew on the stick."

I was going to have to write that one down. I kept a notebook in the drawer filled with tidbits of wisdom from my clients. The best ones were from the children. Like my personal favorite—*the washing machine doesn't like suckers.*

When I got to Sally's, naturally it was packed because it was the lunch hour. I scanned the booths, looking for Alex, but couldn't find him.

"Bernice, over here."

Out of the corner of my eye, I caught a movement. Alex was sitting at the counter, right smack-dab in the center of the retired farmers. On Lester Lee's stool. I hurried over to rescue him.

"You'll have to wait a sec, Bernice," one of them said irritably. "We have to finish our game."

They were playing checkers. Checkers!

Sally sailed by with the coffeepot. "There's a corner booth over there, Bernice. Might as well take it." She lowered her voice. "Hopefully your guy will be smart enough to let him win."

I slid into the booth and Sally poured me a cup of coffee. "He comes in here a few times a week and buys everyone coffee," she said, a reluctant smile tipping the corner of her lips. "He even threw in pie the other day."

I'd had no idea there was a benevolent celebrity in our midst. Candy was a tough sell, but he'd won her over. Now Sally. And, from what I'd just witnessed, the farmers—whose collective weakness was pie, coffee and a good game of checkers. I needed to call Lester Lee about that llama.

A cheer went up at the counter and a few seconds later Alex slid into the empty space across from me. There was a gleam in his eyes that told me he'd been smart enough to throw the game.

"What can I getcha?" Sally asked, pausing next to the booth.

"A bowl of whatever soup you have today."

"Sounds good." Alex smiled at Sally and she smiled back. And I wanted to scream.

"Can you do me a favor?" Alex asked me after Sally deposited two bowls of her famous chicken dumpling soup in front of us.

"I don't know. Can you tell me what the favor is *before* I agree to do it?"

"I've been playing around, working on something. I'd like you to read it and tell me what you think."

"Read it?" I frowned. "Are you writing a screenplay?" I'd seen a high-tech laptop on the coffee table when I was at his house Sunday night but hadn't thought twice about it at the time.

"Right now it's just a…story."

"Like a novel."

"Not quite that lofty."

"A poem?" I must have made a face because Alex laughed.

"You'll just have to read it and tell me what you think it is."

"Okay."

Sally came back to refill our water glasses and she had a sour look on her face.

"What's wrong, Sal?"

"That guy over there," Sally said disgustedly. "Sent his food back to the kitchen *twice*. Reggie is ready to quit on me."

I looked over Alex's shoulder. The man was looking right at me and I couldn't prevent the little shudder that skittered along my spine. He was scarecrow-thin with a scraggly goatee and a serious case of bed head. The kind that always tempted me to put the guy in a headlock, grab a razor and turn him into something that resembled a human being.

"Tell Reggie the soup is great and I'll take a quart home with me," Alex said. "And make that guy pay for his own coffee. I'll take care of everyone else's."

Sally perked up a little.

Now that Sally had brought my attention to the stranger, my eyes kept straying back to him. And every time I glanced at him, he was staring at me. At one point, he even smiled. A creepy half smile that had me looking at my watch.

"I have to get back to the salon," I told Alex. "My lunch break was officially over five minutes ago."

"Coming out this weekend?"

I shook my head. "I can't. Saturday is packed with girls who need their hair done for the Senior Tea. I'll be working from seven-thirty to five that day. Sunday I promised Annie I'd help her and Elise wallpaper the nursery."

"Then I better take advantage of the time I have now and walk back with you."

Don't you get it? I wanted to shout at him. *I miss you when you're not around and I have to get used to it because you're only here on a temporary loan.*

There was a chorus of cheerful goodbyes when we left from the people who'd found out they didn't have to pay for their coffee.

Alex dipped his head as a gust of wind slammed against us.

"Missing California?" I couldn't resist.

"No. You?"

"Sometimes." I had to tell the truth. "You look shocked."

"I am. I never thought you'd admit it. What do you miss?"

You?

"If I tell you, you'll think I'm sentimental."

"Too late."

"What do you mean?"

Alex caught my elbow as I put the key in the lock.

"Look up. Isn't that mistletoe? I think mistletoe is very sentimental."

"It's a tradition." I had to have a talk with Denise. She was the one who told me mistletoe was a tradition. She never mentioned anything about it being sentimental.

"Men don't hang up mistletoe, women do," Alex said,

as if that closed the argument. "You know what else is sentimental?"

"What?" I pulled back slightly but he put one hand over mine and his fingers closed over the key before I could turn it in the door and escape. "Keeping a two-dollar snow globe for twenty years."

I was hoping he hadn't remembered, but he did. Just like he remembered that my mother and I had more issues than the county road had potholes.

"You only paid two dollars for that?" I tried to inject some indignation into my voice and failed miserably. I gave in and laughed.

And then I heard a tiny click and saw the flash. Scarecrow was standing a few feet away, the creepy smile still on his face.

"Alex."

Alex turned and instinctively stepped in front of me, but I had a feeling it was too late.

The photographer lifted his camera in a mocking salute.

"Any particular caption you want me to write for this one, Mr. Scott?" he asked.

"Go inside, Bernice," Alex said quietly. "I'll handle this."

I hesitated, not liking the expression on his face, but the guy lifted the camera again so I quickly turned away and stumbled into the salon.

When Alex came in a few minutes later he looked like he wanted to take something apart. Probably the camera. Or maybe the guy holding it.

"I'm sorry. I have no idea who he is or where that picture is going to show up."

"It was only a matter of time. You should be used to it by now." They weren't exactly comforting words but I was still in denial. The photographer hadn't snapped our picture at Sally's. He'd followed us, hoping for something better. And he'd gotten it. We'd been inches apart, laughing under mistletoe the size of a disco ball. One freeze frame away from a kiss. At least, that's what people would assume.

"I never get used to it. It's one thing when I'm at an awards ceremony or a charity benefit—I *expect* there'll be photographers—but I hate it when they sneak around and steal chunks of my privacy."

"Do you think he'll stick around?"

"He might." Alex raked one hand through his hair in frustration. "It depends on what he's looking for. If he just wants to throw my picture into a collage of shots of celebrities on vacation, he's probably on his way home already. If he's the kind who wants to dig up some dirt, he'll hang around for a while until he figures out it's a waste of time. Just be glad the only thing he can find out about us—if he's really committed to a story—is the fact that we dated twenty years ago."

My mouth went dry. He could find out a lot more than that.

"I'm going to go home and give my publicist a call." He looked distracted but I couldn't offer him any encouragement. Not only because we had a photographer suddenly interested in us but because Alex had just told me he was going home. And I knew he wasn't talking about California.

It was a relief to know I'd be so busy with the girls coming in to have their hair done for the tea that I wouldn't be able to think about the photographer. Not that I hadn't spent a few restless hours during the night wondering where that picture was going to surface. And how long the photographer planned to hang around Prichett. I tried to console myself with logic—that reporters were the ones who dug up the dirt and wrote about it but the photographers just wanted a picture of it. Chances were, this guy wasn't going to do anything more than ask who I was and spell my name wrong in the caption.

I stared at the contents of my closet a lot longer than I should have and then, when I realized what I was doing, I let out a little shriek, which sent Snap diving under the bed.

Rebelling, I put on something guaranteed to give a dedicated photographer something to laugh about. The plaid Western shirt threaded with silver that Elise had bought me to wear while I cheered Bree on at the horse shows. It even had pearl buttons. And dark denim boot-cut jeans. Sure this wasn't the West but it was the *Mid*west. Close enough.

When I got down to the salon, Greta was already there, waiting for me.

"Hey, what are you doing here so early? Or am I late?" I nudged up my sleeve to look at my watch.

"I'm early." Greta followed me inside.

"This is always a big day," I said, deliberately pushing aside my own burdens and silently asking God to carry them for me. "Why don't you put some music on? Sally is going to bring over a few boxes of Danishes in a little while. And I've got some chocolate in the back room. That's a necessity, you know."

Greta wasn't smiling. "Melissa won't come to the Senior Tea."

"She probably doesn't feel well…"

"She's home now. One of her friends told me that she won't come because she's losing her hair and she feels like everyone will be staring at her."

"This has to be hard on Melissa," I said cautiously. "She's dealing with a lot right now. You and I both know what it's like to feel like you don't fit in. Remember?"

"And that's just stupid." Greta frowned. "I wasn't going to go to the Senior Tea for the same reason. Because I thought people were going to make fun of me. Now you know what I think? I think we think too much about what other people think."

I laughed. That was exactly why I looked like a cowgirl today. Because I refused to walk that path anymore.

"Melissa is chairman of the committee. She picked out the theme—*A Winter Garden*. She should be there. Everyone *wants* her to be there."

The door suddenly opened and a trio of teenagers came inside, giggling and stomping the snow off their boots. They were early but I was used to the girls coming in way ahead of their scheduled appointments so they could dream through the style books.

"Hey, Greta. Hi, Bernice," one of them called cheerfully. It was Alicia, one of my nativity angels.

"Are you ready?" I asked Greta. "You're first on the list this morning."

Greta nodded and went over to my chair. I clipped the cape around her neck and picked up her hair, smoothing down the heavy black waves. And wondered what her natural color was. Judging from her coloring, probably auburn…

"Did you decide what you want?" I asked. "I could do a French twist."

Greta stared at her reflection in the mirror.

"I want you to shave it off."

"What?" I couldn't possibly have heard her right.

"Shave it off. All of it."

"Greta…"

The girls must have heard what she said because their laughter dissolved into silence.

"Bernice, I'm serious. Maybe Melissa will come to the tea if she knows she isn't going to be the only bald girl wearing a formal."

Alicia came over and I hoped she was going to talk some sense into Greta. She looked at me.

"Me, too."

The other two were nodding.

"Girls, it's December…" *And your mothers will kill me. They'll boycott the Cut and Curl.* The thoughts tumbled over each other even as my heart swelled with pride.

The door opened and my teary eyes swung toward it, praying that it wasn't one of the girls' mothers.

"Hey, Mama B!"

I blinked and knew my blurry vision wasn't playing tricks on me. It was Heather.

"I know you're swamped so I decided to surprise you and help out today. I could use the practice." She shrugged out of her jacket and grinned. "So, put me to work. What can I do?"

I took a deep breath.

"Grab a pair of clippers."

Chapter Twenty-One

The vision spread. By midmorning, six girls were running their fingers over their bare scalps.

By noon, there were ten.

The buzz of the clippers was nonstop. So was the chatter. None of the girls left—they all ate Danish and watched as the next girl's hair drifted to the floor.

There was only one holdout. Samantha. When she walked in and saw the other girls, she almost fainted. Until Greta filled her in on what was happening.

"I can't." Samantha's eyes were terrified as she stared at Greta.

"You don't have to," Greta said. "It's totally up to you. It's just something we want to do."

"Sisterhood!" someone called out.

"But I'll feel out of place if I'm not bald!" Samantha wailed.

Some of the girls laughed but Samantha turned tormented eyes to them. "I have a…birthmark. My hair kind of covers it up. If I shave my head, everyone will see it."

"Really?" One of the girls sauntered over. "Where?"

Samantha hesitated but then pushed her bangs back, revealing a reddish purple mark the size of a Ping-Pong ball.

"Wow, it's shaped like a heart."

Everyone crowded around and Samantha looked like she was about to cry. Just as I was about to intervene, Greta came to the rescue. Again.

"Cool," she said, and there were murmurs of agreement. "I wish I had one of those. It would make my head more interesting."

Heather glanced at me. "You or me?"

I patted the back of my chair. "Samantha, you're next."

When they left an hour later, I knew it was only a matter of time before the phone started ringing off the hook. So I took it off myself.

"That was the most incredible thing I've ever seen," Heather said. "I wish I could see Melissa's face when they stop by her house."

"It will be the most incredible thing their parents have ever seen, too," I muttered. Maybe the fact that I hadn't charged the girls would score me some points. Fat chance. It didn't matter, though. I was so proud of Greta for finding a way to reach out to Melissa.

"I believe you mentioned something about chocolate," Heather mused.

We'd worked straight through lunch and my stomach growled on cue at the word chocolate.

"In the back. Top desk drawer. Um, middle desk drawer. And…"

"The bottom desk drawer?" Heather grinned.

"You got it."

She disappeared and I sank into the shampoo chair and closed my eyes.

"I knew you'd need a break about now."

My eyes snapped open and I couldn't prevent a low-pitched keen from escaping. Alex. I jumped out of the chair and landed in front of him.

"Where is everyone? Are you finished already?" He looked around the empty room then back at me, his eyes scanning my outfit. "Did I miss the rodeo?"

Oh, I'm finished all right.

"Hey, Mama B!" Heather's voice sailed through the thin wall that separated the front of the salon from my office in the back. "Dark, white or milk chocolate? Or all three?"

Alex put on a polite smile that froze on his face when Heather came into view. She saw him and tilted her head, smiling back.

"Wow. You look a lot like Alex Scott."

"What a coincidence. So do you."

"Alex…"

There was a split second when he looked at me, his eyes so raw with pain that I automatically took a step toward him. It didn't matter. He pivoted sharply and walked out.

"Bernice?" Heather's hand touched my shoulder. "What's going on?"

"That *was* Alex Scott."

"You're kidding?" Heather looked at the door. "Why is he here? Why did he say I looked—"

I knew the minute she put the pieces together. Emotions skittered across her face and she put her hands over her mouth.

"Him?"

"I never told him about you." I could barely say the words, bracing myself for Heather's anger. Or disgust. "I was going to tell you at Christmas." Would she even believe me? "I didn't know *how* to tell you. He's not exactly your run-of-the-mill ordinary guy. It's complicated. You can see why it's complicated."

"You need to talk to him," she said, not a trace of anger in her voice. Or in her eyes. I couldn't believe it. "I'll go up to your apartment for a while and wait until you get back."

I was rooted to a spot on the floor. This was not at all the way I'd pictured Alex—or Heather, for that matter—finding out about each other.

"Alex Scott." Heather looked as dazed as I felt.

"It's a long story."

"I've got time. I don't have to leave until tomorrow." Tears began to track her cheeks. "I could tell you didn't want to talk about him and all this time I thought he'd abused you, or he was in prison or something horrible like that. I even wondered if you'd been…raped."

Lord, help me not to fall apart here. I should have told her when we met the first time.

"He's famous." Nothing like stating the obvious.

She smiled tremulously. "The things I was imagining were a lot worse. I think I can handle famous."

Just like that. Obviously, Heather's backbone had come from another part of the family tree. Certainly not mine.

"You promise not to leave? I should tell you everything."

Heather gave me a quick but powerful hug. "I promise."

It was the only thing that gave me the strength to drive out to Alex's. His truck was angled in the driveway as if it had been abandoned instead of parked.

He opened the door before I had a chance to knock.

"Can I talk to you?"

"*Now* you want to talk to me." Bitterness edged his voice and I couldn't blame him a bit. "Sure, come in."

We went into the living room and I didn't bother to take my coat off. I had a feeling I wouldn't be there very long.

"You were pregnant. That's why you left."

"No. I found out I was pregnant after I left."

He said something under his breath that I was glad I couldn't understand. "Then why didn't you come back? Why didn't you tell me? Bernice, I could just…" He paced the length of the room. "I can't *believe* you never told me."

"I…put her up for adoption. She found me a few months ago," I said.

"You just met her?" I could see he was surprised and realized he'd assumed I'd raised her and deliberately kept her from him.

"She found me," I said shakily, remembering that first phone call. "I… When I found out I was pregnant, I couldn't take care of her." I needed him to understand that it was a decision I hadn't made lightly.

"I could have! *We* could have." His voice cracked and something inside me splintered right along with it.

"I'm sorry. I knew it was wrong not to tell you—that's why I called. Then you showed up in Prichett and I was going to tell you, but when you started talking about obsessed fans, I realized that I had to tell *her* first. Your life doesn't belong to you, Alex. It belongs to everyone. It's the life you *chose* but Heather didn't. She needs to decide if she wants her face splashed all over the front page of the tabloids if the press gets hold of this. That photographer yesterday just proves how different your life is."

"Her name is Heather?"

"I didn't name her. I barely got to hold her…" That was as far as I could get before the tears clogged my throat.

Alex groaned and yanked me out of the chair. I wasn't sure if he was going to shake me or let me lean on him. At the moment I didn't care.

"Why did you go through that alone? Bernice, you always insist on going through everything *alone*. What is it with you? I would never have turned my back on you. Ever."

"I don't do that anymore." Not since that day on Elise's

porch when Annie told me that God loved me with an everlasting love. A simple thought, but I'd grabbed it with both hands and held on tight.

"I would have married you. You know that, don't you?"

I hadn't been sure. Even though he'd told me he loved me, I hadn't trusted it to last. Hadn't believed I was worthy of someone loving me like that. He read the answer in my eyes and let go of me.

"You had a high opinion of me, didn't you, Bernice?"

"I had a low opinion of myself." My lungs felt like they were burning.

"So you walked away. Then you made a decision that I should have been involved in." He walked over to the window and stared outside. "I need some time to think about this."

Alone. The unspoken word hung between us.

"Are you going to leave?"

"I think you're confusing me with you. You're the one who runs away, Bernice."

I don't do that anymore, either. That's what I wanted to say. Instead, I let myself out of the house quietly and drove back to my apartment.

Heather and I stayed up until three in the morning. We curled up on opposite ends of the sofa with Snap purring contentedly between us while I told her everything. How Alex and I had met. How I felt when I'd found out I was expecting her. I didn't need to tell her how much the decision I'd made to put her up for adoption had affected me—the entire box of tissue I used up did it for me.

I tried to explain what his life was like, what hers might be like if word got out that he was her biological father. I even mentioned the photographer who had snapped our picture and the icky need-a-shower feeling I'd had after it happened.

I realized it was easy to take a thing like privacy for granted until someone stripped it away.

"That guy was a slug," she pronounced.

"If the slime trail fits…"

Heather actually giggled and once more I was amazed at how she'd handled the shock of unexpectedly finding out who her father was. When I got back to the apartment, I could tell she'd been crying, but she hugged me and I could see the warmth in her eyes was real. There were a hundred things she could hold against me but I knew that Heather had been taught to forgive, just like she'd been taught to tie her shoes. Or ride a bicycle. It's something I wouldn't have known how to teach her. Not until recently anyway and I still needed practice.

"I'm going to tell Mom and Dad when I get home tomorrow night. I need their advice. This might affect them, too," Heather said, her voice low and drowsy. "Do you think he…wants to meet me?"

I remembered the look on Alex's face when he said her name. "I know he does."

Heather's lips curved into a smile and she closed her eyes.

We went to church the next morning and as soon as I began to see bright yellow crocheted hats everywhere, I wished we hadn't. I was probably standing in the crosshairs of a group of angry mothers.

"They all found matching hats," Heather whispered, nudging me. "Do you think it means that Melissa went to the Senior Tea?"

"I hope so."

Greta ran up to us, looking like a newborn bunny with a cap stretched over her bare scalp.

"She came to the tea, Bernice," Greta said, her eyes sparkling. "And she's in church today, too."

Greta's enthusiasm lifted some of the weight off my chest. "Is she wearing a hat, too?"

"It was her idea. Mrs. Crandall and some of the ladies at the nursing home knit them for cancer patients and Melissa's mom called and asked if they had any more. Mrs. Crandall gave us a whole boxful."

Esther. I should have known. She may have been tucked inside the walls of the Golden Oaks now, but her influence wasn't.

"Greta!" One of the girls called her name.

"This is for you." Greta pressed something into my hand. "I'll talk to you later!"

I looked down at a Polaroid photo of the girls who'd attended the Senior Tea. They were all standing in front of a picket fence decorated with silk flowers and ivy. Melissa was in the middle, smiling, her arms draped over the shoulders of the two girls on either side of her. One of them was Greta.

As much as I wanted to keep it, I knew I could find a better place for it. I'd give it to Sally in the morning. It belonged on the Pride and Joy Wall.

The organ music started, drawing everyone who was milling in the hall into the sanctuary. Heather had attended church with me before and people recognized her and greeted her as if she were one of their own.

The pew Elise and Sam sat in was already filled so Heather and I slipped into one a few rows behind them. I could see Annie's bright red hair toward the front, where she sat with Stephen and Pastor Charles. Next to them were Candy and Mark Fielding. Interspersed throughout the congregation, like the first jonquils that come up in the spring, were yellow hats.

Stephen gave the sermon and as always, he had everyone laughing. No wonder he was so good with teenagers. He had an infectious humor that pulled people in. Until the end.

"I'm sure you've noticed all the yellow hats here today," he said. "But maybe you don't know the story behind them. We've been praying for Melissa ever since she was diagnosed with cancer a few weeks ago. She's gotten lots of cards and flowers, but yesterday her friends gave her another kind of gift. Let me read a passage from 1 John Chapter 4 to you. 'This is how God showed His love among us: God sent His one and only Son into the world that we might live through him.' This is love: not that we loved God, but that He loved us and sent His Son as an atoning sacrifice for our sins. Dear friends, since God so loved us, we ought to love each other."

Stephen stopped for a second and cleared his throat.

"Some people argue that the Bible isn't relevant for today. That it's outdated. That it doesn't work anymore. I want to show you something to remind you that it does."

A picture flashed up on the wall behind him. One identical to the one Greta had given me except for one thing. The girls weren't wearing their hats. They were cheek to cheek. And they were completely bald.

There was a hushed silence in the room as everyone stared at the picture.

"Amen." Stephen stepped down.

Heather had to leave right after lunch and before her car pulled away, I opened the door to the backseat and put something inside.

"Don't open it until Christmas Eve," I said. "Promise."

Heather nodded. "Promise. And, Mama B, I'll call you."

I knew she meant after she'd talked to her parents about Alex. After she left, I drove out to see Esther, feeling guilty for needing her wisdom but hearing Alex's words still ringing in my ears.

You insist on going through everything alone.

I found her in the family lounge, knitting.

"Restocking your hat supply?" I dropped the photograph of the girls on the table in front of her.

Esther studied it and when she handed it back, her eyes were glossy. "That is the most beautiful bunch of girls I've ever seen."

I had to agree.

"Where is John this afternoon?"

"He had a restless night so I didn't want to disturb him with all this clacking," Esther said, smiling pensively. "He's been a little frustrated."

"Frustrated?" It was hard to imagine.

"His health isn't good. Especially in the winter. He's so susceptible to colds and the flu. He'd wanted to sing this morning for the worship service but he's been nursing a sore throat the past few days and couldn't do it."

Esther's knitting needle suddenly rolled out of her fingers and I was stunned to see a tear roll down her cheek.

"Last night I was laying next to him, listening to him breathe, and suddenly I was terrified that I was going to lose him. And I felt so bad, like God had given me a treasure and all of a sudden I just wrapped my arms around it, stamped my foot and said *mine.*"

I put my hand over hers. "What did you do?"

"Trusted Him with my future all over again, just like Mary did with her perfume."

I didn't know that story and it must have shown on my face.

"Mary, one of Jesus's friends, not His mother, took an expensive bottle of nard before the Passover and poured it all over Jesus's feet. Everyone complained—even the disciples— because it was worth a lot of money. Some scholars believe it might have been Mary's dowry—the only thing of value she had to secure her future. Back then, women counted on marriage so they would be taken care of. But Mary, she poured her future security out, not caring what the other men thought of her. Not caring that it might cost her a good marriage. You see, she knew God held her future, not that bottle. Even though it was risky, it was an extravagant gesture, a lavish display of love for the one who'd taught her what love really was." Esther smiled. "Whenever I get scared about the future, it helps when I remember what she did."

Esther was right. It did. But I had the overwhelming feeling that I was going to have to remember, too.

Chapter Twenty-Two

Alex was waiting for me when I got back to my apartment. I couldn't even summon a smile at the sight of him slouched on the sofa with Snap sprawled across his chest.

"You should lock your door."

"*You* should know that trespassing is against the law."

I shrugged out of my coat and dropped it on the nearest piece of furniture, every nerve ending in my body on red alert. I wasn't ready for round two with Alex yet. For some reason, my heart ached and even praying with Esther hadn't made it go away.

"Even though I want to, I know we can't go back and change anything. And I can't blame you without blaming myself, too." Alex hesitated. Then, "What is she like?"

I didn't know where to begin. There was so much I didn't know about Heather, but I knew he needed me to share the things that I did.

"Beautiful, you saw that right away. She looks like you. She's smart. Her parents wanted her to be a doctor but she wants to do hair and makeup. She's a Christian. She's confident and funny and she loves pasta."

"They're good to her, then?"

They're better than good, I thought. They're the best.

"Her dad is a doctor. Her mom stays home but does a lot of charity work. I haven't met them or talked to them but they encouraged Heather to find me."

He closed his eyes and even though he'd said he couldn't change the past, I knew he was trying to imagine what life would've been like if I hadn't walked away. What kind of parents we would have been. If we'd still even be together. I'd already wrestled with those thoughts and finally God had shown me that I was only going to walk away from that particular fight wounded and tired. There wasn't any way I could turn back the clock and make a different decision.

"Would we have made it, Bern?"

I shook my head. "No."

He moved restlessly. "How can you be so sure?"

"Because when all was said and done, I didn't love you enough to stay and you didn't love me enough to leave." We'd both wanted what we wanted. A very shaky foundation for something that has to last a lifetime.

"You know that's not true."

The words hit me like a shot and came out the other side, leaving me filled with tiny holes. "Alex…"

"Let me finish. When I met you, I was ambitious, I admit it. My life was getting crazy and when I saw you, it got steady. You made it that way. I could see that you had some insecurities and I figured with time, you'd get over them. We were practically kids then. But now, you're so much more. You've matured. You know who you are. You've gotten stronger. And softer. You're still brutally honest sometimes." He laughed softly. "But you don't seem as reserved anymore. You have *friends*. You didn't have friends when I met you. Didn't even seem to *want* them, let alone need them. Now you've got people who fall all over themselves to protect you. I'd give up everything for that. I mean it. Maybe I chose that life when we were twenty-four, but right now, I'd walk away from it in a minute to be a part of yours. I'm still in love with you, Bernice."

It was the last thing I expected him to say. All this time, I'd told myself he was staying because of Prichett. Because on some level it felt good to not be the center of attention. To have space to breathe. Even after he sent the flowers, I wouldn't let myself believe that I was the reason he was still here.

Part of me wanted to dive into his arms and lose myself in the moment. I wanted to say the words back. To recapture everything the years had taken away from us.

God, why did You bring him back into my life if it was just to say goodbye to him again? I don't understand why You're asking me to do this!

"You think I'm different because I've matured." I managed to push the words past my lips, which suddenly felt dry and cracked. "I told you that I've changed because of what God's done in my life. If you would've come back six months ago, you wouldn't have seen any of the things that you see now. Because I wasn't this person. I was a train wreck. I wasn't living, I was *surviving*. Leaving you, then giving Heather up for adoption pretty much ripped me apart inside, Alex. For twenty years I lived with the guilt. I didn't think I was worth anyone's love."

Alex was leaning forward, staring at me intently as though he wanted to believe what I was saying, but I could see the skepticism in his eyes.

"It doesn't matter who you were six months ago," he said quietly. "It matters who you are right now."

I closed my eyes because I couldn't look at him. "But who I am right now means we can't be together."

"Why? I can tell you still have feelings for me…"

I love you. I always loved you.

"You aren't a believer."

"I believe in God."

My heart gave a wild leap but his next words yanked it back down to earth.

"Maybe I don't think He's as involved in people's lives as you do, but I'd never stop you from going to church or anything. I told you that a lot of it just doesn't make sense to me. And I don't think you give yourself enough credit. You've always been a strong person, Bernice. Maybe it was just the right time for you to let yourself heal from the past."

It sounded so reasonable but I knew it wasn't true. I'd tried to fix myself but the thread I'd used was too fragile. I knew I'd been slowly breaking from the weight of it. It had only been a matter of time.

"We can't build a relationship on two different foundations."

"We don't have to." Alex moved abruptly, rousing Snap, who sprang away and disappeared under the sofa. I wanted to do the same thing. "Are you sure this isn't just another excuse? Are you sure your old insecurities aren't coming back? Maybe you're afraid of the future and you still don't believe you have a right to be happy so you're just putting up roadblocks. You're really willing to walk away from *us* again just because I'm not sure if I can accept the fact that God came to earth as a baby?"

Afraid of the future… I didn't know I'd need to remember so soon.

"Esther told me a story today about Mary, a friend of Jesus who poured out a bottle of expensive perfume on his feet. The disciples complained that it was a waste. Maybe they thought she should have just given him a friendly slap on the back for changing her life." I drew a slow, painful breath. "If you're that kind of person—the kind who doesn't understand that I owe Him *everything*—then I can't be with you."

The words hung in the air between us as we stared at each other. Then Alex looked away.

"I guess that's it then."

He waited and when I didn't say anything, he grabbed his coat. "If Heather decides she wants to talk to me, you know where I am."

"Are you leaving?"

"You won't give me a reason to stay."

I thought it was going to kill me when I was the one who left Alex. But when the door closed softly behind him, I knew it was no comparison to the pain of letting him go.

The next morning Lester Lee came into the salon. He swept his cap off his head and tapped it against his leg. This lapse into his peculiar brand of Morse code wasn't a good sign.

"He told me to give ya this."

That's when I knew that Alex had really left Prichett.

Fortunately I was between appointments and wouldn't have to wipe myself up from the floor in front of any witnesses.

He held out a small box wrapped in gold foil.

"Thanks, Lester."

He coughed lightly. "Ah, see ya then."

Package delivered, Lester made a break for it.

The box was the size that jewelry usually came in and I wondered if Alex would be capable of that kind of cruelty. Only one way to find out.

I read the card first.

Merry Christmas. I hope it fits.

I felt like one big open wound already so I knew whatever was in the box couldn't hurt me any more. When I opened the lid, there was a key nestled against a backdrop of velvet.

The key to the house.

I picked up the phone and Elise answered on the second ring. "Bernice?"

All she'd heard was a sniffle, so I'm not sure how she recognized it was me. Somehow she must have managed to pick out the words *key, animals* and *gone* because she broke calmly into my ramblings.

"Sam and I will meet you at the house."

I moved in that night. I told myself it was because of the animals. We still needed to use them for the live nativity and it was easier to leave them where they were until after Christmas. It didn't have anything to do with the fact that when I stood in the living room, I could still breathe in the faintest scent of Alex's cologne. Elise asked me if I enjoyed torturing myself. Sam sent Riley over in the evenings to clean out the stall, check the water and make sure Houdini wasn't planning the next great escape.

Every time I faltered, God steadied me. It's just that He used other people's hands. Greta and the rest of the girls in the youth group coaxed me into helping them decorate cookies for the residents at the Golden Oaks. Candy forced me to go to a movie with her one evening. Even Colonel Mustard had his own devious way of keeping me busy at home.

I spent overtime in the salon and my evenings outside, making sure the live nativity would be a night to remember. I had long conversations with Junebug. From a safe distance away. And just in case I might have had time to *think,* Jim kept me busy working on the grant. He even suggested that I convince Marissa to help us, but I figured that if Candy hadn't been able to guilt, scold or otherwise bribe her into joining PAC over the years, I wasn't going to be the one to change her mind.

But I did need to buy Elise a Christmas present, so I decided to stop by Marissa's to see if I could find something.

Marissa is one of those women whose age was hard to pinpoint. Her skin had that dewy, porcelain finish that wrinkles won't stick to. Like Teflon. Add that to a thin, petite figure and hair as dark as charcoal and she could be standing anywhere on the line between twenty-five and forty.

"Merry Christmas, Bernice."

When she greeted me at the door, she was an artist. Sometimes when I walked in, she was a businesswoman in a silk blouse and wool slacks. Today she was wearing blue jeans, hiking boots and a heavy fisherman's sweater. And her hands were dabbed with drying clay.

"Come on up." Marissa motioned me to follow her to the attic, which had been transformed into her studio. While she went to wash her hands, I took advantage of the time alone and wandered around. That's when I saw it. On her desk was a flat stone, embedded with shards of pink and yellow and blue. It looked like the kind of stone you'd use to make a garden path but there was only one of them. I ran my finger across the pieces of china embedded in the clay.

"This is beautiful."

"It was my mother's Bavarian china teapot," Marissa told me.

"Did you break it?" I was almost afraid to ask.

"My mother broke it when she threw it at my dad. It was one of her treasures but it was the closest thing she could grab when he came after her one night. She threw the pieces away but I dug them out of the trash and made this. It was the first piece of art I ever created. When I gave it to her, she cried. That day she packed our things and we went to live with my grandma. She told me a few years later that it was the only thing that kept her strong. Knowing that something beautiful can come out of broken things."

I stared at her until she shook her head.

"I don't know why I told you that," she murmured. "I never tell anyone that. People ask me if it's for sale and I just tell them no."

I knew why. It was like Annie's grace graffiti. Only instead of being written on three-by-five cards, God was writing it on my life. To remind me. God had taken the pieces of my past and was making something beautiful. And new. Even if Alex wouldn't be part of it.

"There are some things we just have to keep." Like a two-dollar snow globe.

For a second our eyes met in perfect understanding, then Marissa smiled. "What else can I do for you?"

"I need a special Christmas present for a special friend."

She helped me find a ceramic tray etched with wildflowers for Elise and while she was wrapping it, she glanced up. "Jim Briggs stopped in the other day."

"He's really excited about this sculpture."

"He asked me if I'd be interested in getting involved in the project."

Go, Jim. I silently applauded. We could use all the help we could get. Neither one of us knew anything about art. I loved my black-and-white movie posters and Jim had confessed his walls were still bare. "What do you think?"

"I don't know." One of Marissa's shoulders lifted and fell. "Are you two…seeing each other?"

"No!" I wasn't ready for the grapevine to send out a new shoot in that direction. "We're friends. And please feel free to squash any rumors to the contrary."

"Oh." Marissa smiled slightly.

A smile that was clearly relieved. Wow. I hadn't seen this coming. Now I was clearly relieved.

"He has nice hands, doesn't he?" she mused.

"To tell you the truth, I've never noticed." I tucked the package under my arm and headed toward the door. When I looked back to thank her, Marissa was still smiling.

I was just closing up the next day at noon when Irv hurried in, setting the mistletoe in motion.

"Didn't know if you'd be here on Christmas Eve. Special delivery. Wasn't sure if I should leave it upstairs or take it out to your new place," he said.

It was probably the cheese box from my parents, although it looked larger than usual. I reached for the package but Irv made me sign for it first.

When I saw the postmark was from Minneapolis, I ripped off the brown paper and saw a huge message taped to the front: Do Not Open Until Christmas Eve.

Heather, the scamp. She was getting revenge. Now I had to wait until tonight to open it.

Elise had managed to convince me to spend Christmas Day with them but this evening being the final night of the nativity, I knew I needed to be alone. I was tired and although I'd been spending the past week and a half on autopilot, I knew it was time to engage again. Heather's unexpected gift had thrown the switch.

The first two nights of the nativity had been successful—probably because people were hoping to get a glimpse of Alex Scott—but I had a feeling that tonight—Christmas Eve—was going to be our busiest night.

And I was right. The unending stream of headlights winding up the driveway proved it.

No matter what the motivation, no one ended up being disappointed. The kids were wonderful in their parts. Melissa was able to be the angel of the Lord for one night and Greta had made her a flowing headpiece—lined with fleece.

Junebug, diva that she was, hung around the barn and allowed people to admire her. Lester was offended but we'd hung up a Beware of Cow sign anyway.

The best thing that happened was when Annie showed up. We stood next to each other, watching another impromptu snowball fight between the shepherds and the angels while they waited for the next group to come in.

"The kids love it out here," she said. "There's so much room."

I loved sharing it with them.

Elise joined us and for a moment we soaked in the sounds of the kids' laughter. When a pair of headlights scored the darkness, everyone ran back to their posts.

"I'll bet there was a lot of laughter that night." Annie burrowed closer to me and Elise until we were huddled in a small circle.

"Sure you won't change your mind and come over tonight?" Elise asked.

I shook my head. "Not tonight. I've got a present to open."

When everyone left after the final performance, I found Snap sleeping on the package Heather had sent me. I made myself a cup of hot cocoa, enjoying the anticipation of opening her gift. And wondering what she'd think when she opened mine and read through twenty years of letters.

"Heather." When I opened the box, I breathed her name even though she couldn't hear me.

She'd made copies of photos—from her baby pictures to her high school graduation—and put them in an album for me. I saw her smiling at the piano. Glowering in her leotard and ballet slippers. Dressed in a formal gown, hand in hand with a smiling teenage boy. Arms around her parents. In the midst of a huge family around a Christmas tree.

She'd lovingly filled in the missing pieces. And even if

it was a few hours early, it was the best Christmas present I ever received.

Happy birthday, Heather.

Chapter Twenty-Three

"Watch out for the puddle!"

Annie squealed and I put one hand under her elbow and carefully guided her around the tiny lake in the church parking lot.

"I can't see anything within a three-foot radius around my stomach!" she wailed.

"Oops, another puddle." That one I stepped in and felt the freezing water slosh into my shoe. April was always a temperamental month. There was still the occasional snowfall but winter was fighting a losing battle against longer days and a mellow sun.

"Annie!" There was a cheerful chorus from the women who were keeping watch by the door and I gave them a stern look behind Annie's back. The only thing Annie knew was that this was a Mission Circle meeting and she'd been asked to give a brief update about the upcoming youth mission trip in the summer.

"Hi," Annie said breathlessly, then winced and anchored both hands against the small of her back.

"Are you all right?" I couldn't believe anyone could be so *heavy with child*. Annie had looked as if she'd been ready to give birth in February and she'd still had two months to go. I was beginning to think we should have bought three of everything instead of two.

"I've had a backache all morning," Annie murmured.

No wonder, with all that weight dragging at her front! I was as anxious to hold those babies as she was but knew that every day they stayed put added precious ounces to the weight they needed. In an attempt to keep her spirits up, Esther had taught her to knit and I kept her supplied with the cozy mysteries that she loved to read.

We went down to the fellowship hall in the basement and I paused for a second, pretending to dig in my purse for something. When we reached the door a few seconds later, I made sure Annie was in front of me.

"Surprise!"

She stopped dead in her tracks, a look of amazement on her face.

"Bernice!" She turned to me, her eyes wide, and I smiled smugly.

"I know. You can't believe we managed to keep this a secret."

She shook her head and pointed to the floor.

Her water had broken.

Elise and I paced the waiting room at the hospital for four hours until a nurse finally shooed us down to the cafeteria to have a cup of coffee.

"She's got at least another three hours to go," we were informed.

"She's three weeks early." I tapped my fingers against the table while I waited for the coffee to cool from scalding to drinkable.

"The doctor says the babies will be fine," Elise reminded me. But I could tell she was reminding herself, too. Annie's doctor had been confident that she didn't need to deliver by cesarean or that they needed to slow things down. Not that they could have at this point. The twins had decided they didn't want to wait three weeks to see their presents.

Immediately, Jeanne had put Annie and Stephen on the prayer chain. Elise called Bree and I made a quick call to Heather. One of the big surprises would be if Annie's babies were girls, boys or one of each. Annie subscribed to the "there aren't many surprises left in life and I don't want to ruin this one" philosophy. Dr. Meyer knew and a few times I'd been tempted to make him talk, but the truth was, I wanted to be surprised, too.

When we got off the elevator, I saw Stephen roaming the hall. He was still wearing scrubs and his face was several shades whiter than usual but he grinned and waved when he saw us.

"Babies?" Elise asked.

"Babies." He nodded happily. "Two of them."

Elise and I held our breath. Stephen kept grinning.

"What *kind* of babies?" I had to ask. "Pink or blue?"

"Pink *and* blue."

Elise and I both squealed. "One of each!"

"Joanna Ruth and Nathaniel Stephen. I have to call my parents now, but Annie wanted me to tell you right away."

Elise and I lurked around the nursery window for another hour until two new cribs were wheeled into the room. The nurse recognized us and obligingly brought them to the window for our inspection.

"They're perfect," I whispered, pressing so close to the window that the glass fogged up. The babies were wrapped snugly in little flannel cocoons but I could see their tiny faces peeking out. They both wore a color-coded cap.

Elise tapped her finger against the glass to get the nurse's attention, then pointed to her head.

With a good-natured smile, the nurse lifted the corner of the pink cap. The glint of red was unmistakable. Joanna was a redhead, just like her mother. Elise gave a whoop and we slapped our hands together in a very undignified high five. When she did the same thing to Nathaniel we saw there was nothing underneath but a bit of blond fuzz. We whooped again.

The nurse put her finger to her lips and we slunk away. When we finally got in to see Annie, she was almost asleep.

"I'm sorry I ruined the surprise shower," were the first words out of her mouth.

"Are you serious? This is better than eating cake and trying to figure out how many words we can make out of the word 'twins.'" Elise laughed. "Which, by the way, isn't that many."

"Tin. Win. Snit," I muttered, and nudged her with my elbow. That will teach them to put me in charge of games next time.

Then I reached down and hugged Annie. "You did good, kiddo."

"I did, didn't I?" Annie smiled radiantly. "Did you see them?"

"Yes, until the nurse made us leave." I glanced at Elise.

"Not that we were making a fuss or anything."

We giggled.

There was a light tap on the door and a woman wearing a volunteer's uniform came in, her upper body almost completely concealed by an extravagant bouquet of pink and white roses.

"Who are those from?" Annie said, shocked. "Will you read the card, Bernice? I'm so tired my eyes are crossing."

"Sure." I tore open the tiny envelope and scanned the message.

"Are they from the church?" Elise prompted.

I shook my head slowly, staring at the words. "They're from...Alex."

"Alex!" Elise plucked the card out of my hand as if she didn't believe me. "'God bless your new family. Alex.'"

"That was sweet of him," Annie said.

"How did he find out?" Elise slid a look at me and I shrugged helplessly, still trying to get my heart back into its normal rhythm. Just when I thought I'd been doing all right the past few months, just seeing his *signature* had the power to push me off balance. I was pathetic. No doubt about it.

"Don't look at me," I managed. "The only person I called was Heather."

Like a punctured tire, I suddenly felt the air leak out of my lungs. I knew that Heather had called Alex just after the New Year. She told me that she'd left a message and he'd called her back within the hour. And he'd asked her how I was doing. Her parents still weren't sure they wanted her to become fodder for the tabloids, so they decided that when they met it would be in a place where there was no chance of a slimy photographer jumping out from behind a rock. I'd been tempted to say that I didn't know we were launching shuttles to Mars yet, but then decided that wouldn't sound very nice, even though it came from my desire to protect Heather.

She and I called each other weekly but that was the only time she mentioned that she'd talked to Alex. If she'd called him so quickly after finding out Annie was in labor, maybe they'd been in closer communication than I'd thought.

I waited to see what kind of emotion that stirred inside me and was surprised that it was contentment. I wanted them to know each other. I wanted Alex to appreciate and love Heather. She was just that kind of person. The one who makes your life better because they're in it. And I had no doubt that Alex would do whatever he could to protect her, too.

"We better let you get some rest," Elise said.

"I'm fine," I said automatically, then realized how far I'd strayed from reality when Annie snickered and Elise rolled her eyes.

"I meant Annie." Elise's hand closed around my wrist and she pulled me toward the door. "We'll be back tomorrow."

When we got in the elevator, Elise leaned against the wall and a blissful smile crossed her face.

"The marquee has to change now. Twins definitely beats the pageant."

"I don't know. The Spencers' fiftieth wedding anniversary didn't replace you."

"That's right." Elise chewed on her lip, and then her eyes took on a mischievous sparkle. "We may have to take matters into our own hands. To give Annie's babies top billing, of course."

"Of course."

Our minds linked together in the way only best friends' minds can.

"It has to be after dark," Elise plotted.

"It's almost dark now," I pointed out as we stepped into the front lobby. I knew we'd been at the hospital most of the day but I was still surprised to see the evening shadows had snuck in.

"It has to be *later* than dark. Meet me in the alley behind the theater at ten o'clock."

"You are really getting into this." I chuckled. "How are we supposed to reach the marquee? It's going to be hard to miss two women up on a ladder on Main Street."

"You could shoot a cannon down Main Street after nine o'clock and no one would notice," Elise argued.

That was true.

"I'll be there."

Even though Candy would shoot me on sight if we got caught. Or worse yet, sentence me to ten more years on the PAC.

"Elise?" I crept around the corner and called her name softly. While I waited for it to get darker, I'd watched *To*

Catch a Thief, which inspired me to change into a pair of black jeans and a black turtleneck sweater.

Which made Elise double over when she saw me.

"And you accused me of *getting into this,*" she choked.

"We have to blend," I said in my defense.

"I brought Sam's truck and there's a ladder in the back."

"What about the letters?" I hadn't thought of that before. Candy probably had them locked up in a safe somewhere.

"I finally found a purpose for the scrapbooking kit my mother-in-law gave me last Christmas," Elise said. "I cut letters out of black construction paper and covered them with that see-through stuff. We'll just tape them on." She reached in her pocket and waved a roll of duct tape two inches from my nose.

"For a farmer's wife, you're pretty scary. A genius, but scary."

We hauled the ladder around the front and I volunteered to be the one to climb it since Elise had spent the last few hours cutting out letters while I sat on my behind and pretended I was playing opposite Cary Grant.

"It's kind of wobbly," I gasped, feeling the ladder shudder as I took the first few rungs.

"I had to get one from the garage so Sam wouldn't notice it was missing. He never uses this one."

And she didn't think there was a reason for that?

I reached the top and started to pull off the letters that were already there, dropping them down to Elise, who hummed happily as she picked them up and stuffed them in her pocket.

"What is this supposed to say?" I opened the envelope and saw enough new letters to rewrite *Gone With the Wind* on the marquee.

"Joanna Ruth and Nathaniel Stephen. Welcome to the World. And to Prichett. Population Now 1534."

The ladder creaked and just as I finished the word Welcome, we heard a rumble down the street.

"What is that? A plow?" I clutched the ladder and saw the sweep of headlights in the distance.

"It can't be a plow," Elise hissed back. "There's no snow."

Good point. Panic has a tendency to short-circuit a person's brain.

"Should I come down?" Even as I asked, I knew there was no time. The enormous vehicle turned the corner and its lights glared at us, shining on me at the top of the ladder and on Elise clutching the bottom of it.

I was already mentally rehearsing my speech to Candy. "It was Elise's idea!" Then I heard a familiar voice.

"This would be an interesting picture for the *Prichett Press*."

Jim. I almost fell off the ladder in relief.

"What are you doing here?" I yelled.

Elise shushed me.

"Funny. That's what I was just about to ask you two."

"Um, we're just changing the marquee. For Candy." Technically it *was* for Candy. She just didn't know about it yet.

"At ten-thirty at night."

"Right."

The ladder creaked again and I felt one of the rungs weaken underneath my foot.

"Bernice Strum, get off that death trap," Jim demanded.

"I can't." I gulped. "I still have another chapter to write."

Elise shook the ladder and I squeaked.

"You're going to fall and kill yourself and the marquee is going to be posting the time of your funeral service," Jim said.

I clung stubbornly to the ladder until I heard him sigh. "Fine. I'll help you."

His idea of helping was to hoist Elise and me into the bucket of his front-end loader and lift us up to the marquee. With the two of us working on the letters, we were safely back on the ground in less than ten minutes.

When he got a good look at me, he laughed. "Taking this life of crime a bit seriously, aren't you?"

I ignored him and we loaded Sam's ladder back into the truck. Elise had told Sam she'd be home by eleven so she took off, leaving Jim and I standing in the middle of Main Street.

"Want a cup of coffee?" he asked.

My fingers were numb because I hadn't had a pair of black gloves and didn't want to ruin the look. Wrapping them around a cup of coffee was tempting. "Where are we going to find a place that's open this time of night?"

"Jim's Café." He pointed to the cab of the truck. "We also have our day-old crème horns on special."

"Now that's an offer a girl can't refuse." I climbed into the truck.

"I stopped by the hospital earlier," Jim said, pouring me a cup of coffee from a metal thermos. "Those two are going to keep them busy."

"Annie's been waiting to be busy."

"Her room already looks like a garden," Jim said.

Which immediately made me think of Alex's bouquet. *God bless your new family.* What did that mean? Was he just being polite because he knew Stephen was a pastor? I prayed for him on a daily basis and knew a lot of other people were, too. Every time I was tempted to claim him, I made myself put him in God's hands. He was safer there.

"I should be jealous."

"Of what?"

Jim gave me a half smile. "That I'm not the one making you miserable."

"I'm not miserable." It was the truth. Fragile, maybe. Counting every minute as one closer to the point of healing, yes. Knowing that I did the right thing, definitely. No one ever said the right thing would be the easy thing, though. Esther hadn't been too far off when she'd compared the Christian life to bungee-jumping. I knew I was never going to hit bottom again but there were still times I felt like I was hanging upside down. The only thing that kept me from complete terror was that I knew Who was holding on to me. It was the only thing that had kept me from falling to pieces after Alex left.

"If you're not miserable, then how about dinner tomorrow night? I make a mean blackened steak."

I hesitated. Jim and I had met several times over the past month with PAC and the friendship that had started to grow between us was the solid kind. Still, I didn't want to lead him into believing it would ever be more than that. My heart stubbornly refused to consider it.

"I'll throw in cheesecake."

"You know the way to a woman's heart."

"I hope so." He winked at me.

"All right." I slanted a glance at him. "Why don't you ask Marissa to come, too? Cheesecake just might tip the balance in our favor, you know, to get her to join the PAC."

Jim's cheeks got a little pink. "Marissa?"

I'd never seen Jim blush before. Interesting. "You don't like Marissa?"

"It's not that. She's an…artist."

"It's a career, Jim, not a disease."

His eyes suddenly narrowed. "You're not trying to play matchmaker, are you, Bernice?"

Of course I am.

"I'm just saying we could use her help."

The suspicious look faded but the red tint on his face remained. He shrugged. "I guess I could ask her."

Chapter Twenty-Four

I knew the twins were going to make their debut at Faith Community on Easter Sunday but I didn't know there'd be a line of loyal subjects waiting to get a peek at them. The line started in the foyer and wound all the way to the second-grade Sunday school room.

"Look at that," I grumbled. "I hope no one has a cold."

"You held them yesterday for two hours," Elise whispered. "You need to learn to share."

True.

"And you'll get to hold them after church when they come for brunch."

Also true. Elise had invited us all over to the farm for Sunday brunch. This time I'd stepped out of my comfort zone and offered to bring a dessert. Made with my own hands. I'd been designated to pick up John and Esther after church and bring them out while Elise put the finishing touches on. Bree was home on spring break. Which meant that Riley would be there, too. I frowned. Maybe I *wouldn't* get to hold the twins that much.

The organist delayed the prelude for an extra ten minutes, just so the twins' fan club could get a glimpse of them. When we made our way to the pew, sunlight streamed through the stained-glass windows and Easter lilies formed a fragrant hedge around the altar.

For a few minutes I didn't do anything but soak up the setting. I loved Christmas now, but secretly admitted that my favorite holiday was Easter. No less a story of beauty and power than Jesus's birth, but to me it connected the circle that Christmas started.

"Hi, Bernice!" Greta touched my shoulder as she walked past. I would have stood up to hug her but it would have meant hugging Kyle, too, because he was holding her other hand. I still couldn't get used to Greta's hair. It had started to grow back in a very pretty shade of russet-brown and so far she hadn't dyed it black again.

I watched as they made their way to the group of teenagers who sat together in the front. My eyes burned a little when I watched Melissa's face light up when she saw Greta approaching. Kyle stepped dutifully to the side while the girls laughed and wound their arms around each other. Melissa's cancer had been zapped into extinction by the chemo and a heavy dose of loving prayers.

You do things well, don't You, Lord?

Candy sang a special solo that had everyone in tears and Pastor Charles gave a stirring message about new life. I could have been the poster child.

After the service, I made my way over to Annie.

"First dibs when we get to Elise's."

Annie's nose wrinkled. "I'll give you first dibs now if you change Nathaniel's diaper."

I caught the unmistakable fragrance and backed away.

"I have to pick up Esther and John."

Annie laughed. "Coward."

I couldn't argue the label. "I'll see you at Elise's."

Esther and John were waiting for me in the lobby.

"He is risen," Esther sang out cheerfully when she saw me.

I'd been coached with the proper response. "He is risen, indeed!"

It was a greeting that early Christians had used and the words took wing inside me. I repeated it, just to savor them again.

The drive out to the farm was beautiful. I opened the window an inch just to let the moist, sweet air drift in.

Everyone was on the porch, soaking up the sun, when we pulled up. Annie was sitting on the swing, empty-armed. Bree held Joanna but Nathaniel was nowhere in sight. Sam immediately bounded over to help John out of the car while I rescued my berry cobbler from its bumpy ride in the trunk.

"Just put that in the kitchen," Elise directed, closing her eyes as I cruised past her. "Oh, that smells great."

Clancy, Elise's golden retriever, followed me into the house, eyeing the dish in my hands hopefully.

I put it down and decided to look for Nathaniel. I loved both the twins, but that little boy and I had really bonded. He had officially become my sweetie. Joanna was the rambunctious one, always in motion, but Nathaniel would lie quietly in my arms for hours, looking at me with wise brown eyes that held secrets he promised to share as soon as he could talk.

Someone had him and it was *my* turn!

I heard a noise and followed it to the little, glass-enclosed room that Elise called the sleeping porch.

"Aha! Hand him over…"

"Surprise."

Heather stood near the window, cradling him in her arms and I launched myself across the room.

"You're here! How did you get here? I thought you were in Florida!"

"I was." Heather laughed, keeping a secure hold on Nathaniel while she brushed her lips against my cheek. "But I begged Mom and Dad to let me leave early. And someone was nice enough to bring me here."

She looked over at the high-backed floral chair in the corner. That's when I realized we weren't alone.

"Hi."

My heart stopped.

Heather gave my arm a bracing squeeze. "I'll be back in a little while."

Alex stood up but didn't take a step closer. I could hardly comprehend that he was here. But that explained why everyone was on the porch outside. A conspiracy.

"Hi." It got stuck, so I tried again. "Hi."

Alex's hair had grown a little since the last time I saw him and the two-day growth of stubble that shadowed his jaw gave him a reckless look. Like a rugged backwoodsman. Minus the flannel. He looked better than the chocolate rabbit waiting for me on the kitchen counter. Except, I reminded myself ruthlessly, he wasn't mine.

"I know you love me."

I gaped at him. "What?"

"You love me," Alex repeated, as if he knew I needed to hear it again. "I saw it in your eyes the last time we talked. When I went back to L.A., I asked myself why—if you loved me—wouldn't you want us to be together? What were you choosing instead of us? Then I remembered that story you told me, about the woman and the perfume, so I bought a Bible and tried to find it. I ended up reading the entire New Testament and by the time I finished it, I knew what you'd chosen. And why. You'd chosen God, Bern, because you couldn't walk away from what He'd done for you. That's what you were trying to tell me that day. I finally understood what you were talking about. And all of a sudden, it wasn't about you and God. It came down to God and *me*. What was I going to do? So I gave my life to Him. Everything.

"If you don't believe me, ask John. We've been on the phone a few times a week ever since I left. I made him promise not to tell you because I didn't want you to think I was using it to win you over, but he thought today would be a good time for me to tell you. So did Heather. So here I am."

This was absolutely not happening. I was going to wake up any minute in my apartment. Alex looked like he was waiting for me to say something but all I wanted to do was cry. And laugh. Only I wasn't sure what I should do first. My emotional circuit board was totally confused.

"There's more." Alex looked a little uncertain now. "Even though *some* people may be skeptical, I've decided to step out of my life."

I wasn't going to assume anything. But now I needed to use my words. "Where are you going to go?"

"Actually, I was hoping there'd be room in yours."

The way my heart was swelling, I figured there was. Okay, maybe now I was going to assume a tiny bit. But that was all. The tiniest, teensiest little bit.

"Um, for how long?"

Alex took a step closer and pushed his hands into his pockets. "Until we're old and gray?"

"You know, that might not be that far away." I felt obligated to point that out.

"It doesn't matter how long it is. I'll take it."

The last of my defenses crumbled. "So will I."

Epilogue

"Smile, Bernice! We've got a Kodak moment here." Bree held up a camera and I tried to hide behind the towel Heather had draped around my neck. An electric-green beach towel with bikini-clad penguins marching from one corner to the other. Other than the towel, I was barefoot and wearing a slip.

The flash went off and Bree collapsed against the wall, giggling. "How much do you think we can sell this for?"

"Oh, at least a few thousand dollars," Heather said. "But if she drops the towel, I'm sure we could get more."

"Girls, behave," Elise admonished.

Heather and Bree grinned and once again I felt a monumental relief that they hadn't grown up together. Elise and I wouldn't have survived the obstacle course they would have put us through growing up.

As if she'd read my mind, Elise looked at me and nodded.

There was a light tap on the door and Annie slipped into the room. "It's almost one. We have to get ready."

There was a mad clamor as everyone collected their things and headed out the door. Elise paused at the door.

"Are you sure you don't need anything else?"

"I'm sure." My heart had begun to dance to a crazy rhythm and my palms were sweaty. With Alex in my life, I figured I was just going to have to get used to it.

Elise smiled knowingly. "Alex is nervous, too. Sam told me that Lester and some of the guys cornered him at Sally's yesterday and told him he better treat you right. Apparently there's some doubt as to whether or not he's good enough for you."

Tears gathered in my eyes and Elise wagged her finger at me. "None of that. You'll smear your makeup." The door closed softly behind her.

The soft strains of a harp beckoned me to the doorway. Dad tucked my arm under his and we walked slowly down the aisle, where Alex was waiting. Everything melted away when I saw him smile. The music. The lights. Even the friends and family that had gathered to celebrate our wedding day.

God, if there's ever a time in the future that I wonder if You know what You're doing, remind me of this moment.

When we reached the front of the church, Alex stepped forward to meet us and reached for my hand. Dad sniffed, which got me going all over again. Fortunately, Elise was close, a handkerchief tucked in her bouquet for emergency breakdowns.

Pastor Charles opened his Bible.

It was a verse Alex had chosen. The one he'd read that day on the card he'd found in my apartment. And the one he'd heard on the radio when nothing else would come in. He told me he'd never forgotten it.

"You're my treasure, Bernice," he'd told me a few days after Easter. Right before he'd slipped a stunning diamond and sapphire ring on my finger. "How long are you going to make me wait this time?"

"I want the lilacs to be in bloom," I told him.

And they were. The church was full of them, mixed with garlands of ivy and white roses. The heady scent wafted out of the windows and mingled with the May sunshine. My bouquet was a simple spray of long-stemmed white roses, wrapped in satin. Greta had helped me choose my dress and when she brought it to me to try on, I immediately dismissed it as too frothy, too romantic, too…soft. I loved it. Next to me stood Elise, Annie, Heather and Bree, now dressed in pale pink organza.

As we finished saying our vows, I caught Esther's eye. She gave me a playful wink that clearly said, *This day brought to you by God—who wants you to live an adventurously expectant life.*

I winked back.

"What do you give as a token of your affection and love?" Pastor Charles asked.

That was my cue to pay attention again. I slipped the gold band on Alex's finger and when it was his turn, he kissed my palm first and then slid the ring on.

"Ladies and gentlemen." Pastor Charles smiled at us. "It is my privilege to introduce to you for the first time—Mr. and Mrs. Alex and Bernice Scott."

I barely heard the applause because I was waiting for what would come next. Pastor Charles was grinning and didn't realize he'd forgotten something *very* important.

Until Alex coughed meaningfully.

"Oh! I'm sorry. You may kiss your bride."

"You're beautiful," Alex said softly, his lips skimming my earlobe.

Just before he kissed me, I looked into his eyes and saw my reflection.

I smiled. "I know."

* * * * *

QUESTIONS FOR DISCUSSION

1. Can you remember a time in your life when your past "caught up" to you? What happened?

2. Why does Bernice assume that because she is a believer, her life will be "peaceful and full of tranquility"? Do you think that's a common assumption? What is the danger in having that perspective?

3. Bernice lived above the beauty salon even though she dreamed of owning a house with a picket fence. What do you think this ideal represented? Why hadn't she pursued it?

4. Alex confronted Bernice when he realized she hadn't been honest about the range of her talent as a hairstylist. God wants us to use the gifts and abilities He's given us. Is there an area where you feel He's calling you to serve but you've been hesitant to step forward? Why?

5. Candy Lane came to the salon, hoping Bernice could "make her beautiful." Have you ever had a makeover? How did you feel afterward? How long did that feeling last?

6. What do you think is the greatest obstacle that Bernice and her parents will have to overcome in order to move forward?

7. With whom do you identify the most in this book? Why?

8. If Bernice had stayed with Alex, he wouldn't have been forced to seek God on his own. Have you ever had

to make a difficult choice like this? What was the outcome?

9. Think about the ways Bernice grew in her faith over the course of the book. How did God use her to encourage others? In what areas of your life have you been able to encourage other people?

10. The theme verse in Ephesians 3 says that God is able "to do immeasurably more than all we ask or imagine…" What has God done with your dreams?

Steeple Hill Café™

Superwoman doesn't live here

MARILYNN GRIFFITH

Happily Even After

MARILYNN GRIFFITH

life faith ...

Tracey Blackman never thought she'd get married. One hundred extra pounds and one wedding later, she wonders why she did so. Now it seems all she gets from her husband is voice mail. Throw in a mother-in-law, aptly named Queen Elizabeth, who can't stand her, and you can see why Tracey needs a visit to the Sassy sistahood for some much-needed advice about men, marriage and motherhood!

Steeple Hill®

www.SteepleHill.com

Available wherever books are sold!

SHMG598

Back to Russia with Love

SUSAN MAY WARREN

Newly married Josey Anderson will be the perfect wife. She just has to find the perfect cape-style house while learning how to bake and sew. That shouldn't be too difficult, right? However, when her husband, Chase, lands a new job in Moscow, Josey's dreams disintegrate. After all, she's been there, done that as a missionary, and moving back to a city without year-round hot water—or decent maternity clothes—leaves much to be desired. But what's the perfect wife to do?

Steeple Hill®

Chill Out, Josey!

Available wherever books are sold!

www.SteepleHill.com

SH585

HARLEQUIN

More Than Words

"Changing lives
stride by stride—
I did it my way!"

—**Jeanne Greenberg,** real-life heroine

*Jeanne Greenberg is a Harlequin More Than Words
award winner and the founder of **SARI Therapeutic Riding.***

Discover your inner heroine!

SUPPORTING CAUSES OF CONCERN TO WOMEN

HARLEQUIN

WWW.HARLEQUINMORETHANWORDS.COM

MTW07JG1

HARLEQUIN

More Than Words

"Jeanne proves that
one woman can
change the world,
with vision, compassion
and hard work."

—**Linda Lael Miller,** author

*Linda wrote "Queen of the Rodeo," inspired by Jeanne Greenberg,
founder of **SARI Therapeutic Riding**. Since 1978 Jeanne has devoted her
life to enriching the lives of disabled children and their families through
innovative and exciting therapies on horseback.*

Look for *"Queen of the Rodeo"* in
More Than Words, Vol. 4,
available in April 2008 at eHarlequin.com
or wherever books are sold.

SUPPORTING CAUSES OF CONCERN TO WOMEN ‖ HARLEQUIN
WWW.HARLEQUINMORETHANWORDS.COM

MTW07JG2

Only she could redeem him…

RUTH AXTELL MORREN

He was tall and dark with eyes as blue as cobalt, and in a glittering ballroom Hester Leighton saw a man she knew she should not keep company with.

Hester was the only woman who'd ever made Gerrit feel truly worthy of love, and he would not lose her. Separated from her by her father—and an ocean—Gerrit had to decide whether he would risk his life and his soul to earn a home in Hester's arms forever.

The Rogue's Redemption

"Ruth Axtell Morren writes with skill and sensitivity about things that matter most."
—*New York Times* bestselling author Susan Wiggs

Available wherever books are sold!

Steeple Hill®

www.SteepleHill.com

SHRAM600